A MILES DARIEN DETECTIVE THRILLER

HUMAN COLLATERAL

HARRY PINKUS

BQB

North Carolina

Human Collateral: A Miles Darien Detective Thriller
© 2022 Harry Pinkus. All rights reserved.

This is a work of fiction. All of the characters, names, incidents, organizations, and dialogue in this novel are either the product of the author's imagination or are used fictitiously.

Published in the United States by BQB Publishing
(an imprint of Boutique of Quality Books Publishing Company, Inc.)
www.bqbpublishing.com

Printed in the United States of America

ISBN 978-1-952782-63-3 (p)
ISBN 978-1-952782-64-0 (e)

Library of Congress Control Number: 2022935044

Book design by Robin Krauss, www.bookformatters.com
Cover design by Rebecca Lown, www.rebeccalowndesign.com
First editor: Caleb Guard
Second editor: Andrea Vande Vorde

PROLOGUE

It was one of the few slow days at the Gary, Indiana Coroner's office when the body of a Jane Doe arrived in the hands of medical examiner Lois Turner. It was a young woman, one could say a girl, whose face looked troubled even in death. Lois cradled the limbs of the body gently in her arms, as she always did, identifying the unhealed marks that remained. There was a large scar across the abdomen, too recent not to matter. In her arm was a small, yet very notable, puncture.

"Appears to be pulmonary edema, likely heroin-induced, given the needle track on her right arm," she noted, "which is unusual, given the muscle development of that arm indicates she was right handed." She turned the arm over so her assistant could see the track mark.

"So, you think a right-handed person would shoot up in the opposite arm?" her assistant, Bill, asked.

"I do, but it's not relevant to her cause of death. We'll add the anomaly of the right-arm needle mark to the report. Maybe the police will find it important. For now, let's get blood and tissue samples to the lab to confirm the cause of death."

While Lois acquired the tissue samples, Bill drew two vials of blood from the deceased woman. He then took the tissue samples and vials of blood to a lab technician in the adjacent room for analysis. When he returned, his boss was still examining the body.

"Find anything else interesting?" he asked.

"Interesting, yes, but again not something I see as a direct cause to her death. Look here." She pointed to a badly infected area of the Jane Doe's abdomen at the site where her left kidney had been removed. "She was obviously in a weakened condition from this poorly executed surgical procedure. Look how jagged the incision is. It certainly contributed to the infection and likely compromised her body's chance of surviving the overdose. We can't be sure, but it's worth noting."

An hour later the toxicology report came back, confirming a heroin overdose as the cause of death. The results were added to the coroner's final report. The infection related to the kidney removal and the location of the needle mark were also recorded.

"What now?" asked the assistant.

Lois shook her head. "Move her body to the morgue and send the report to the police department. It's up to them to try and locate her next of kin. If they're unsuccessful, she'll be cremated and buried with numerous other unidentified corpses."

Lois could see Bill shivering. Apparently he had not yet become accustomed to seeing someone so young and so alone die in such a gruesome manner. It was not how young the Jane Doe was, or her anonymity, that bothered Lois this time. It was the needle mark and the scar. Both were likely a sign of what this girl died for, and if it was true, she feared there would be other young women destined to suffer the same fate.

CHAPTER 1

The case load at Miles Darien Investigations had increased dramatically over the past six months. Nothing like solving a couple of high profile cases to generate a flow of new business. Particularly considering their scope and diverse nature. The one that received the most notoriety required thwarting a corrupt political party's efforts to discredit an opponent's campaign by framing Jack McKay, its campaign manager, for a horrible crime he didn't commit. In the other, Miles unraveled a complex scheme by a team of arsonists to defraud RightStone, a Lakeview based insurance company. In each case, Miles was the force that exposed the wrongdoing. That string of successes necessitated today's first order of business: seeking applicants for a badly needed assistant's position.

Miles began reading some of the help wanted ads on the Lakeville Examiner's website for help with creating his own. He grabbed a couple of sentences from an ad for a dental receptionist and then posted a reworded version to fit the job he was offering.

That task completed, he turned his attention to the three new cases he had been hired to solve: missing merchandise from a retail store, an identity theft, and finding a potential witness to a car accident.

Just as he began reviewing his notes, the phone rang.

"Miles Darien," he answered.

"Hello, Mr. Darien." The caller's voice was deep and authoritarian. "This is Christopher Chapman of Chapman's Department Store. We spoke a couple of weeks ago about the rash of unsolved retail thefts at our store. I'm concerned that I haven't heard back from you about this." The air of impatience in Mr. Chapman's voice was unmistakable.

"Well, Mr. Chapman, the good news is I've uncovered the 'how it was done' part of the case. Someone turned off the surveillance cameras for about ten minutes several times over the past month. Each time between midnight and two am. The question I'm still investigating is the 'who'."

"How did you uncover the gap in the camera footage?"

"In reviewing recent footage of each camera, I saw the clock on the wall shown on one of the rooms didn't match the timer on the camera recording. Unfortunately I could only check the last two weeks as the previous footage had been recorded over. Can you get me a list of all of your employees, former employees, or anyone else who may have had access to the office where the cameras are controlled?"

"Of course. You'll have it by the end of the day."

"Thanks. I'll get moving on the list as soon as I get it."

Mr. Chapman's voice had taken a softer, more relaxed tone. "Please keep me posted on your progress. I'm sure you understand that it's not so much the loss of the merchandise that concerns me. It's having a thief under our roof."

"I do understand. I'll be in touch soon."

Returning to the other two cases he had been working on, Miles noticed his red email icon showing the number 24 highlighted in white on the top of his computer screen. In the short time he was on the phone with Mr. Chapman, his inbox had exploded with emails from numerous prospective applicants for his assistant's position. He decided to turn his attention to them, rationalizing that getting an assistant would allow him the time to devote his full attention to his cases.

After reviewing all of the emails, one stood out. Anne Jeffries had been a legal assistant for a criminal defense attorney who was retiring. He replied to her email offering a couple of times the following day for an interview and then turned to his case reviews.

Once again he was interrupted by his phone ringing. This time, he immediately recognized the caller's number displayed on the screen. It was his boyhood friend, Ryan Duffy.

"Hey, Ryan. What's up?" Miles asked.

"I'm calling with a request." There was a definite excitement in Ryan's voice. "I'm working on a project that's due in a few days. Once I've submitted it, I'd like to come for a visit. I really could use some time away."

"Not sure. Let me check my reservation log to see if the guest room's going to be available," Miles joked.

"I haven't even given you any dates yet!" Ryan shouted in mock anger.

This type of back and forth had been a mainstay of their relationship going back to elementary school.

"Just let me know your dates and flight information," said Miles. "I'll do my best to open up my schedule so we can have some quality time to hang out."

"Great. Does the need to clear your schedule mean your PI business has taken off?" Ryan asked.

"It really has. Bringing down Randall Davies and his corrupt political cronies was like setting off fireworks."

"That gives me a great idea for my next article. 'Gay, Jewish Private Investigator from New York City becomes the go-to detective in Lakeville, Wisconsin. I'm sure the *Times* will eat it up."

"Very funny. Listen, I couldn't be happier that you're coming. I've been working non-stop for weeks. I'm not complaining but I could also use some time off and it'll be great to share it with you."

"Perfect. I'll keep you posted as my travel plans crystalize. Bye."

Ryan hung up. He had won this round of their ongoing competition as to who gets the last word.

No more stalling, he thought as he returned to the case files in front of him. He had to finish them or there would be no time off to spend with his old friend.

CHAPTER 2

R yan couldn't sleep. Deadlines always reminded him of the night before a big exam in college, one he hadn't studied for, which then required a night of cramming to make up for his procrastination. This Sunday night was no exception. The *Times* was expecting his piece on the dilemma of jobs versus the environment in coal country by Friday morning no later than ten a.m.

It was actually the kind of story he loved. Opposing positions with valid arguments from each side. His trips to West Virginia had been both enlightening and disheartening. He had all the research in hand. Now the hard part: taking all of that and building a compelling essay. Most importantly, he hadn't yet found a solution to the problems facing the coal industry. Without a solution, his essay would simply be another recounting of a seemingly hopeless stalemate between two forces whose interests never aligned. He had paced the floor for hours searching for the answer. Even though he hadn't found one, it was time to start writing. Hopefully, the answer would somehow mystically appear.

Just as he sat down at his computer to begin, his phone rang.

"Hi, Ryan. It's Ted."

"What's up, Ted?" Ryan was annoyed by the disturbance, and the tone of his voice made sure his editor knew his call was a nuisance. He was at an impasse with his essay, and the call was just another roadblock since he had just begun getting his essay down on paper.

Undeterred, Ted said, "I need a status check." Ted wasn't asking, he was commanding.

Ryan didn't like the sound of that at all. "Are you worried?" he said in a rather forceful voice, which he hoped would provide cover for his uncertainty.

"Truth is, with the election behind us, we're a little light on content this week. We really need your 'Coal Jobs Versus the Environment' story this week. Without fail." Ted sounded genuinely concerned, which wasn't like him. Normally, he resembled one of those brash newspaper editors in a 1940s film noire crime drama.

"Not to worry, you'll have it in plenty of time. I have more than your pleadings driving me to the finish line."

"What's your extra motivation?" Ted asked in a much more relaxed tone.

"I'm taking a break from all this starting next Sunday." Ryan wasn't asking permission.

Ted started in with the *where-are-you-going-when-will-you-be-back-I-have-slots-saved-for-your-next-series* line of questioning.

"Ted, now you know why I'm a freelancer. I like my free-dom. Don't get me wrong, I'm extremely grateful that you have published so many of my essays, but I need my time to be my own. I'll be on break for a couple of weeks. When I'm back, I'll call you and we can discuss another assignment. Okay?"

"Okay. But promise me you'll have that essay to me by Friday at ten a.m."

"I already promised you that. Goodnight, Ted." Ryan hung up.

He wrote for another hour and then decided to get some air, stretch his legs, get something to eat, and find the elusive solution for his story. The wonderful thing about the Upper

West Side of New York City was that there were so many cool places to walk to, particularly on an unseasonably warm May evening. Tonight it was the world-famous hot dog stand, Gray's Papaya. It was about ten blocks away, which allowed him sufficient time to get good and hungry on the way. It also afforded some time on the way home to reset his mind and work off the Recession Special: two hot dogs, topped with sweet red onion relish, and a tropical juice of choice. Ryan always had the iconic pineapple juice.

After polishing off "the special," he started home to resume the battle of the coal miners versus the environmentalists. He hadn't made it a block before his cell phone rang again. *It better not be Ted again*, he thought. Thankfully, the Caller ID said it was Rebecca.

"You horny again?" Ryan teased, immediately regretting his response.

"Not anymore," Rebecca shot back.

"Sorry, my humor suffers when I'm facing a deadline," he said in the most sincere, apologetic tone he could muster.

"Truth be told . . ." she kidded. They both laughed. Ryan and Rebecca had a long-standing, no-strings-attached relationship. They each coveted their own unattached lifestyle, so the relationship worked. They occasionally enjoyed a meal or a concert, but mostly it was all about satisfying their libidos a couple of times a month.

Ryan never really understood what she saw in him. She was smart, funny, an accomplished actress, and an absolute knockout. He was astute enough not to question the relationship. Rebecca obviously felt the same way. It worked, and that's all the analysis either of them needed.

"Hey," she said, "I actually called because I need a different kind of favor from you. My agent, Tom Crowley, is having a cocktail party on Friday night and I'd like you to be my date. I hate showing up alone, and I think it might be fun. I guarantee the refreshments will be amazing."

Considering what he had just consumed, he was sure the refreshments would be a major step forward. "My deadline is Friday morning, so a party that night sounds great to me."

"Wonderful. Suit and tie, of course. Pick me up at seven."

"Perfect." Ryan finished his walk and headed upstairs to his apartment and his essay. Her invitation was just the incentive he needed to get back to work.

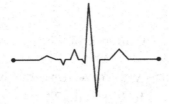

CHAPTER 3

M iles arrived at the office around eight-thirty to prepare for his nine o'clock interview with Anne Jeffries. He made a list of all the tasks he expected her to perform, followed by a list of talking points including compensation, work hours, confidentiality, and so on. Lastly, he added questions about her work experience, specifically her current employment with a defense attorney.

She walked through the door at eight fifty-five, which meant she already had one gold star for punctuality.

"Good morning, Anne. Thanks for coming in," Miles said with an approving smile.

"Nice to meet you Mr. Darien," she replied.

"Please call me Miles." He gestured to a nearby table and the two of them took a seat. "So tell me a bit about yourself."

"Well, I've been divorced for fifteen years. My daughter lives in Burlington with her husband and eleven year old son. They're only a thirty minute car ride away so I spend a lot of time with them as I do with my women friends. I've been working for Jerry Slater for a little over ten years. He's retiring, as I mentioned in my email. What else would you like to know?" she offered.

"I'd be interested to know what appealed to you about this job," he asked.

"I read all about that case and the work you did uncovering the conspiracy," she said enthusiastically. "I was intrigued by the possibility of working on cases like that."

"What questions do you have for me?" Miles asked.

"What brought you to Lakeville?"

"The Lakeville Police Department needed a forensic specialist, so they hired me to work on a one-year contract. Shortly after I moved here, I met Robert and we became a couple. It worked out fine for a while but when Robert and I broke up, it seemed the perfect time for me to strike out on my own. While I have a degree in forensic science, it was the non-scientific side of investigating that interested me most."

"Must have been hard leaving the security of the police department though with, I assume, only minimal local connections."

"It was, but liberating at the same time. My being gay wasn't always looked upon favorably at the department. This allowed me the freedom to pick my cases and use techniques my narrow forensic lab work at the department never would. Through my friendship with Mickey Martin, a retired judge, I started to build my practice. My involvement in the high profile case of Jack McKay being framed for child pornography is what has created my burgeoning workload and need for an assistant."

Switching back to the job interview, Miles asked her to explain her current job duties, which pretty much aligned with what Miles needed her to do. He laid out a few additional tasks from his list that she'd be asked to do. She acknowledged her agreement with a nod. The conversation then went to the subject of compensation.

"Jerry pays me by the hour," she explained. "He doesn't need me full time, which is good for me too. It affords me plenty of time with my family and friends and my hobbies. He pays me twenty five dollars an hour and I'm averaging about thirty hours a week. He also gives me an additional two hundred fifty dollars a month to offset some of my health insurance premiums. With my alimony payments, I'm good. Speaking of my financial wellbeing, do I have a chance at getting this position?"

Miles really connected with Anne's honest and straightforward manner.

"Yes," he said with a smile. "When can you start?"

"Well, that's the rub. I promised Jerry I'd stay on until all of his cases are completed. That may take a month or so. Does that change your offer?"

"No, provided you can help me out in one way between now and then."

"What's that?"

"My phone system allows me to forward incoming calls to another number. Would you be amenable to me forwarding those calls to you when I'm out of the office?"

"Sure, no problem."

"Good. Then I'm fine with continuing your same compensation program to start. What's your mobile phone number?"

Anne picked up his phone and added herself to his contacts. Her take charge attitude made Miles chuckle. He had obviously found the right person for the job.

Ryan was awakened at eight a.m. by the sound of a garbage truck collecting the trash in front of his apartment. He accepted noise being a constant factor in New York City and normally the hour wouldn't be an issue, but he had worked on his essay into the wee hours of the morning after getting home from Gray's Papaya. Only half awake, he made his way to the kitchen to get some much-needed coffee going when his cell phone rang.

"Hi, buddy boy!" It was Miles.

Ryan and Miles met in third grade. Their teacher seated the class in alphabetical order, so Ryan Duffy sat behind Miles Darien the entire year. They'd been best friends ever since.

"Hey, Miles. I was going to call you later to talk about my travel plans for Sunday. Hold on a second while I get my itinerary." Ryan reached for his notebook. "Okay. Are you going to write this down?"

"We private investigators are good at remembering details. Give it to me," Miles replied in mock anger.

"Delta flight 762. Arrives MKE at 11:35 a.m."

Miles explained he would be waiting for him in the cell phone lot and said to call him once he had retrieved his bags.

"I've been working non-stop for three months on my latest piece, and I'm ready for some R&R."

"R&R is my specialty. Your vacation is in good hands. See you Sunday." Miles hung up without a formal goodbye.

Ryan flipped on the coffee pot and sat down to assess what he still needed to do to meet his deadline. Between his notes and what he had already written, all the pieces were there. He just needed to splice it all together. The key to making his article more than just the retelling of two opposite positions was finding a solution. Could he come up with an idea that could lead to a positive outcome for both sides? It dawned on him that any solution would, at the very least, have to include two key elements: Elimination of the demand for coal, and then new jobs for the coal industry workers. He decided to call Roger Jamison, his parents' former colleague and close friend at Columbia University. Professor Jamison was the former head of the Economics Department who was now frequently seen offering his views on cable news shows. If anyone could lead him in the right direction, it was the professor. He decided to give him a call.

The professor seemed genuinely pleased to hear from him and listened intently as Ryan explained his essay problem.

"Outlining the pros and cons is fairly straight forward," he said. "I'm struggling to find a satisfactory path towards a mutually acceptable solution. Can you give me any guidance?"

"So much to be said. Why don't you come over this afternoon so we can discuss it at length? Say, about two?" Offered the professor.

Ryan was elated at the prospect of getting expert guidance in resolving his dilemma. "I will. Thank you for the generous invitation. Are you still on 89th Street?"

"Yes, see you then. I'll have tea ready."

The path to Professor Jamison's apartment led Ryan through his old Upper West Side neighborhood. It was still basically populated by middle class families, although the cost of living in that part of the city had grown significantly over time. It still had a large Jewish population, but there had always been many other ethnic groups represented. Case in point were Ryan's great-grandparents, who emigrated from Ireland and settled there in the early 1900s.

Along the way, he passed the house where he grew up. The small brownstone looked very much the same. It took him back to his childhood, playing kick-the-can and stick ball in the street with the neighborhood kids. A couple of blocks further, he passed Miles's childhood home, a red-brick apartment building with a large lobby and numerous mailboxes lined up on one wall. He remembered the first time he was invited over to play. How he had questioned Miles about the metal thing that was nailed to the doorway entrance to the Darien's unit. The explanation of the significance of the Mezuzah was his first lesson in Jewish customs. Miles would further Ryan's Jewish education frequently over the years, particularly the food culture. The Darien family's religious affiliation was much more ethnic than religious, which mirrored Ryan's own religious experience. His Irish Catholic heritage showed up mostly symbolically but not ceremonially, like having a Christmas tree but seldom attending church services.

Just before reaching the professor's apartment, Ryan passed the corner where the men's clothing store owned by Miles's father had once been. The storefront was now another convenience store, just like the thousands of others that catered to New York City's multitudes of on-the-go inhabitants. Ryan and Miles had been part-time workers at the clothing store when they were kids. If Miles's mom, Helen, needed a break, she'd send the two of them to the store so Miles's dad, Ben, could keep them occupied. The boys did odd jobs like breaking down the boxes the suits arrived in, sweeping up the remnants in the tailor's workshop, or running to the bank to get some change for the cash register. Ben always referred to the boys as "the odd couple" since they looked and acted so differently. Miles was tall and wiry with dark hair, Semitic features, and an introspective personality. Ryan was quite a bit shorter, looking every bit the Irishman with reddish-blond hair and a slightly turned-up nose. He had the stereotypical gift of gab, which he displayed at every opportunity. Another difference between them was the gender of the people they were attracted to. No jealousy over each other's dates had eliminated that typical boyhood conflict.

As he rounded the corner onto 89th Street, Ryan returned to present day and the task at hand. When he arrived at the professor's building, he rang the bell and was buzzed in. As he climbed the creaky wooden stairs to the third-floor apartment, he was struck by how much the place smelled like old books, the way a library smelled. He assumed the building was likely populated by numerous members of the Columbia faculty, past and present.

"Welcome, Mr. Duffy. So nice to see you." The professor seemed genuinely pleased by Ryan's arrival. He was just as Ryan had remembered him. Short, balding, and round with smiling eyes peeking through his horn-rimmed glasses.

"Been a long time, Professor Jamison. Thanks for inviting me over to chat."

"It is I who should be thankful. It's so nice to see a new face. These days I only seem to see the other inhabitants of this building, and they're mostly former colleagues whom I've been seeing for decades." Ryan had been right about the reason behind the pervasive smell of old books.

"Happy to be of service," Ryan said with a wry smile.

The professor retreated to the kitchen to fetch the teapot. The tea bags, milk, sugar, cups, and a plate of cookies were already positioned on the coffee table. Once he returned, each poured themselves a cup and added their other ingredients.

Once settled, the professor began. "Bring me up to speed on where you are with your essay."

Ryan filled him in on his basic premise. The two factions, the coal industry and the environmentalists, were in a stalemate with no real solution in sight. The essay outlined the positions of both sides: How the coal industry was providing jobs and filling an existing demand for their product and how the environmentalists sought to break the cycle of pollution and hazardous workplaces. The essay went on to explore the ongoing efforts to make coal cleaner and the workplace safer, concluding only modest gains had been made in those areas. The missing piece, he explained, was a path to resolving the stalemate. Eliminating the need for coal by replacing it with an alternative or alternatives while avoiding the destruction of regional economies and putting tens of thousands of mostly unskilled workers onto the rolls of the hopelessly unemployed, seemed to be an insurmountable goal.

After a short pause and a few strokes of his beard, the professor spoke. "Well, Ryan, like most complex economic problems, there is no singular solution. I'd approach it as a series of small steps that could eventually lead to a new paradigm. Eat the elephant one bite at a time, so to speak. I'd begin by developing a plan that includes new jobs for the coal industry workers. Remember their primary objection is to prevent job loss, not a love of coal. If they can find good paying jobs above ground, they'll likely jump on board. The real trick is what you come up with to decrease the demand for coal."

"I agree. But finding that alternative has eluded me."

The professor again paused and stroked his beard. "One bite at a time, my boy. One bite at a time. I suggest you come up with a series of alternate measures that could be implemented to help phase out coal. Just to flip a switch and the light goes on won't work here." He smiled, enjoying his own analogy.

"I understand. Luckily, I still have three days to come up with those alternatives," Ryan said, making light of his impending deadline.

They spent the rest of the visit reminiscing about Ryan's parents. How the three professors became friends serving on a faculty budget advisory committee for the school of liberal arts at Columbia. About their visits to jazz clubs in the village and the dinner parties they took turns hosting. Ryan had fond memories of being included in several of their outings.

Before he left, Ryan promised to stay in touch. He really

enjoyed the professor's company and felt like, in a way, it kept him connected to his parents, who had both passed more than ten years ago.

He headed home and straight to his desk to tackle his seemingly impossible quest for solutions to the coal dilemma. The rest of the day and evening was lost fitfully searching for possibilities which could move the opposing factions towards a mutually beneficial outcome. He gave up and went to sleep hoping a new day would deliver new options.

Ryan awoke the next morning with a renewed enthusiasm for his quest. As he downed a bowl of cereal, the first good possibility came to him in a sudden moment of clarity. Use tax incentives to lure a major heating and cooling equipment manufacturing company into opening a plant in West Virginia. Sweeten the pot by adding a private equity investment in the company aimed at developing new technology to convert existing coal-burning furnaces into alternative fuel consuming devices. The third piece would be funding for vocational training, which would provide the new skills needed to convert coal workers into factory workers. The revenue generated by the economic boost the job shift would provide pays back the tax incentives the state provides upfront. This one multifaceted solution would address the needs of each of the stake holders.

Ryan would use this concept to demonstrate how, if all sides of the issue are considered, solutions could be found that would provide benefits for each constituency. It was not *the* solution, but rather highlighted one of many possibilities which could ultimately solve the problem. He was so excited he left his bowl of cereal on the table, mostly uneaten, and literally ran to his desk. He didn't look up until he had finished a complete draft of his essay many hours later. It was just after midnight, so Wednesday night had become Thursday morning. For the first time in days, he'd get a good night's sleep.

CHAPTER 4

Having finished a complete draft of his essay before turning in, Ryan started his day relaxed and able to turn his attention to more mundane tasks. He treated himself to breakfast out at Sarabeth's for eggs benedict and then off to Zabar's for some groceries. After dropping off the groceries at his apartment, he headed to the dry cleaners to pick up his shirts and the suit he would wear to the party Friday night.

With his morning chores completed, he returned to his desk to transform his draft into a finished essay. No sooner had he switched on his computer than his cell phone rang. It was Rebecca.

"Hello, Ms. Bartoni. What can I do for you?"

"Well, Mr. Duffy. This is about what I can do for you." Her reply was incredibly provocative. Easy for an actress of her experience, he thought.

"Okay. I'm in, whatever it is," Ryan said, playing along.

"Turns out you won't need to pick me up on Friday after all."

"Are you canceling on me?" Ryan hoped he hadn't had his suit cleaned for nothing.

"No, silly. My agent has splurged on a limo for us, so I'll pick you up at seven."

"Obviously sounds like this party is going to be quite a celebration. Do all of his guests get the same VIP treatment?"

"Nope, just us. I guess I should have told you he's throwing the party for me. He just signed me to a contract to star in a network TV series. The actress who was originally cast had to drop out for medical reasons. Rather than delay production, I was signed for the part. We start working on it right away."

"That's wonderful. Details!" Ryan demanded.

"I'll fill you in when I see you on Friday. Got to go." She hung up.

It was so like Rebecca to tell him about the party in such a matter-of-fact way. For a successful actress like her to have such a subdued ego was quite rare. Though, from what Ryan knew of her background, it seemed fitting. Her father worked in the hotel industry. Her mother was in the States as staff with the Argentinian delegation to the UN. They had met while he was the assistant manager at the UN Plaza Hotel where her delegation housed its visiting diplomats and where they had many of their events. One of her jobs was to interface with the hotel staff to arrange accommodations and the events. Her interface with Mr. Bartoni evolved into love and a forty-year marriage. Hardworking, down-to-earth parents molded a talented yet modest daughter. Ryan was captivated by her unique combination of "star power" and humility.

Ryan had used the rest of the day on Thursday to polish his essay. Just to needle Ted a little bit, he waited until five minutes before his Friday deadline to press Send on the email with the essay attached.

An hour later, his cell phone rang. As he expected, it was Ted calling to admonish Ryan for making him sweat.

Ryan decided to come clean. "Just having a little fun. Have you read it?"

"Yes." Ted deadpanned. Now he was having some fun.

"And?" Ryan answered, knowing how this was to play out.

"Okay. Enough screwing around. It's really well done. The writing is, as usual, extremely engaging and smart. The beauty of it, though, is how you laid out the positions of each faction in the conflict without bias and then offered a possible solution. Workable or not, you gave both sides some food for thought on how to resolve their differences with benefits for all. Ryan, this is the best piece you've ever done for us. I'd really like to nail down the next project now if we can."

Ted was in full pitch mode. Ryan had dealt with pushing from Ted before and knew just how to handle it.

"Ted, as I told you when we last spoke, I will be in touch as soon as I return from my vacation. I promise not to commit to an assignment from anyone else before talking to you. Okay?"

"All right. Call me as soon as you get back." Ryan's message that Ted had pushed things as far as he could had obviously been received.

"Will do. Bye, Ted." With that out of the way, Ryan was truly able to wind down for the party tonight, only to spend Saturday packing for his trip on Sunday morning. He'd spend the next two weeks in Lakeville, Wisconsin bumming around the Midwest with Miles.

His thoughts returned to preparations for his date with Rebecca. Should he shave or have that cool five-o'clock-shadow look? Did his shoes need shining? Should he change the bedsheets just in case? He chose "yes" on all three and added one more. After lunch, he'd go the grocery store on the corner and pick up a rose.

Ryan was showered and dressed by six thirty. He spent the next few minutes tidying up his place in case Rebecca would be stopping by after the party for a nightcap. Just before seven p.m., he received a text from her. *Be there in 5 minutes.* After a brief glance in the mirror to be sure his tie was straight, he checked his pockets. Phone, wallet, keys, all good. As he was about to head downstairs, he remembered the rose. He quickly grabbed it out of the glass of water it was resting in. Forgetting it was a rose, he was instantly reminded by the sting of one of its thorns. No blood, just another of life's reminders to slow down and smell the roses.

When he walked out of the lobby onto the sidewalk, there was a large black town car parked outside. The rear passenger window opened slowly, and a woman's arm appeared. Her index finger made a beckoning motion. Rebecca's sense of the dramatic was on full display. As he approached the car, she opened the door and invited him to join her.

"For me?" she asked, looking at the rose.

"Actually, it's for the driver," Ryan teased. "I should have gotten one for you too, I guess."

She gave him a light slap on the arm, then leaned in and gave him a huge kiss.

"So, tell me about this TV series you're going to be in," he said.

Rebecca explained that the show was about a Hispanic doctor, played by her, who runs an inner city clinic for the underserved in the neighborhood. People came in with problems that went way beyond their medical issues. Her character enlisted the aid of friends and other do-gooders to help. Her eyes lit up as she described the premise.

Ryan listened intently and realized how perfectly she had been cast in the role.

Rebecca seemed particularly pleased that the stories would shine a spotlight on a wide range of the real-life dramas people are confronted with and possibly provide some impetus for change.

Ryan was quickly on board. "I love the altruistic side of the show. Can't wait to see it. By the way, you look stunning!" He couldn't take his eyes off her in that figure-hugging sapphire blue evening gown. She looked fully prepared for a red carpet entrance.

"Why, thank you, sir. You look pretty dashing yourself." She gave him a wink as the limo pulled up to Tom Crowley's swanky East Side apartment building. It was a beautiful older building with an elevator and rooftop deck. A rare find in Manhattan.

Rebecca grabbed her handbag and the rose, then took Ryan's hand as she exited the limo. Then she slipped her hand through his arm and the two of them headed inside where there was a group of party guests waiting for the elevator. Rebecca greeted one of the couples, a director she had worked with and his wife. She then introduced the couple to Ryan.

With that, the elevator door opened, and the group ascended to Tom's penthouse apartment. Inside the door to the penthouse was an unattended table full of ladies' designer handbags. Only in the residences of the New York elite would they find such a display. Rebecca added hers to the pile, and they headed inside to find their host.

When they found Tom, he was holding court next to his baby grand piano. After Rebecca introduced Ryan, Tom politely swept her away to make the rounds. Ryan retreated to the bar set up in the corner. Frankly, he was just fine with simply standing off to the side, drink in hand, observing the crowd. He was sure he recognized a couple of actors, although he couldn't put names to the faces. There were a few others he recognized—a former Congressman, a news anchor, and a retired coach of the New York Knicks. It was likely that all were, or had been, clients of Tom's. It struck Ryan how much the scene reminded him of a classic Hollywood movie.

The sound of a spoon clinking a wine glass quieted the

room. Tom held up his glass and proposed a toast. "To Rebecca Bartoni. The star of the new TV series, *Compassion Clinic*."

A "Here! Here!" was followed by Rebecca's polite bow and waves to each side of the room. After that very brief ceremony, she made her way back to Ryan at the bar.

"Buy a girl a drink?" she proposed.

"Sure, ma'am. What'll you have?"

"Three fingers of bourbon." She stared seriously at Ryan. "Rocks please," she said, turning to the bartender. Returning her gaze to Ryan, she said somewhat apologetically, "I'm not usually a bourbon drinker but it sometimes helps me relax."

"Rebecca, the formal portion of the evening is over. I would think you'd already be relaxed."

She picked up her glass that the bartender had poured. "The festivities are nothing. It's the weight of the task ahead of me that's got me on edge. Carrying a network series is quite a responsibility." She punctuated her point with a healthy gulp of the bourbon.

The buzz in the room was replaced by someone playing the piano. Undoubtably one of Tom's musically talented clients. Suddenly, a medley of Broadway showtunes followed. A number of the guests joined in forming a chorus. Rebecca chose to stay with Ryan by the bar. She had obviously had enough of the spotlight for one evening. They took a time out from their drinks to sample some of the fancy hors d'oeuvres. A sound strategy to balance the 80 proof bourbon.

They stayed in the corner for another hour and then called for the limo to pick them up. Rebecca retrieved her handbag and the rose as they left the penthouse and boarded the elevator. Once they reached the first floor, Rebecca hurried out of the elevator, her spike heels clicking on the marble lobby floor as they made their way out to the street. They hopped into the limo that was already waiting there.

"Back to my place," she commanded both the driver and Ryan. She took his hand, leaned on his shoulder, and let out an audible sigh of relief. Ryan hoped she'd continue doing that when they arrived at her apartment.

Her apartment's decor was a reflection of her personality: tasteful but elegant. Unlike Ryan's place, everything was neat and tidy.

"Something to drink?" she asked.

"Just water, thanks. I think I've had enough alcohol for one night," Ryan conceded as he loosened his tie and took his customary seat on the sofa.

"Same for me." She conceded as she disappeared into the kitchen.

She returned quickly with two glasses of ice water and joined him on the couch.

Ryan noted the look of concern on her face. "You seem troubled."

"It's this new role. Besides the weight of the show on my shoulders, properly representing my Hispanic heritage is critical to me." She seemed uncharacteristically overwhelmed. Her eyes looked straight at the ceiling, clearly revealing her trepidation.

"You can be yourself. Your mother has given you that gift, hasn't she?"

"Yes, as far as my DNA goes, but I grew up in white America without ties to my Argentinian roots in any way. I don't even speak fluent Spanish." Her voice was a mixture of frustration and sadness.

"Do what you've trained to do. Take what you know, study

what you don't know, and then create the character. In short, be an actor!"

"You should be a director." A smile had finally come to her face. "Let's see how well you can direct a love scene." She took his hand and led him into the bedroom.

CHAPTER 5

Saturday was spent packing and doing a few last-minute errands. A two-week vacation posed some unique clothing challenges. Not wanting to do laundry on the trip, Ryan packed fresh underwear for each day, enough shirts of various varieties so he wouldn't need to wear any of them more than twice while also having sufficient variety to cover multiple occasions. Hopefully, he had the right stuff for his two weeks in Lakeville. He figured two pairs of jeans, one pair of slacks, and a pair of shorts should suffice. In any event, Miles had a house with laundry equipment if needed.

The rest of the packing was easy. Basic toiletries and charging cables for his electronic stuff. He'd take his laptop, notebooks, and other writing supplies in his shoulder bag. He'd wear a spring jacket on the plane, so that should about do it. With his packing complete, it was time to make arrangements for his mail and newspapers. As always, it was his plan to bribe Fred, his neighbor from across the hall, to bring those things in for him. He'd stock the refrigerator with deli and beer, which Fred was free to pillage for his trouble.

All of the preparations were complete, and it was only four p.m. What to do with the rest of Saturday? He thought about calling Rebecca, but since the night before had been so perfect, he chose to let that memory last until he returned from Lakeville. He decided instead to take a walk down Broadway to Lincoln Center. *If something good's playing tonight, I'll get a ticket and catch dinner in the neighborhood before the performance,* he decided. The exercise would be a good way to channel the nervous energy that had built up in anticipation of his trip.

Walking down one of New York's major commercial streets was always a treat for Ryan. Peeking into the storefronts and restaurant windows provided a colorful texture to the land-scape. The people-watching was special as well, adding a film-like quality to his walk. The diversity of passersby provided a cast of characters of all shapes, sizes, ages, and manners of dress: a human tapestry of sorts.

When he arrived at Lincoln Center, Ryan was thrilled to find there was a ticket available for that night's performance of Dvorak's *New World Symphony* by the Philharmonic Orchestra. Even though he wasn't up to speed on most classical music, he enjoyed it and had at least heard of this symphony. He bought a ticket and headed over to a nearby restaurant, The Smith. It offered a broad range of American favorites and a seemingly endless array of cocktail options. He took a seat at the bar and ordered a Gray Goose Martini. It seemed a fitting choice as he was, after all, going to Lincoln Center for a concert. He had about an hour and a half before heading to the performance, so he took some time to savor his drink before ordering.

Ryan loved dining out in New York. Every restaurant and bar seemed to have a unique buzz all on their own. This was no exception. Young, hip, and sophisticated wrapped into one upscale package. He was seated at the bar, staring at the vast collection of beer tap handles lined up in front of him when he felt a hand on his shoulder.

"Mind if I join you?" It was Ted.

"If you promise not to talk shop," Ryan said firmly. He wondered if Ted had somehow purposely tracked him down.

"Of course. We're both off duty. What are you doing here?"

Ryan was tempted to say something snide like "Having

a drink," but he opted for, "I'm going to a concert at Lincoln Center. What are you doing here?"

"I'm meeting Brenda here shortly. She's having her hair done and this place is nearby." Brenda was his wife, a powerhouse in her own right. She headed a division of the publishing giant, Random House. They were truly a New York power couple.

Ted beckoned the bartender and ordered a single Glenlivet on the rocks, then turned to Ryan. "I promised I wouldn't talk shop, but I assume that means no discussion of your next essay. Correct?"

Ryan hesitated but then conceded. "Correct."

"Listen, I just want you to know all of us at the paper hold you in the highest regard. Your last piece drew great comments on social media, so if you ever—"

Ryan held up a hand. "Thanks, Ted. But as we discussed before, I'm very happy freelancing."

"Okay. I'll stop. How do think the Yankees will do this season?"

"I'm a Mets fan," Ryan deadpanned. They both broke out laughing.

Brenda arrived shortly thereafter, and Ted introduced her to Ryan. Ted paid for Ryan's drink along with his own and headed to a table with his wife. Ryan ordered another drink and the pot of mussels with fries for dinner. He finished both in plenty of time to take the leisurely walk to the concert hall.

As he entered the building, he couldn't help but notice the diversity of the crowd. A broad range of ages, ethnicities, and apparel choices were represented. Quite a contrast to the audiences of his parents' day and age. He found his seat in the first balcony and settled in. The drinks had mellowed him out a bit and the music took over his attention. The people seated around him were obviously regular patrons of the symphony.

They knew exactly when to *ooh* and *aah* or when to look at one another and nod. He wondered if they knew he was a one-night intruder.

The concert concluded with the customary standing ovation and bows by the conductor and musicians. As soon as the house lights went on, Ryan exited the hall onto the plaza and unmuted his cell phone. He saw he had two missed calls, each with a voicemail. The first was from Miles.

"Hey, there. Give me a call back. I have some special instructions about what you need to bring with you tomorrow." Ryan assumed he wanted a Kosher salami or something equally New Yorkish. Miles answered the call back on the first ring.

"Were you too preoccupied with your actress friend to take my call?" Miles emphasized the word "preoccupied" in mock disapproval.

"No. Turns out I missed a call from her as well. What's up?"

"I need you to pack a warm jacket and a sweater." Miles's request came without an explanation.

"What for?" Ryan wondered aloud as he pushed through the crowd and started walking up Broadway.

"We're going fishing on Monday."

"Well, that raises a whole set of questions. The usual 'who, what, where, and how' ones to start with. Enlighten me."

"I did a favor for a guy named George Willis who runs a charter fishing boat on Lake Michigan. He's offered us a couple of spots for Monday."

Ryan assumed correctly that Miles had already accepted the invitation.

"You'll love it. The lake is filled with all sorts of great fish to catch. The charters focus on three species of lake trout and two species of salmon. Some of the salmon weigh in at twenty pounds or more. They can put up quite a fight, especially this early in the season when they begin spawning. It's a fun morning."

Ryan chuckled. "When did you become such a fishing enthusiast?"

"When I did a bit of work for George. He was in some trouble not of his making. I helped him clear things up and agreed to take fishing trips in return for cash. Best deal I've made in years."

"Okay. That brings us to the 'why'. Why the cold weather gear? It's supposed to be in the sixties there."

Miles explained that in spring the water temperature of the lake is still cold from winter. It would be particularly cold a couple of miles out where they would be fishing. Any added wind and Ryan would be glad to have brought along a warm jacket.

Ryan realized he had put himself in Miles's hands for his two-week stay so he ended the call by simply saying, "Okay, then. See you tomorrow." It was fortunate he'd decided to take his largest suitcase. There would be room for the sweater and jacket Miles had recommended. Adding a hat and gloves seemed to make sense as well.

He walked into his apartment shortly after hanging up. Once inside, he called Rebecca back.

"Hot date?" she teased.

"I'd hardly call Dvoák a hot date," he replied.

"You mean the composer, don't you?"

"I was able to secure a ticket for tonight's Philharmonic performance. Just got home."

"Then I'll stop being jealous. Seriously, I called to thank you for being the perfect date last night. You helped me through my emotional distress over the whole TV show thing and, well, the other part was pretty wonderful too." The tone in her voice was noticeably relaxed, a welcoming change from the tension it contained the night before.

"Thank you for inviting me. It was a pleasure. *All of it.*" He had to stress that he wasn't just referring to the bedroom part.

She wished him safe travels and made him promise to call when he got back or, preferably, before.

Ryan promised to stay in touch. Then he went to his front hall closet to select a warm jacket to take on his trip. The down-filled ski parka was a bit much, so he opted for his fleeced-lined, full-zip hoodie and added a Columbia University sweatshirt, a pair of wool gloves, and a knit hat to round out his fishing ensemble. Fortunately, as he anticipated, there was ample room in his suitcase for all the additions.

Ryan was heading to Wisconsin knowing he would be leaving two significant relationships unresolved. The idea of continuing his work with the *Times* was certainly enticing. It paid well and he was allowed to pick his own topics. On the other hand, Ted wanted Ryan's essays to be available almost on-demand. Even as a freelancer, his time wasn't his own.

He was also conflicted over his relationship with Rebecca. It had been quite a while since his last committed relationship and, like the dilemma with the *Times*, escalating his relationship with Rebecca would certainly command his undivided attention.

CHAPTER 6

Ryan was up by seven a.m. on Sunday morning. After showering and getting dressed, he headed to the kitchen. Everything in the refrigerator that wasn't payment for Fred and wouldn't survive the two-week absence had to be thrown away. After finishing off the bottle of orange juice, a hard-boiled egg, and a piece of toast, he filled a garbage bag with the remaining perishable items.

The last few things which needed packing were added to his suitcase and shoulder bag. He decided he'd take a cab to the airport. The ride services were fine, but he felt a responsibility to use the NYC cabs from time to time. Those drivers needed to make a living, too.

Grabbing his suitcase, shoulder bag, and the sack of garbage, he headed to the street to hail a cab. No sooner had he put the garbage into the container than a cab spotted him standing on the sidewalk with his luggage. The cabbie pulled up and asked, "Where ya headed?"

"La Guardia," Ryan replied.

The cabbie, a man about sixty, leaped from his seat and ran around to open the cab's trunk. He was obviously excited to have a morning trip to the airport with the prospects of a return fare shortly after. Once the luggage was loaded, they both assumed their respective places in the cab, and were off.

"Airline?"

"Delta."

"Delta terminal. Got it. Flying somewhere exotic?"

"If you consider Milwaukee exotic."

"Always thought *Laverne and Shirley* were cute." The cabbie was tickled with his own version of New York superiority.

"That they were," Ryan replied offhandedly.

The driver turned his attention to crossing the Triborough Bridge and the mass of cars that seemed to converge from all directions. *Amazing that all of these people have someplace they need to go this early on a Sunday morning,* Ryan thought. The rest of the ride was quiet, giving him time to erase unwanted emails from his phone and check his Weather Channel app for the Lakeville forecast. Sunny with seasonal temperatures but cooler near the lake.

The new Delta terminal was a tremendous improvement over the old one. It was also the first one completed during the massive La Guardia renovation. It was a quiet Sunday at the airport, so he breezed through both the ticket counter processing and security checkpoint. His flight was set to depart at 10:45 a.m. and was posted as being on time. He had almost an hour before boarding, so he headed to the newsstand to pick up the *Sunday Times*. Back at the gate, he felt a little self-conscious sitting there reading his own essay even though no one there could have possibly realized it was his. He finished reading a couple of other articles and then packed the paper away in his bag. He'd leave it discretely somewhere in Miles's house and see if he discovered it.

The flight was short and uneventful, just over two hours from wheels up to landing. With the time zone change, it was barely an hour later local time from his New York departure time. Just enough time to read the Lakeville Examiner's series on the trial of Jack McKay, who had been framed in a child pornography case. Miles had solved the case and implicated the corrupt local political party in the process.

The airport in Milwaukee was even quieter than La Guardia had been. His suitcase was already making its way around the belt in baggage claim when he got there. He collected it and dialed Miles.

"Hi. I'm just heading out of Door Three, bags in hand."

"Great. I'll be there in a minute or two."

Ryan walked out the door from baggage claim and quickly discovered what "cooler near the lake" was all about. A stiff easterly breeze served to authenticate Miles's request that he bring some warm clothes for their day on the lake.

A moment later, Miles pulled up and popped open the trunk without getting out of his well-worn '97 Toyota Camry. Dirt and a few well-placed dents brought the seldom-used term "jalopy" to mind. Ryan hopped in and gave his old friend a hearty handshake.

"Good flight?" Miles asked.

"About as easy as they come. On time and only half full. Read the series of articles about you single-handedly bringing down the mob-like political party. Quite a feather in your cap, I'd say."

"It's certainly brought in a few new cases. Hungry?"

"Actually, yes. It's after one p.m. where I came from. What do you have in mind?"

Miles suggested a little place in Bay View that made their own sausages of all different kinds. Miles sounded particularly enthusiastic about his recommendation.

Ryan gave him a thumbs-up. Miles smiled and headed to Bay View.

They shared a brat, a hot chicken sausage, and an order of crispy fries. Between bites they caught up on the current events in each other's lives.

Ryan told him about the party he and Rebecca had attended

to celebrate her new TV show. He left out the events of the after-party at her place. The two of them had always had one unwritten rule: accounts of their respective sex lives were kept to themselves.

"That's a big deal for her," said Miles, impressed. "Her star is obviously on the rise."

"It is and she's a little insecure about the whole thing. The perception that she's carrying the show on her back is frightening for her."

"Understandably so. What's going on with your career?"

Ryan reached into his shoulder bag, retrieved the *Sunday Times*, and handed over the section containing his article.

"This is very cool. You've obviously been quite busy." Miles noted.

"I have been busy, and having the deadline behind me is a huge relief. This getaway comes at a perfect time."

"I promised you R&R and you shall have it. Our fishing expedition tomorrow will be a great change of pace for you." Miles sounded excited to share his newfound passion for fishing with his friend. He explained the fishing charters normally carry six to eight passengers, but tomorrow's trip would just be the three of them. They'd have the whole morning on the water, and with any luck, manage to catch a few fish. As a bonus, his friend George would take whatever they caught home with him and return the fish in a couple of days, all ready to eat.

"What time does our adventure begin?"

"We cast off from the dock at six a.m."

"You're kidding, right?" Ryan reacted, obviously stunned.

"Nope, that's the drill. Cast off at six a.m. and return around one p.m. Hopefully with a boatload of fish and a few tall tales in tow."

Who is this guy? Ryan wondered.

They finished their lunch and were off to Miles's house in Lakeville. Along the way, they mostly reminisced about their childhood together. Ryan provided an update on New York politics and changes in their old neighborhood. Miles went on at length about how much he loved his new hometown. He had previously shared that when his friend Mickey passed away, his daughter Bobbie allowed Miles to move into Mickey's house at the same rent he was paying in his little apartment. Miles would have to continue providing storage for some of the things Bobbie wanted to keep, and take responsibility for Mickey's dog, Molly. A great deal for all concerned, including Molly. Miles had accepted without a moment's hesitation.

Miles chose to take Highway 32, which ran along Lake Michigan instead of the Interstate. Along the way, they passed a mixture of cottage-like homes and small farms. Many of the homes had a well-used basket attached to the garage, which reminded Ryan of a scene from the movie *Hoosiers*. The farmland showed the signs of early Spring with crops barely peeking up through the soil.

As they entered the city limits, the differences between Lakeville and New York were obvious. The streets here were quiet, lined with tall trees and sturdy single-family houses set back from the street, each with a well-manicured lawn in front and a driveway that led to a garage, which explained why the streets were empty of parked cars. There were a number of people on the sidewalk enjoying an afternoon stroll, in stark contrast to the hustle and bustle of New Yorkers who always seemed to be in a huge hurry to go somewhere.

When they arrived at the house, Molly greeted them at the door and, after a quick pee in the yard, began getting to know Ryan as only a dog could. Miles showed Ryan to his room on the second floor. It was small and tidy with furniture that reminded

Ryan of his grandmother's apartment. The guest bathroom was directly across the hall with fixtures which appeared to be of the same vintage as the bedroom furniture.

After depositing his bags in the guest room, Ryan took a self-guided tour of the house. It was a well-kept Tudor with small rooms and a lot of ornate woodwork. *Miles must certainly have some form of cleaning help, given all of these dust catchers,* Ryan thought. The kitchen was also small with some dated appliances, but again, all was in order. Miles joined him in the kitchen and offered him a beer.

"It's only three o'clock, but I'm on vacation," Ryan said, accepting the offer. Miles wasn't having one.

"Why don't you take the next couple of hours to get settled and then we can discuss our plans for dinner?" suggested Miles. "We should turn in early, though. It'll be an early morning. If you'd like to get some exercise while I'm gone, feel free to grab the leash and take Molly for a walk."

"Where are you going?"

"I have to go to my office to meet a prospective client. I'll be back before dinner time."

"No wonder I'm the only one having a beer."

With that, Miles was out the door. Molly looked up at Ryan as if she had heard the suggestion about Ryan taking her for a walk. He got the message and grabbed the leash.

———

Miles's office was downtown, only a ten-minute drive away. He had opened the office as the result of an influx of new business, which grew from the notoriety he received for his work solving the McKay case. A proper office was a much more professional setting to meet with clients than his living room had been. It also provided space for him to set up his forensic lab equipment. He particularly loved the frosted glass window on the front door to the office with the words "Miles Darien Investigations" printed on it. It looked as if it was right out of a 1950s melodrama.

He managed to straighten up his desk and his lab equipment before his appointment showed up. Cora Sims was a woman in her mid-sixties, he figured. Based on her attire, he guessed she had come directly from church. He invited her to sit in the chair across the desk from him.

When she made the appointment, she mentioned needing his help to locate her daughter. Before delving into the specifics of her case, he offered her a bottle of water, which she declined.

"So, please tell me about what's been going on with your daughter."

"As I told you, I believe my daughter, Olivia, is missing because I got this in the mail." She handed him an impound notice for an automobile issued by the Chicago Police Department.

Miles looked up from the paperwork. "I assume you are the owner of the car. Correct?"

Mrs. Sims explained she had received the notification because the vehicle was registered in her name. "When my husband, Louis, passed away three years ago, I gave Olivia use of the car. She was still living at home at the time. One day, about six months later, I came home from the store and there was a note saying she was going to Chicago to look for a job and would be in touch as soon as she got settled. She hasn't been home since."

"And she took the car?"

"Yes." Cora began to tear up.

Miles offered her a tissue and continued with his questions. "When did you last hear from her?"

"She called me on my birthday, a little over a month ago. Said she was fine but was still trying to find her way. Told me not to worry, which of course I did anyway." The sadness in her voice hadn't let up.

"Do you know anything about her working in Chicago?"

"She never mentioned a job, or money for that matter, except for the insurance money."

"Insurance money?"

"Louis had her as a beneficiary in a small life insurance policy, $12,000."

"While we're on the subject of money, does Olivia have any particular training or skills which she could be using to earn a living?" Miles was looking for any possible way of tracing her.

Before answering, Mrs. Sims paused briefly to compose herself, wiping fresh tears from her eyes. "Olivia has artistic ability. Talked about art school but never went. Loves to sing. She was a nanny part-time, which I guess is a skill you can make money with."

Moments like these were the most difficult part of Miles's job. He was totally comfortable with the actual detective work he was hired to do, but he often struggled right alongside his clients as they tried to cope with the emotional turmoil their cases caused. Forcing himself to return to the clinical part of his job, he asked Mrs. Sims if she had the car's title, keys, and a recent photo of Olivia, as well as some forms of identification such as a copy of her driver's license or a social security card. She acknowledged having the photo and the car keys, and she promised to check her late husband's file cabinet to see if it contained any of the other items Miles had requested.

"Gather up what you can and bring it here tomorrow, say two o'clock?"

She nodded.

Before she left, Miles told her he'd have an attorney friend draw up a letter for her to sign, authorizing him to retrieve her car. He explained that while it may not be needed, it would be insurance for him to go to Chicago and get the car without her having to make the trip. He also asked her to bring a credit card so she could pay the fine online and receive an emailed receipt he could take to Chicago. In addition to having everything he might need, Miles wanted the opportunity to spend some time investigating in Chicago without having Mrs. Sims in tow. He'd take Ryan along to keep him company.

She agreed to meet there again the next day, made a failed attempt at a smile, and walked out.

As soon as she left, Miles called his attorney friend, Carl Rafferty.

"Hi, Miles. How are you doing? Don't tell me you're working on a Sunday." Carl was always so cheery. *Odd for a defense attorney*, Miles thought.

"I'm fine. Listen, I need your help."

"Sure. What's up?"

"I have a case where I'm trying to track down a client's adult daughter. Turns out she has a car, owned by her mother, which turned up in the Chicago Auto Pound yard. Daughter is nowhere to be found. I need you to draw up an authorization so I can retrieve the car for her and see if I can get a line on her daughter."

"Seems simple enough. When do you need it?"

"Can you meet at my office at two o'clock so she can sign it and you can notarize it?"

"Email me her name and address and I'll be there tomorrow, paperwork in hand."

"Thanks, Carl. See you tomorrow."

Miles was concerned about this case. He had a sixth sense about these things and this one had him worried. His training and experience had him translating an estranged daughter and her abandoned car into some form of foul play. For now, though, he'd turn his attention back to his house guest and their plans for dinner.

CHAPTER 7

R yan was startled by the alarm going off at 4:45 a.m. The room was pitch-dark and he was disoriented at first. Finally remembering where he was and the order of the day, he flipped on the bedside light, grabbed his clothes, and headed to the bathroom to wash up. When he finished, he started down the stairs only to be greeted by Molly heading up in the opposite direction. After he stroked her head, she let him pass.

Miles was busy in the kitchen setting out travel mugs, sweetener, and milk so they could take their coffee to go. He looked up. "There's a banana in the basket on the counter. I suggest you eat a little something before we head out onto Michi Gami. George will have lunch on board, but it'll be a good while until he brings it out."

"Michi Gami?" Ryan asked.

"Native American for 'Lake Michigan'."

Ryan wasn't hungry yet but decided to follow Miles's advice, adding a banana to his coffee carryout as they walked out the door. Lakeville was still asleep for the most part as they made the ten-minute drive through town to the marina. They arrived dockside right on time. There was George, who looked ever so much like a stevedore, unloading a cooler from his truck. Miles introduced them while they lugged all the gear to the end of the pier and loaded it all onto the vintage Christ-Craft 33 fishing vessel. George pointed out that the end slips at the marina were reserved for the commercial fishing boats, as they ventured out far more often than the pleasure cruisers.

As they left the marina, Ryan began to understand the allure of the lake. The sun, barely up over the horizon, peeked through a few wispy clouds. The reflection of its bright yellow rays on the rippling blue-green water was spectacular. Feeling ever the newbie, he pulled the phone from his pocket and snapped a few pictures.

"The beauty of the lake this time of day never gets old," said George. "Particularly when the wind is calm like this. Best part is, it's different every day," he added.

After about twenty minutes they lost sight of land. Only water and gently rolling waves in every direction. They might as well have been out in the middle of the ocean, Ryan thought. About five few minutes later, there was a pull on the line. After a short tussle, Miles skillfully reeled in the fish and brought it close enough to the boat so George could use the net to bring the good-sized steelhead trout on board. Ryan was dutifully impressed.

George attached the fish to a hand-held scale and declared, "Nice fish. Just under nine pounds. Should be good eating."

The next few hours were only mildly rewarding. Other than spotting a gigantic cargo ship in the distance, the only other activity was adding a couple of small brown trout to the fish container. George brought out three turkey sandwiches and a large bag of potato chips. There were several bottles of water and a six-pack of beer in the cooler. Ryan and Miles each grabbed a water. George, being a native Wisconsinite, opted for a Pabst Blue Ribbon.

Sure enough, as they took the first bites of the sandwiches, they were interrupted by the unmistakable whirring sound of the fishing reel giving up its line at a frantic pace. George ran to take control of the rod. Once he had it in hand, he called for Miles and Ryan to assist.

"Looks like we have something big on the hook. Which one of you wants to take on the battle?"

Miles motioned to Ryan, "It's all yours!"

"I'll hold on to it with you until you have a secure hold," George said as he extended the rod toward Ryan, who dutifully added his hands to share the grip. Once the rod was firmly in Ryan's control, George removed one hand and then the other, leaving Ryan in sole control of the equipment.

George never left Ryan's side, coaching him on when to reel in some line and when to let the fish run. The back-and-forth scuffle lasted more than fifteen minutes. Finally, their catch was close enough to the side of the boat so George and Miles could net the large fish and haul it up onto the deck while Ryan held on to the pole for dear life.

"Wow!" George exclaimed. "That's one big Chinook." He was right. The salmon weighed in at 23½ pounds.

Ryan felt a sense of having achieved a great victory. He also felt as if his arms were no longer fully functional.

Miles patted his friend on the back. "Nice work, my boy."

They spent the balance of their time on the boat finishing off their lunch and reliving Ryan's epic bout with the Chinook. Miles couldn't stop laughing at Ryan's level of exhaustion and loss of arm strength. Ryan couldn't stop smiling over his accomplishment.

Once they returned to shore and had the boat securely tied up at the dock, George asked Miles about how to divide up the day's catch.

"George, why don't you keep the three trout," Miles offered. "How about we split the salmon, provided you'll smoke it for us?"

"Good plan. I'll have a nice big filet for you by the end of the week. I'll text you when it's ready to be picked up. How about a picture?"

The two friends shared a pose, holding the enormous fish. Their triumph was now memorialized. After shaking hands with George, Miles and Ryan grabbed their gear and headed to the parking lot, leaving George to wrap up things on the boat.

Before they drove off, George shouted, "I'll email you the picture."

They got in the car, having had a wonderful morning on the water. "Miles, that was so much fun," Ryan declared. "Far exceeded my expectations. I really like George, too."

"So glad you enjoyed it. The first time I went fishing with George, I was hooked. Pun intended! Listen, when we get home I have to wash up quickly and head to the office for a short follow-up meeting with the client I met with yesterday. I'll fill you in on all the details when I get back. It will likely lead to a road trip for us tomorrow."

When Miles got to his office, Mrs. Sims was waiting outside his door with a small box in hand. Once inside, she handed him the box and then pulled a credit card from her wallet and handed that to him as well.

"Everything Louis had is in this file box along with the citation, title, and car keys."

After briefly examining the contents, he pulled out a picture of Olivia. "How current is this picture?" he asked.

"It was taken about three years ago, just before Louis died."

It was a photo of a beautiful young woman: tall, early twenties, dark brown eyes, light brown skin and a dazzling smile. He sure hoped he'd find her well and looking just like her photo. Just then, Carl arrived. Ever the fashionista, Carl showed up in a three-piece suit with a bright blue tie that matched his eyes.

Miles introduced Mrs. Sims to Carl, and they all sat at the small round table in the corner of the office. Carl explained the authorization letter to her while Miles looked over the contents of the box.

After signing the letter and then paying the impound fee online, Mrs. Sims asked if there was anything else they needed from her.

"Would it be all right if I kept the box for a few days?" Miles asked. "I'd like to examine the contents some more to see what else might be helpful."

"Of course. You'll keep me informed of your progress, I hope?" She was understandably anxious for word of her daughter.

"Absolutely. In fact, I hope to have information for you when I bring the car back to your house. It may be tomorrow evening or Wednesday morning, depending on the time I get back from Chicago," Miles promised.

"Just call me before you come by. And thank you for everything you're doing."

"Of course." Miles walked her to the door and then returned to the table to talk to Carl.

"Nice of you not to mention the main reason you're keeping the box a while," Carl noted.

"Oh, so you saw the plastic bag with the little girl's pigtail in it?" Miles was impressed with Carl's power of observation.

"I sure hope matching the DNA to a body isn't going to be needed." Carl had been around criminal investigations his entire career and knew full well the value of DNA evidence and the often unfortunate circumstances when it was needed in establishing an identity. Miles gathered up all the items he'd need for the trip to Chicago the following day. He thanked Carl for his help as they left the building together.

When Miles pulled into his driveway, he saw Ryan and Molly coming up the street from a walk. Once inside the house, Miles filled Ryan in on the details of the case. He rationalized that since Ryan was being informally deputized as a participant in the investigation, he was entitled to be fully informed. They would take the 8:35 a.m. Amtrak to Union Station in Chicago on Tuesday. An on-time arrival and a short cab ride should get them to the Auto Impound lot around ten a.m. After extricating the car from the lot, they'd head to Olivia's last known address to begin tracking her down.

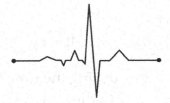

CHAPTER 8

T hankfully, the train pulled into Lakeville on time. The stop consisted of an automated kiosk which dispensed tickets and a small trackside covered platform. Once on board, Miles and Ryan each selected seats and settled in for the short ride. Miles spent the next few minutes reviewing the background information Mrs. Sims had dropped off. He hoped he might just find some clues buried in Olivia's letters and documents. His concentration was interrupted by Ryan.

"So, have you been seeing anyone?" Ryan inquired.

"Nothing significant since Robert and I split. There are plenty of options in Lakeville, believe it or not, but none have clicked recently." Miles's response was rather matter-of-fact, but there was a twinge of sadness in his voice.

"Do you have a theory on what's become of Olivia Sims?"

"Only bits and pieces so far. If she went away without her car, it's likely she took a cab or ride service to her destination. If the destination was an airport or train station, we'll have a much tougher time following her trail."

"Why would she take a cab if she was staying in town?" Ryan asked naively.

"Parking, of course," Miles said, stating what he deemed to be obvious. "If you owned a car in New York, you'd use it sparingly. Parking in a big city, even if you can find something convenient, most often costs more than the ride."

"Of course," Ryan conceded.

As they approached Chicago's outskirts, Ryan stared

intently out the window, watching the rural landscape turn into the city of Chicago, its tall buildings rapidly coming into view.

"Incredible skyline," he remarked.

"Chicago is the home of the skyscraper. The first ones were built here, not in New York as most people think."

"You should be a contestant on Jeopardy." Ryan was only half kidding.

Miles smiled and nodded. The screeching of the train's brakes meant they were pulling into the station. After a seemingly endless walk down the platform, they reached the escalator taking them to the Adams Street exit and the cab stand.

Miles instructed the cabbie, "Chicago Auto Pound, 701 North Sacramento, please."

Ten minutes later, they reached the lot which was situated adjacent to a maze of rail lines for the Metra commuter system. The noise created by dozens of trains constantly passing by was almost deafening. Once they were inside the Auto Pound office, Miles took a place in line. After about twenty minutes he reached the clerk, who was positioned behind a counter fronted by a glass partition. Miles handed the paperwork to the clerk through the slot. After a quick review of the documents, he asked Miles if he had keys to the car. Affirming that he did, the clerk handed the paperwork back and told him to wait outside for a lot attendant who would escort them to the car. Five minutes later the attendant arrived. Miles and Ryan followed him as he walked through rows and rows of impounded automobiles, finally arriving at Mrs. Sims's 2011 Ford Fusion. After signing the receipt for the car, they got in and Miles turned the key. Fortunately, the car started right up.

They made a right turn out of the lot and, using the GPS app on Ryan's phone as a guide, headed to Olivia's last known address on Wentworth Avenue, near Chinatown. There were no parking spaces on the block of Olivia's apartment, so they parked in one of the many lots used by Chinatown visitors. As they walked the three blocks back to Olivia's building, they agreed a lunch of authentic Chinese food would have to be the next order of business once they checked out the apartment.

When they approached the front door of the building, they saw a woman in the lobby retrieving her mail. They knocked on the glass, and she opened the door a crack.

"What can I do for you?" she asked politely.

"We're looking for Olivia Sims," Miles said. "Her mother hasn't heard from her in several weeks and she isn't answering her phone. Mrs. Sims is very concerned about her and asked us to see if we can find her. I'm a licensed private investigator." He showed her his badge.

She put her hands on her hips and took a moment to size up the two men before finally deciding to respond. "I haven't seen her in about two weeks. I did see the city towing her car away a week or so ago. I'm Alice Winters, the building manager. Her mail's been piling up, and I was just going to drop it off at her apartment. Under the circumstances, I guess it would be okay to let you in to look around a little."

Obviously, Miles's badge had somehow convinced Ms. Winters of the validity of his request. It wasn't okay legally, but Miles wasn't one to stand on ceremony, particularly when they needed information and this could very possibly provide some sort of important lead. Ms. Winters stood in the doorway as they looked around. Miles's experience led him directly to the bathroom. If people were leaving for any amount of time longer than for the day, there would be important items they'd take from their bathroom. Sure enough, there were no toothbrush, toothpaste, or hairbrush present. Obviously, Olivia was planning to be gone, at least overnight. Miles also noticed a picture of Olivia and her parents, which she kept on the top of her dresser indicating, at least circumstantially, that there had not been a major falling out with her family.

"Ms. Winters, do you know what Olivia did for a living?"

"Nope. Kept to herself mostly. She did often leave late in the afternoon walking. I've seen just one woman friend stop by a couple of times. Always paid her rent, occasionally a day or two late. Paid it in cash." From the tone of her voice, Ms. Winters thought paying the rent in cash was odd. It led Miles to believe that whatever Olivia did to earn money, she was paid in cash.

"How did you notice she left on foot?" Miles asked.

"Because I'd often see her head down Wentworth and leave her car parked in front of the building." Obviously, Mrs. Winters had some detective in her as well.

Ryan looked at the pile of papers on the coffee table in the living room. There were two very interesting documents there. One was a deposit slip from fifteen days ago at BMO Harris Bank for $2,500. The other was a detailed health assessment from a clinic in South Chicago. It contained details of an examination and blood tests she had undergone less than a month ago. He took a picture of both with his cell phone camera.

Finally, they looked at her unopened mail. Knowing Ms. Winters would certainly draw the line at letting them open any of the envelopes, they simply wrote down the senders' names and return addresses of two notable ones which were from what appeared to be collection agencies. Once they finished looking through the apartment, they thanked Ms. Winters and took down her phone number should they need to contact her again. Miles also left her his business card and asked her to call him if either Olivia or her friend showed up.

They left the apartment building and headed into Chinatown to pick a spot for lunch. They selected MCCB Chicago on South Archer Street, a bustling hot spot teeming with Asian customers, always a good indicator of authenticity and quality.

While they waited for their food to arrive, they went over what they had found at Olivia's place. Miles started with his hypothesis that she'd left planning to at least be gone overnight. Also, whatever she had been doing to earn cash hadn't been enough to keep her afloat, based on the collection agency letters they saw. From the $2,500 deposit into her bank account, it appeared she had found some income from somewhere, presumably to pay off a portion of those debts.

"What do you make of the information from the clinic?" Ryan asked.

"Could be routine or tied in some way to her disappearance," said Miles. "It sure would be helpful to know what the results of her tests were. I'll look into the clinic to see if they specialize in anything that might help us." The smile on Ryan's face proved to Miles that Ryan's journalist curiosity was now fully engaged and he was onboard to the end. Lunch arrived and their attention turned to the exotic Szechwan dishes they had ordered. The food was spicy and delicious. After finishing their food and an entire pot of tea, they walked back to the car.

"What now?" Ryan asked.

"I think we just head back. We may need to return at some point, but we have some research to do by phone or online back at my office. Mrs. Sims will be glad to have the car back, and knowing we didn't find any evidence of foul play at Olivia's apartment will be comforting for her."

"Could we head back through the city a little way? I've never been here before."

"Sure, we'll take Lake Shore Drive north a ways and then jump on the Kennedy Expressway after we pass through downtown." Miles had come to know Chicago well since moving to the Midwest. The city reminded him in many ways of his hometown, New York. So many wonderful things and too many not-so-wonderful things all bundled into one enormous package.

He and Robert used to come in often, sometimes to attend performances at the Lyric Opera House, usually making a night of it with dinner and an overnight stay at a nice hotel. Other times they'd make the trip solely to shop for clothes on Michigan Avenue. Miles also spent considerable time in the greater Chicago area investigating a broad range of cases. It was fascinating, he thought, how so many of his Lakeville clients' troubles had a connection to Chicago.

Driving north on Lake Shore Drive, known to the locals as the Outer Drive, they passed many of the city's most famous lakefront landmarks. Miles pointed out each one by name: Soldier Field, the Museum of Science and Industry, the Natural History Museum, the Shedd Aquarium, the Adler Planetarium and finally, Navy Pier.

"You should have been a tour guide," Ryan teased.

"It would be a fun job, but there's no money in it," Miles shot back.

They exited the Outer Drive at Fullerton and drove west to the Kennedy Expressway. They took the northbound onramp and headed back to Lakeville. A little over an hour later they pulled into Miles's driveway. As expected, Molly greeted them at the door, squealing and turning circles to show her excitement. Miles took her for a walk around the block and, when he returned, asked Ryan to play with her so he could call Mrs. Sims without interruption.

"Hi, Mrs. Sims. It's Miles Darien. We're back in Lakeville and we have your car. May we come over to drop it off?"

"Did you find out where Olivia is?" She asked hopefully.

"I'll fill you in on what we found when we get there. The good news is, we found nothing bad. We'll be there in about twenty minutes." Miles tried his best to be reassuring.

He took a few minutes to look over the day's mail and wash up before he and Ryan left to drop off the car. Miles decided to let Molly go with Ryan in the Camry. She'd been alone quite a bit the past couple of days and loved riding in the car, her head poking out of the partially open back window.

When they arrived at her house, Mrs. Sims was already anxiously waiting for them on the front porch. Miles pulled into the driveway and Ryan parked on the street. They met her on the porch and Miles handed her the keys to the Ford. After Miles introduced Ryan, he shared what little information they had come up with so far.

"Olivia's building manager was kind enough to let us into Olivia's apartment. There were absolutely no signs of foul play or any indication of trouble. The mail that had accumulated seemed to indicate she'd been gone for several days."

"Anything else?" she asked.

"That's all we have now, but we've just begun our investigation. I promise to let you know as soon as we have any important developments. One question, though. Does Olivia have any distinguishing features like tattoos or scars?"

Mrs. Sims expression turned from concern to fear. "Why? Do you think she might need to be—?"

Miles stopped her before she could finish her question. "No, not at all. Just covering all the bases." It was important to ease her mind.

"She has one tattoo that I know of. Her father's face on

her left arm. She got it at someplace downtown a month or so after Louis died." She tapped the spot on her left arm near the shoulder to demonstrate.

"Thanks. That's all for now. We'll let you know the moment we have something more definitive to share."

"Thank you both so much. Having the car back and knowing you didn't find anything scary at Olivia's is comforting. At least a little." She was obviously appreciative, but the sadness and fear in her voice spoke volumes.

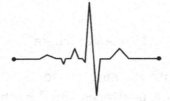

CHAPTER 9

After breakfast, the two of them headed to Miles's office to continue their investigation of Olivia Sims's disappearance. Ryan's investigative skills, while totally on the journalistic side, were still valuable in looking for information. His first task on this Wednesday morning would be to make calls to Chicago area hospitals to see if Olivia was a patient at one of them. He'd use a little subterfuge to avoid resistance searching for her name on their computer.

He'd open with: "Hi, would you kindly connect me to Olivia Sims's room, please?"

"And what is your relationship to the patient?" was the most common response.

"I'm her brother, Sidney," he'd answer.

"Let me check." After a moment, the response would typically be, "We do not have a patient here by that name."

"Sorry, I must have the wrong hospital."

This went on hospital after hospital.

While Ryan was going through the long list of Chicago area hospitals, Miles called his friend, Jim Rathburn, a pathologist at the county medical examiner's office. They had worked together on numerous cases when Miles was with the Lakeville Police Department's crime lab.

"Hi Jim, it's Miles."

"Been a long time. To what do I owe the pleasure?"

"I'm working on a missing person's case. One of the few things I have to go on is a recent medical bill. If I email you a copy, can you decipher the exam details from the CPT procedure codes? I guess I could look them up online, but I was hoping you could expand on the possibilities for me."

"Sure. Send it over. I'll buzz you back when I have some information for you. By the way, are you and Robert still together?" he asked.

"No, that ended a while back."

"Sorry to hear it. You guys seemed great together." Jim was a really nice guy and one of the more open-minded members of the department. Miles appreciated the sincere condolence.

"Thanks, Jim. I'll send the email right away."

Miles turned his attention to the local police. He could file a missing person's report, but that seldom bore fruit. A more expedient approach would be to go to the Lakeville Police Department and ask if they would check the national database on Olivia to establish if she had been recently arrested or charged with anything, or if she might be in custody somewhere. As a licensed private investigator, he felt comfortable he'd get cooperation. Besides, he still had a couple of acquaintances on the force who, like Jim, might assist him.

He grabbed his coat and notebook and was on his way out the door. "Hey, Ryan. I'm going over to the police station to see if they'll run Olivia's name through their computer system. It's tied to a national database so we may be able to get a line on her if she's been in any trouble with law enforcement. See you in a couple of hours. By the way, you're doing a great job of masquerading as 'Sidney.' Your girlfriend would surely be impressed."

Ryan responded by flashing Miles the finger before dialing the number of another hospital.

Miles headed out the door, hopped into his car, and headed to the Lakeville Police headquarters. He had walked into this building a thousand times, but it seemed strangely unfamiliar now that he was simply a citizen. So many new faces were populating the squad room. There was even a new metal detector added to the entrance way.

"Miles Darien, are you here looking to get your old job back?" Sergeant Rita Hernández teased. She was a twenty-year veteran of the force and one of the few Lakeville officers he had actually gotten along with.

"Nope. Unfortunately, I'm here investigating the disappearance of a client's daughter. I was hoping I could have someone here run a check to see if she had been arrested recently and if she might even be in custody somewhere."

"Wait one," Sergeant Hernández said as she headed over to a clerk seated at a desk in the back of the room. After a brief conversation with the clerk, she motioned for Miles to join them.

"Miles, this is Richie. He'll help you out."

"Thanks, Rita. Nice to meet you, Richie." Richie's bookish appearance was certainly befitting of his job description.

Miles briefed the clerk on Olivia Sims's personal information so he could do a proper search. "Also, please check for any Jane Does who fit her description. If you come up with one, I have a picture we could scan and send over."

"Got it. Have a seat," Richie instructed without even a glance up from his computer. "I should have something for you in a few minutes."

Miles took a seat at an empty desk and spent the next couple of minutes looking for familiar faces in the large room filled with cops. Finding none, he pulled his phone from his pocket and began checking emails and texts. The only important message he found was an email from Jim Rathburn asking him to call to go over the information on Olivia's medical bill. That would have to wait until after he had the results of the computer search. There was also a text from Anne saying Mr. Chapman had called to thank him for the information which led to the arrest of a security guard who had been the one stealing merchandise.

After about ten minutes, Richie motioned for Miles to rejoin him. "No recent arrests for Olivia Sims," Richie said. "Also, no unidentified suspects in custody. There is an unidentified body of a young African American woman at a morgue in La Grange. Give me the photo and I'll send it over to them."

"Here it is." Miles handed him the photo. "Also, let them know she has a tattoo of a man on the upper part of her left arm."

"Got it. It may take a while before they get to my email and respond. Leave me your number and I'll call you when I have something."

"Thanks, Richie." Miles handed him his business card.

As he left the station, Miles waved and said "thank you" to Rita, who was busy with one of the detectives. She waved back without looking up. Once in his car, he called Jim Rathburn.

"I've gone over the codes, and it appears that while the examination was quite routine, the bloodwork was far more extensive than what I would have expected," Jim said. "Without getting too technical, they ran several tests on liver and kidney function. Not typically called for in an otherwise healthy young person. They may have expected to find that something might be wrong with her. She would've had to have displayed some symptoms for them to explore to this extent."

"So, they were looking for a diagnosis?" Miles said.

"Or confirmation of one before planning a course of treatment."

"One more thing, Jim. Can you run a DNA test for me? I have some of her hair from a few years back." Miles wished he'd thought to bring it along.

"I thought you had a lab put together in your new office."

"I do, but I don't have what I need to do the DNA sequencing."

"Well, then drop it off and I'll run it."

Miles hated the idea of needing the DNA sequencing on Olivia. It was his job to look into all possibilities, and this one was unavoidable.

Ryan was still doing his 'Sidney' routine when Miles returned to the office. Miles sat down at his desk and opened the box Mrs. Sims had given him, taking out the plastic bag with the pigtail in it and placing it along with his notebook into the satchel he used as a briefcase. It resembled a carpet bag but with a shoulder strap. It was his favorite memento of a month spent in Costa Rica a little over three years ago after leaving his job at the police department. He'd drop off the pigtail at Jim's lab on the way home.

"Any luck with the hospitals?" Miles asked.

"Nada. I asked every single one and they all checked. No one by that name was a patient."

"Since she only used cash and didn't have a credit card, it's going to be nearly impossible to see if she booked travel," Miles lamented.

"Is there any way to see if she withdrew any cash from her bank account after making the deposit we saw on the receipt in her apartment? It did show a balance of about $2,800."

"The only chance for that is if her mom somehow has access to the account. I'll check with her to see." Miles turned his attention to new text messages on his phone. There was one from Richie at the police department. *No tattoo on the body.* Miles was relieved but not happy to still be at square one. "Good news, Ryan. The police search didn't turn up anything."

Ryan looked confused. "Why is that good news?"

"If the police did find something, it would likely have meant something bad. Like she was in big trouble with the law or even worse, deceased."

"I see your point. What now?"

"I'll call Mrs. Sims to fill her in on their progress or, unfortunately, lack of it. I also need to ask her about the bank account."

He dialed the phone. Mrs. Sims answered on the first ring.

"Have you found her?" she asked anxiously.

"Not yet, but we've eliminated some possibilities. She isn't a patient in any of the Chicago area hospitals. We also did a national police check, and she hasn't been arrested and isn't in custody and, thankfully, she's not an unidentified person in any of the area morgues. We have a lot more investigating to do, but so far we haven't uncovered anything unpleasant."

"So, you haven't really uncovered anything at all." She was obviously frustrated and growing more fearful with each dead end.

"I know how worried you are, but these investigations often take considerable time. Hopefully, you can take some comfort knowing these potential consequences have been eliminated. One avenue we're trying to pursue is the activity in her bank account. Do you have access to it?"

"I do. I'm a signer on that account." Her muffled response was a mirror of her sadness.

"If you have a deposit slip, could you go to the local BMO branch and make a small deposit into that account and ask for a printout of the last month's transactions? I'd do it for you, but it's very likely they'll only give the information to a signer on the account." Miles hoped having her help out with the bank information would give her the sense that she was doing something. Much better than sitting around the house brooding.

"I'll go there first thing in the morning and call you when I've got it."

"Thanks, see you tomorrow."

With that checked off the to-do list, he decided to call it a day at the office. He and Ryan would head to Jim's lab to drop off the hair sample, then home to tend to Molly and the comfort of a cocktail.

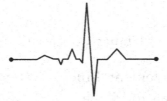

CHAPTER 10

After a long day working followed by an evening of reminiscing over cocktails and leftovers, Miles and Ryan decided to turn in early. When they met the next morning at the breakfast table, Ryan was already prepared with a few new questions.

"I suppose there are many ways to earn a living paid in cash. Doesn't leave much of a paper trail, does it?"

Miles set down his empty cereal bowl. "There are a few things we can try. If she's singing at clubs or bars, we can check out those places. Chicago has hundreds. The nanny angle, like cleaning help, will be tough to crack without uncovering some direct evidence of a connection. Artists can make money in a number of ways from painting signs to becoming a tattoo artist. If she works in a massage parlor or another sex worker job, it'll be difficult to find her unless she advertises. Besides, with her clean arrest record, that possibility is quite unlikely. Sometimes catering companies hire part-time wait staff and pay them cash. Again, numerous possibilities."

"Where do we begin?"

"Good question. Before we go bar hopping and checking out massage parlors, let's see if we can find a clue that helps narrow the search. If we can find what she was doing, then we can look into where she might be doing it. The bank statement Mrs. Sims is getting us will likely only confirm our supposition that she's in 'cash only' mode."

Their conversation was interrupted by a call from Mrs. Sims.

She had the bank statement. Miles told her they'd pick up the statement on the way to his office. She was leaving soon and offered to leave the statement in her mailbox.

Just before they left the house, Miles received an email from Jim including the DNA information, which would really only be helpful if it were needed for the positive identification of a body. They first stopped to pick up the bank statement, then headed to Jim's office to pick up the pigtail. When they arrived, Miles first introduced Ryan to Jim, who was seated at a large white table full of surgical instruments, test tubes, and a microscope. He stood up, all six-foot-six of him, and acknowledged Ryan with a handshake.

"Nice to meet you," Jim said as he handed the plastic bag with the pigtail back to Miles.

"Jim, I really appreciate your doing this for me. Did you find anything unusual in the DNA?"

"You're welcome. The DNA was very straightforward with nothing that could be tied to her genetic background. Do you think the information on the blood tests will lead you any-where?"

"Don't know yet. Unfortunately, it only creates more questions that need answering. Thanks again."

Miles left Jim's office feeling like they hadn't really accomplished anything, so he decided to go back to his office to pursue other leads.

Once back at the office, the first order of business was to examine the bank statement. As suspected, it contained several entries for small cash deposits during the month as well as the larger one for $2,500. Interestingly, it was a check that was deposited. If they could determine who issued the check, they'd have a concrete lead. Hopefully, Mrs. Sims could get the bank to give her the check information over the phone or even send her an image of the canceled check. Assuming she was still at her hair appointment, he decided to call her in a couple of hours.

"Do you think she might be pursuing a career as a tattoo artist?" Ryan offered.

"What's your theory?" asked Miles, looking for an explanation.

"She's an artist. She has a tattoo. She was paid for whatever work she did in cash. Why not look into a tattoo parlor apprenticeship or something along those lines?"

"We don't have anything more solid to go on at the moment." Miles was impressed with Ryan's reasoning, even if it was a stretch. "Why don't you check with the local tattoo places in town and see if you can find the one Olivia went to. If you're successful, see if they remember her showing a particular interest in tattooing as an art form. If you can establish that, we'll have something in that line of work to pursue further."

"I think I should take a copy of the picture of her when I visit some of the shops. I'll look for their locations online and then see if they've been in business long enough to have been her place." Ryan's investigative skills were coming in handy.

"Good plan. The keys to the car are in my jacket pocket when you're ready to leave." Miles handed Ryan his private investigator's badge. "Flashing this might help you convince people you're legit." Just then, his cell phone rang. It was Bobbie Martin, the woman who owned his house.

"Are you calling to let me know you're kicking me out?" Miles said with tongue in cheek.

"I'd do that in writing if it were the case," teased Bobbie. "I'm a lawyer, you know. Actually, I have a deposition in Lakeville at one o'clock tomorrow and thought I'd stop by to see you and collect a couple of things from the basement."

"I'd like that. You could join Ryan and me for dinner if you'd like."

"Who's Ryan? Your new boyfriend?"

Miles quickly clarified his status. "Ryan's my best friend who's here visiting from New York. By the way, he's much more your type than mine. Speaking of types, have you heard from Jack recently?"

"We talk from time to time," she said. "Nothing's happening there romantically if that's what you're asking." Miles detected definite disappointment in her answer.

"So, dinner?"

"Sure, I'll stop by after the deposition."

"If we're not there, just let yourself in. I assume you still have your key. Molly will be so happy to see you."

Ryan had finished researching tattoo parlor locations. He was taking the car keys from Miles's jacket and was about to leave as Miles finished his call with Bobbie.

"As long as you're heading out with the car, please fill up the tank. The gas gauge isn't working properly, and I don't want you to run out of gas. I'll reimburse you when you get back."

Ryan laughed, shook his head, and waved as he walked out the door.

Ryan's first three inquiries were not only dead ends, but the people were downright hostile. He had the distinct feeling the badge had turned them off. "No more badge flashing," he decided.

The fourth place, Pinky's Artistic Tattoo, bore fruit. The place was very small and dark with the customary tattoo options displayed on all the walls. The guy behind the counter, who he assumed was Pinky, acknowledged having done the tattoo on Olivia's arm.

"Nice gal. I remember her well. She was real emotional about the ink being a proper likeness of her dad and spent a lot of time admiring the pictures of our handiwork before deciding to go for it. Seemed to have a real artistic point of view. Wanted to understand the process. Hope you find her."

Ryan was elated he had uncovered a lead. It was entirely plausible that Olivia could be working part-time at a tattoo parlor and very possibly be off the books for cash. After stopping for gas, he headed back to the office, quite proud of his work.

Miles looked up from his computer as Ryan walked into the office.

"Got some gas. It took eleven gallons." Ryan decided to wait a moment before sharing his success.

"Nothing at the tattoo parlors?"

Ryan handed the badge back and said, "This was no help. It only seemed to antagonize people. Anyway, I scored some valuable information at the fourth place I stopped." He went on to relay the conversation he'd had at Pinky's.

Miles congratulated him on the news. "Your theory may well prove to be a sound concept to pursue. Unfortunately, there are likely hundreds of tattoo places in Chicago. It'll likely take us days there to find the right one, if there is a right one. Not sure Mrs. Sims could afford it on top of my fee. Any ideas for narrowing the search?"

"Well, for starters, we could assume the place is within walking distance of the apartment. With her being cash-strapped, Olivia wouldn't be too keen on paying to park or for transportation," Ryan theorized.

"Taking the bus wouldn't be that costly for her, but I think working her neighborhood makes sense as a starting point. It could be handled in a one-day trip so Mrs. Sims could likely handle that cost. By the way, you're pretty good at this." Miles gave Ryan an approving wink.

Ryan reminded his friend that detective work was not at all far afield from his investigative reporting work. Miles nodded and proceeded to call Mrs. Sims to ask her to return to the bank to request an image of the check. He also asked her to approve an additional day in Chicago investigating. She agreed to find out what she could about the check from the bank. She also gave Miles the green light for a second day trip to Chicago. Once that was approved, he instructed Ryan to compile a list of the names and addresses of tattoo parlors within a mile or so of Olivia's apartment. They would stop there first to see if Ms. Winters had seen or heard anything new.

"I have some other stuff to take care of on another case here tomorrow," said Miles. "Then we're getting together with Bobbie tomorrow evening. We could head to Chicago the day after tomorrow. I'm sorry that you're spending so much of your vacation working on a case rather than relaxing and having fun."

"This is fun for me," said Ryan. "Hanging out with you and trying to find Olivia is a great adventure, which I hope will turn out to have a happy ending. Besides, relaxing is overrated. What's the other case all about, the one you're working on tomorrow?" Ryan was really getting into his role as a private investigator.

"It's for a divorce. The lawyer who hired me wants to find out if his client's husband is having an affair. Not my favorite type of sleuthing, but these cases help pay the bills. I hate to leave you home all day without a car."

Ryan thought for a moment. "Do you own a set of golf clubs?"

"There's a set of Mickey's old clubs in the basement you could use."

"Perfect. We passed a nice looking course on the way back from the train stop. I'll take an Uber there and back. Golf, fishing, and a missing person's investigation all on the same vacation. You really know how to show a guy a good time!" Ryan obviously wasn't being sarcastic. This was apparently just what the doctor ordered.

After about an hour, they agreed to call it a day and head back to Miles's house. A quiet dinner and a couple of beers would be just the right reward for the day's accomplishments.

CHAPTER 11

Ryan immediately saw that Miles was right when he called Mickey's golf clubs old. When Ryan discovered them in the corner of the basement, they were covered with dust. After wiping them off, he discovered they were a set of original Ping Eye2 irons from the early 1980s. They were in decent enough shape to be usable, and so were the driver and putter. He'd buy some golf balls and a glove at the course.

He brought the clubs upstairs, set them by the back door, and joined Miles in the kitchen for breakfast. Miles was pouring the remaining contents of a milk carton down the drain and apologized that they would have to drink their coffee black today. At least the bread was still fresh so there was something to eat. Miles promised to stop by the store later to refresh the pantry.

"Coffee's fine," Ryan said. "If I get hungry there's likely to be a snack bar at the golf course. As long as you get milk, we should be okay. Unless you want us to cook one night or have something to serve your landlord when she comes over tomorrow night."

"Almost forgot about that," said Miles. "I'll pick up some cheese and crackers or something else to serve. By the way, I'd be happy to drop you at the course on my way to the office."

"Thanks. How long before you're ready to take off?" Ryan asked.

"Half hour work for you?"

Ryan gave him a thumbs-up, finished his coffee, and headed back upstairs to grab his wallet, phone, and the house key.

"You're starting to look at home here," Miles commented. "Even Molly accepts you as part of the place." Ryan acknowledged Miles was right. Molly no longer followed him around wherever he went or continually nudged him to pet her.

Once outside, Ryan dropped the golf clubs into the trunk of the car, and they were off. The ride to the golf course was only about fifteen minutes. The course was one of the many high-quality public ones operated by local communities in Wisconsin. Most generated enough revenue to be self-sustaining. Besides providing a recreation for the locals and visitors, the courses employed a good number of area residents. As they approached, Ryan marveled at how green it all was. In spring, the grass was a glowing green that matched the leaves, which had just made their debut on the trees lining the fairways.

"Thanks for the ride," Ryan said as he closed the trunk.

"What, no tip?" Miles replied.

Ryan flashed him the finger and headed towards the clubhouse.

After leaving Ryan at the golf course, Miles was off to get the goods on an adulterous husband. He was glad that Ryan had taken the opportunity to do another vacation activity on his visit, particularly since the search for Olivia Sims was likely to intensify. This investigation was soon going to become all consuming, and he didn't want to completely spoil his friend's trip.

His first stop was at the office to check the mail, pay a couple of bills online, and plot his strategy for catching the cheating husband in the act. As he climbed the steps to the second floor, he was surprised to find Mrs. Sims pacing in front of his office door.

"Good morning, Mrs. Sims. I'm glad I decided to stop by the office first thing, or we would have missed each other."

"I think I've found Olivia alive." She was ecstatic.

"That's great. Did she contact you?"

"Not exactly. I went to the bank to get a copy of the check, like you asked. Thought it would be a good idea to also get another current statement. There was a $50 ATM withdrawal on the statement from two days ago. Must have been her." There was real hope in her voice, a welcome change from the worried tone she'd had on previous visits.

"Let's hope so," said Miles. "While there's always a chance someone else had the card and the pin number, we'll assume for the moment it was Olivia. May I see the statement and a copy of the check?"

"Of course." She handed over the papers.

Miles first looked at the copy of the check and realized it wasn't going to be helpful. It was a cashier's check, with only the name of the bank and the payee as identifiers. He turned his attention to the ATM entry. The withdrawal was made at the same South Wabash Avenue branch Olivia had used for her other in-person transactions. This was certainly a positive development.

"This ATM entry is good news," he told her. "It likely means Olivia, or whomever she gave her card to, is staying in the neighborhood of her apartment. As we discussed, Ryan and I are planning to head back to Chicago tomorrow to continue our investigation, and this gives us another lead to run down." Miles was doing his best to be encouraging even though the fact that she apparently hadn't been staying at her apartment did not bode well. He hoped she was in a relationship and happily living elsewhere.

"You'll call me as soon as you have something," said Ms. Sims. It was a statement, not a question.

"Of course," Miles said, offering her his hand.

She smiled, shook his hand, and turned to leave. Miles thought he heard her whispering a song as she left. Now they at least had a little something positive to go on. It appeared that Olivia's life, if she still had one, was focused in a relatively small area, which would narrow their search considerably. Miles figured he could have Ryan focus on the tattoo parlor search while he'd return to her building to talk to Ms. Winters and, if permitted, do a more thorough search of the apartment.

Today, however, he'd be focusing on the divorce case involving Claire and Sidney Hansen. On behalf of his client, Claire, he headed over to Sidney's office to await his departure for lunch. A noontime rendezvous would surely jumpstart his investigation and likely lead to its rapid conclusion. Unfortunately, on this day the husband left his office with two other men. They headed two blocks down Thompson Street to a café. About an hour later, he saw them leave the café together and head back to the office. He sensed this one was going to take a while.

Ryan said goodbye to the three older gentleman he had been paired with at the golf course. He was surprised by how well he played, considering it had been quite some time since he his last round, and pleased with how friendly his playing partners had been. Golf was like that most of the time, particularly when paired with people who simply enjoyed the having-fun part of the game.

"You headed back into Lakeville?" asked Rick, one of his playing partners.

"Yep. Just about to call an Uber."

"What part of town?"

"Point Ridge."

"Perfect. It's on my way. I'll drop you off." Rick waved to Ryan to bring his clubs over to the car.

"This is very kind of you."

"Not at all. I'm excited to have a one-on-one conversation with someone who's been published in the *Times*."

Ryan could have been knocked over with a feather. He hadn't mentioned the *Times* during the round, so Rick must have actually read his article. He was immediately embarrassed by his assumption that this older man from small-town Wisconsin hadn't read it. This trip had become a real learning experience in so many ways.

On the way to the house, they chatted about his article, national politics, golf, and the world at large. It turned out Rick was a retired teacher with a collection of a wide range of interests he continued to pursue. Ryan took his number and promised to call if another golf date fit into his vacation schedule. When they pulled into Miles's driveway, there was a car parked there. Ryan assumed correctly that it was Bobbie's.

Ryan grabbed the clubs, thanked Rick for the round and the ride, and walked through the back door. Molly came running and accompanied him down the basement stairs. After returning the golf clubs to their familiar resting place, he headed back upstairs to introduce himself to Bobbie, who was sitting on the couch in the living room reading emails on her phone. She was dressed in a stylish business suit that befit her role as a successful lawyer and having come from an important meeting.

"Hi, I'm Ryan Duffy."

She looked up and smiled. "Nice to meet you, I'm Bobbie Martin." She stood up and held out her hand. It was then that he noticed how attractive she was.

"If you'll excuse me, I'm going to head upstairs to wash off the golf course residue. Thanks for lending the clubs, by the way." Not only did he need to rid himself of the remnants of the round, he wanted to look presentable for the very attractive woman he'd just met.

"Glad they were put to good use," she said as he disappeared up the steps.

Ryan returned freshly washed and in a clean shirt and jeans. He sat down on the leather armchair across from the couch. "Miles told me all about your work on the McKay case. Impressive!"

"Thanks, but the fact my client was innocent, and Miles got the goods on the bad guys, made my job pretty easy," Bobbie said, deflecting the praise. "By the way, you're pretty praiseworthy yourself. I found your article on the coffee table and just finished reading it. You portrayed both sides as well-meaning which, given the circumstances, is hard to do. And most exposés I read fall short of uncovering or offering solutions. But you did so quite thoughtfully."

"Very kind of you. Am I blushing?" he said playfully.

"We Irish blush easily, don't we?" Bobbie replied. Her strawberry-blonde hair and green eyes provided further evidence of her heritage.

Just then Molly starting barking and ran to the door. Miles had come home. Once he saw Bobbie, he gave her a big hug. After joining her on the couch, he filled her in on the case he and Ryan had been working on and then added today's revelation about the ATM withdrawal.

"I hope you're planning to stay for dinner," Miles implored her.

"Sure, but not too late. I have a ninety-minute drive back to Madison."

"Why not stay over and drive back in the morning? I know you love Italian wines, and I have a superb Amarone in the cellar. It will go beautifully with a carryout from Scarfido's."

"How can I say no to Amarone and Scarfido's?" she asked, not needing an answer.

"One condition," Ryan said. "I'm buying the food." He wasn't going to take no for an answer.

After another hour of small talk, they got down to the business of ordering dinner. Following intense negotiations, they agreed to share an order of spaghetti and a pizza. After Miles called in the order, Ryan got directions to the restaurant and took off.

As soon as Ryan was out the door, Miles could see Bobbie had questions. After giving her the abridged version of the boys' history together, he gave her the nod to begin her questioning.

"Is he in a relationship?"

"Not really a relationship," Miles answered coyly.

"What does that mean?"

"Well, he has a fuck buddy," Miles said matter-of-factly.

"I hate that expression," she scolded, giving him the evil eye as punctuation.

"What do you prefer?" Miles was enjoying the sparring.

"How about a passionate companion?" she offered.

Miles broke out laughing. "Call it what you will, bottom

line is they get together primarily for sex. Sometimes a meal or another form of entertainment, sure, but the main objective is physical gratification. By the way, you seem interested beyond just curiosity."

Bobbie smiled and nodded her head, apparently accepting the explanation. "He seems very nice and he's kinda cute. Have you met his 'companion'?"

"No, but I've read about her and seen pictures. She's an actress. Been in a lot of notable stuff, Broadway, TV, movies and so on."

"Is she beautiful?"

"Yes, with a most exotic look."

When Bobbie concluded her line of questioning, Miles could see there was a definite attraction, but it was plain to him that even putting aside the competition, there was really no future for her in pursuing anything beyond a friend-of-a-friend relationship. Chalk up another potential relationship discarded due to incompatible geography.

Miles opened the door for Ryan when he arrived with the food a few minutes later. Over dinner, he and Ryan took turns telling funny stories about their childhood exploits. At least they thought the stories were funny. Miles told Bobbie he was really glad she had decided to stay and be a part of the reunion. They all had to get moving early the next day, so they reluctantly called it a night around ten p.m. Before turning in, Miles stopped by Ryan's room for a brief chat.

"Listen," he said in a concerned tone. "It appears to me that the Sims's case is about to become a full-time investigation for me. I hate that your vacation time is being interrupted by it. Please feel free to do whatever you want for the rest of your time here. You are under no obligation to continue helping out."

Ryan smiled. "Miles, helping you find Olivia Sims would

be, by far, the best possible way for me to spend the balance of my time here. Count me in full-throttle until I have to get back to New York." He replied, offering Miles his hand.

"Welcome aboard! I have a feeling it's going to be an interesting ride."

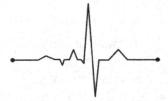

CHAPTER 12

T he next morning Bobbie said a quick goodbye and was on her way before seven a.m. Ryan hoped he'd get the chance to see her again. He and Miles took their time before leaving. No sense being included in hordes of commuters fighting the rush-hour traffic they would encounter heading into downtown Chicago, even on a Saturday morning. Since he had some time before they departed, Ryan decided to check in with Rebecca.

"Good morning. How are things in the Heartland?" Rebecca's voice was cheery. Ryan hoped that meant her anxiousness over the responsibility of carrying her new show had passed.

"I'm having a fun adventure."

"An adventure?" She seemed surprised.

"I'm helping my friend Miles with a case. Trying to locate a woman whose mom suspects is missing and in trouble."

"Aren't the cops supposed to do that?"

"Sure, but there is a limit to what they can or will do as far as devoting resources to a missing person's investigation when the missing person is an adult and no foul play is indicated. That's where Miles comes in. I'm simply along for the ride, so to speak." He was being modest knowing full well he was doing more than simply being along for the ride. "And how are you doing?"

Rebecca sighed. "I'm still learning my character, but I've been rehearsing with my drama coach and I'm getting there." There was definitely a newfound confidence in her voice, a marked change from the last time they spoke.

"Glad to hear it. I was sure once you really got into it, you'd be fine. I miss you, by the way." By breaking their no-strings-attached rule, Ryan knew he might be skating on thin ice with that admission.

She paused for a moment before responding. "I miss you, too." Her reply was a welcome surprise.

He decided this was a perfect time to sign off while the positive vibes were still floating between them. "Glad all's well. I'll call again soon."

"Please do," she said before hanging up.

Ryan had to believe something was changing in their relationship. He wondered if that's what he wanted or if he was simply lonely for their passionate companionship. He laughed to himself at the term. Bobbie would certainly approve of his use of the revised terminology she had shared with Miles.

Miles was ready to go so they packed up their briefcases, grabbed a couple of water bottles, and took off for Chicago in search of Olivia Sims. Given Ms. Winters's observation that Olivia went to work on foot, they'd begin their search of tattoo parlors and bars in her neighborhood and expand from there if need be.

The ride to Chicago in Miles's car provided quite a different scenery from what they'd discovered on the train. The train ride had sort of a pastoral feel with quiet farmland and suburban neighborhoods rolling by. By car, they were surrounded by concrete roads, shopping malls, factories, and office complexes. Even an amusement park. The Chicago skyline also seemed to Ryan to be even more imposing as they approached the junction of the Edens and Kennedy Expressways.

Once they made their way through town and arrived on the

South Side, their first stop was a tattoo parlor on West Cermak Road. Ryan grabbed his briefcase and hopped out of the car. Before Miles drove off, they agreed that unless one of them were on to something, they'd plan to meet up again around lunch time.

Miles was able to find a parking space close by Olivia's apartment building. As he approached, he called Ms. Winters to let her know he'd be there shortly. He had called the day before to alert her of his plan to visit and to be sure she'd let him into Olivia's apartment. She was waiting for him at the door when he arrived.

"Hi. I really appreciate your help."

"No problem. Olivia's a nice young lady, and if she's in trouble I'd like to help out in any way I can." She seemed much more at ease with Miles this time.

He headed to Olivia's apartment. After letting him in, Ms. Winters said goodbye. He was pleased she wasn't going to wait around to watch over him while he hunted for clues. Before she left, Miles promised her he'd lock up when he was finished and to let her know if he uncovered any significant developments in the search for Olivia.

On his last visit, he had noted a few of her missing toiletries. A second look in the bathroom yielded nothing else that would be helpful. He shifted his attention to the bedroom. Since the closet had only one empty hanger and her underwear drawer was nearly full, Olivia had, by all account, only planned to be gone a short time.

The kitchen was clean with nothing unusual in the cupboards or refrigerator. The living room yielded one helpful bit of potentially significant evidence. There was a computer charger and cord still plugged into the wall with no computer in sight. It was either an oversight, or Olivia had left without expecting to be gone long enough for the computer to need recharging. The computer could also have been picked up by a friend who simply forgot the charger.

Once he examined the new mail that had accumulated since the last visit and finding nothing useful, he decided to check in with Ryan over the phone.

"Any luck?" Miles asked.

"Not really. My first stop was IlluminInk. The storefront operation was small, but clean and tidy with bright lighting and colorful tattoo artwork covering the walls, a welcoming environment in light of what I suspect is painful work done there. The proprietor, Victor, was accommodating and didn't recall ever seeing or talking to Olivia. He did offer the names of some other operations that might pay part-time help in cash. I pressed on using the suggestions Victor had given me as a guide. I've been to three of them so far without a nibble. Did you find anything?"

Miles filled him in on his findings, scant as they were. He suggested they meet at a Greek diner he'd passed after dropping Ryan off earlier in the day. When Miles arrived there, Ryan was already seated in a booth poring over the seemingly endless list of menu items.

"What looks good?"

"Can't decide between the chicken tetrazzini or the chorizo frittata or the Greek salad with gyro meat."

"Sounds like a tall task," said Miles sarcastically.

Ryan handed him the menu. "Here. Your turn to be confused."

The waitress arrived, order pad in hand. Ryan decided on the Greek salad and Miles chose beef stew. Those monumental decisions out of way, they began strategizing their afternoon.

Ryan would continue his tour of the neighborhood tattoo parlors while Miles decided to pursue a whole new possibility.

"Remember when her mom said she loved to sing? Well, I know this is a long shot, but maybe she was working for tips at one of the neighborhood bars that feature live entertainment." Miles thought it might be a stretch, but it was a something he could easily pursue while they were working the neighborhood.

"Could be worth checking out. Have you given up on the sex worker angle?"

"Not entirely, but since she's had no issues with law enforcement, it's down on my list of possibilities. We may get there, but let's run the other options to the ground first. Come to think of it, I need to spend some time tomorrow pursuing a possibly adulterous husband. While I'm doing that, you could spend some time checking online ads for Chicago-area escorts. Perfect job for a well-respected investigative journalist from the *Times*."

Ryan accepted the challenge with a sardonic smile. Now that each of them had their next steps planned, they could concentrate on the lunch the waitress was about to put on the table.

When they finished eating, they agreed to meet up at Olivia's apartment in a couple of hours to compare notes.

Ryan started back down his list of tattoo parlors. He found the lead he was looking for at his second stop. The owner explained that Olivia had worked there from time to time and, after an assurance from Ryan he was not with the police or other law enforcement agency, the man reluctantly admitted Olivia had been paid in cash. He was confused as to why she hadn't been in for a couple of weeks since she recently told him about her need for some "serious money." Ryan had accomplished about all he could expect from exploring tattoo parlors and called Miles.

"Find anything?" Miles asked.

"Yes, but not much. Found a place where she worked and was paid in cash. The owner said she admitted to needing, and I quote, 'some serious money.' He hasn't seen her in about two weeks. Seems strange she would have stopped working if she needed money so badly."

"I suspect she decided to find a better way to get that serious money. Now that we have the tattoo angle covered, why don't you join me? I'm on the corner of Canal Street and Archer Avenue."

"Turns out I'm on Archer Avenue a couple of blocks from you. Be right there."

About five minutes later the two men were walking into Jake's Jazz Bar. It was one of a few places Miles had uncovered in the neighborhood that featured live music at night. The bar had just opened when they walked in. The place was dark and virtually empty. It had an unmistakable stale-beer smell, which further added to its rather creepy atmosphere. They headed to the bar to talk to the bartender who was busy restocking the beer cooler behind the counter. He turned to greet them.

"What can I do you for?"

Noticing a familiar tap handle behind the bar, Miles responded, "Two Lagunitas IPAs, please."

Ryan threw a $20 bill on the bar to cover the drinks. Once they had been served, Miles approached the subject of Olivia with the bartender.

"Do you know a singer named Olivia Sims?"

"Sure. She works here occasionally. Why do you ask?"

"We're looking for backup singers for a band we represent." Miles thought a little subterfuge might get them more information. "Do you know how we might get in touch with her?"

"I don't, but our other bartender might. They're friends."

"When will the other bartender arrive."

The bartender looked at the clock, which read 4:15. "She'll be here in about forty-five minutes. Gives you time for a couple more beers," he said with a smile.

Perfect timing, Miles thought. No reason to head back to Lakeville much before seven o'clock, as that timing would allow them to avoid the bulk of Chicago's brutal northbound rush-hour traffic. Besides, a couple of beers seemed like the perfect reward for having made some meaningful progress in their investigation.

They spent the few minutes before the new bartender would arrive reminiscing about their childhood. They laughed out loud over the time they hid all of Ryan's sister's bras so she didn't have one to wear to school the next day, knowing full well one borrowed from her mom would not fit at all. Or the time Miles created a distraction so Ryan could steal the new *Watchmen* comic book from Winkle's Drug Store. This could have gone on for hours but they were interrupted.

"Sammy said you're looking to hire Olivia." Apparently this attractive young woman with short-cropped hair and a collage of tattoos and piercings was the new bartender and friend of Olivia.

"Yes, we'd like to talk to her. And you are ...?" Miles replied, trying not to tip his hand.

"I'm Janine Banner. Olivia's been a little under the weather.

Can I have her call you in a day or two when she's feeling a little better?"

Miles sensed Janine was hiding something and decided to probe. "Listen, Janine. We're actually here on behalf of her mother. Olivia's car was impounded and she's nowhere to be found. Her mom is beside herself with worry. We're not cops, just a couple of friends trying to help." Miles was hoping his sincere concern would get Janine to open up.

She looked stunned but gathered herself quickly. "Maybe she doesn't want to be 'found.'"

Miles was right about Janine hiding something. Now he needed to convince her to let them help Olivia. "If she's in trouble, maybe we can help her. What can we do to get you to trust us? Her mom is willing to do anything she can for her daughter, and we're here on her behalf to do whatever is necessary to secure Olivia's safe return."

Janine just stared at Miles, obviously deep in thought. Suddenly, she broke down. Tears started flowing out of her eyes like rivers. "She's at my place and really sick. I don't think I can take care of her much longer. She needs help."

"What sort of sick?" Miles asked.

Janine gathered herself. "I'd better let her fill you in on that. I'll take you to her after my shift."

The guys passed the remaining time on Janine's shift drinking Diet Coke and listening to the jazz quartet performing on the bar's small stage. It would be a long night and the caffeine would come in handy. Her shift ended at two a.m.

The neighborhood was still lively as the bars emptied out. It had been years since Miles left a bar at closing time. Looking around at all the young faces, it was clear why. His bar-closing days had long passed.

Miles showed Janine his car keys, indicating there was no need to hail a cab. They walked two blocks to the car, and Janine got into the front passenger seat and directed Miles to head west on Cermak. They crossed the Chicago River and were soon in Cicero. They turned down a side street and, after a few blocks, Janine signaled for them to park. Even in the darkness, the area looked downtrodden.

Janine led them into her apartment building. Given the early morning hour, the halls were quiet and uninhabited. When they entered the small apartment, they saw Olivia sleeping on the couch. The apartment was warm, but she was covered in a heavy blanket. Janine flipped on a small lamp in the corner of the room and walked over to her friend.

"Olivia," Janine said, gently touching Olivia's shoulder. Only a groan came out. "Olivia, this man is there to help you."

Miles approached slowly and spoke softly. "Hi, Olivia. I'm Miles Darien, a friend of your mom's. She asked us to find you and bring you home to Lakeville."

Olivia was awake now but barely able to speak. Her face was ashen and her limbs were limp and motionless. The beads of sweat on her brow were telltale signs of a high fever. She stared at Janine, looking angry at first. She had, after all, been discovered by her mother's hired hands. But then she sighed and looked almost relieved.

"Tell them," was all Olivia said.

Janine motioned for them to sit, and each of them took a spot around the dining table, leaving Olivia to remain on the couch.

"Olivia needed a substantial amount of money, both to cover

her existing debts and to enroll in art school. Her goal is to be a graphic artist. She didn't want to take money from her mother, who's living on modest savings and social security. Her bank wouldn't help. She had no real collateral. The loan companies, you know the paycheck-type ones, turned her down. She didn't know where to turn until she got a call."

Olivia then spoke up in a whisper. "A guy said he'd heard I needed money and he could help. They offered $15,000 with my—" She couldn't finish the sentence.

Janine finished it for her. "Her kidney as collateral."

Miles and Ryan looked at each other in disbelief. How could this young woman be so desperate as to give up her kidney to pay a debt?

"Has she had any postoperative medical attention?" Miles asked, addressing her obvious need.

"Not since they released her."

"Why not?"

"Let's just say these were some bad people. She knew she had no way to pay back the loan, so she told them to just take the kidney and give her the money. They've withheld the bulk of it for thirty days to make sure she doesn't alert the authorities, which includes not going to a hospital and having them ask questions about what happened." Janine's eyes were filled with anger as she spoke.

Olivia spoke again, this time with some newfound strength in her voice. "They said they'd kill me."

"We need to get her to a doctor. Now!" Miles was more than emphatic.

"They've convinced her that any medical help around here would tip them off. We can't risk it." Janine obviously believed the danger from these people was real.

After a momentary pause, Miles offered an alternative.

"Let's take her to Lakeville. I have resources there who can provide her the medical care she needs while we keep her off of the bad guys' radar."

Ryan smiled at Olivia in endorsement of the plan.

Olivia nodded her approval, which set the wheels in motion. Janine, obviously relieved, packed up Olivia's things while Ryan carried her to the car. Janine gave her friend a kiss on the forehead, then gave a pillow and blanket to Ryan and Miles to help make Olivia as comfortable as possible in the back seat. Almost as soon as they had secured Olivia's seat belt, she dozed off. Miles and Ryan climbed into the front seat and they headed off to Lakeville without speaking.

At that time of night, there was no traffic to impede their progress. In an hour and a half they'd be in Lakeville. Miles selected some soft music on the radio to help everyone relax a little. Even though it was a little past four o'clock in the morning, he knew he'd soon have to call Mrs. Sims. Miles decided to postpone the call for a little while so they wouldn't disturb Olivia, who was now sound asleep.

After thirty minutes or so, he knew he just had to call Mrs. Sims.

"Hello?" she answered, barely awake.

"Mrs. Sims, it's Miles. We have Olivia with us and we're bringing her home to you."

"Oh my God!" she yelled, obviously overjoyed by the news.

Miles waited a few moments to allow her to calm down before continuing. "Listen, she's very sick and will need medical care, but she's alive. We should be there in a little over an hour."

"Can I speak to her?" Mrs. Sims begged.

"You have been. I had the phone on speaker. She's too weak to talk but she heard you and is smiling."

"I love you, honey. Mama's going to take care of you."

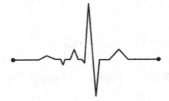

CHAPTER 13

After Olivia's tearful reunion with her mother, the two men went back to Miles's house to sleep for a couple of hours. Miles woke up around seven a.m. and immediately called Jim Rathburn. He apologized for calling so early on a Sunday morning but needed to ask Jim for a huge favor. He explained that they'd found Olivia but she was in a most tenuous medical state. She was currently at her mother's but needed professional care.

"Why haven't you taken her to the hospital?" Jim said.

"It's like this," Miles explained. "She was desperate for money, so when a loan shark offered her the money she needed in exchange for one of her kidneys, she took the deal even though she knew it was likely against the law. Now she's deathly afraid that the bad people involved will come after her if she goes for treatment at a hospital or is asked to recount the circumstances behind her missing kidney."

"Wow. Being terrified and in medical distress is an awful place to be. What would you like me to do?" Jim asked, concern in his voice.

"I need a doctor who'll come to her mother's house and treat her without divulging her whereabouts or the circumstances of her condition. Any ideas?"

"How about this? As you know, even though I'm a clinical pathologist, I am a licensed MD. I could come over to examine her and bring some medications I think might be in order. If I can at least perform some triage and get her stabilized, it'll buy some time to decide what the next steps need to be. Does that work?"

"Jim, you are literally a lifesaver."

Miles texted Jim the address and he agreed to be there in an hour. Miles heard noises from the kitchen, and when he went downstairs he found Ryan making coffee and Molly busy at her bowl. He updated Ryan on Jim's offer to help and then asked him to take care of Molly while he went to Mrs. Sims's house to check on things.

"It'll keep the commotion to a minimum," he suggested.

Ryan agreed and, after gulping down a cup of coffee, Miles took off. Along the way, he called Mrs. Sims to let her know he had a doctor meeting him there. She was obviously appreciative but very frightened about her daughter's condition.

When Jim arrived, Miles was waiting for him on the front porch.

"Good to see you, Jim. Thanks again for helping out. I see you came fully prepared."

"I still keep my medical bag handy at home. Stopped by the lab to pick up a few things I thought I might need."

Miles grabbed the extra satchel of supplies Jim brought in addition to his medical bag and they went into the house. Once inside, he introduced Jim to Mrs. Sims. The two went in to see Olivia while Miles stayed in the living room. He used the time to catch up on his emails. There was an important one from his lawyer client with the allegedly cheating husband:

"Good news. My client's husband has admitted his bad behavior and has agreed to a divorce. Thanks for your help. Feel free to send me a bill for your time."

"Well, that clears my calendar," Miles said to himself.

Soon after, Jim emerged from Olivia's room with a solemn expression on his face. "She has a very bad infection in the area where the incision was made. I gave her an injection of antibiotics and some pain medication. I've instructed her mother to push liquids all day. I'll come back tonight and see where we're at. If she doesn't seem to be improving, or at least stabilized, she'll need to be hospitalized."

"Jim, I—or should I say *we*—can't thank you enough," Miles said offering his hand.

"Happy to help. Promise me you'll leave no stone unturned in finding the bastards who did this." Jim was now fully engaged in resolving Olivia's predicament.

"You have my word." The two men shook hands and Jim was on his way.

Miles waited in the living room for Mrs. Sims to emerge from her daughter's room. When she did, she wrapped her arms around him in a huge embrace. There were tears of joy in her eyes and a look of relief on her face.

"You have saved my baby's life. How can I ever thank you?" she asked.

"Your hug just did," Miles said with a smile.

Before heading off to his place, he promised to check in with her later in the day after Jim had been back to see Olivia.

When Miles arrived home, Molly was under the table and didn't seem the least bit interested in his arrival.

Ryan was at the kitchen table on his laptop. He looked up attentively when Miles entered. "How is Olivia doing?"

"Too soon to tell. Jim got there almost as soon as I did. He gave her antibiotics, something for pain, and treated her wound. Promised to stop by and check on her this evening. He's a godsend."

Ryan nodded. Then he shared what he'd found online

about the totally illegal black market acquisition and sale of human organs, particularly kidneys. And particularly kidneys for African Americans where the prevalence of kidney failure is substantially higher than for the general population. Ryan's voice carried a combination of sadness and anger as he explained his findings to Miles.

"Are you going to write about it?" Miles inquired.

"Not exactly. I'm thinking about a much broader examination of the real problem. The extent people will go, and the illegal opportunities they will take, to overcome hopeless debt." Ryan had obviously shifted into full journalist mode.

"That's a big subject. How do you attack such a thing?"

Ryan grinned. "Like a professor friend of mine says, 'one bite at a time.'"

"So, a series?" Miles was getting the picture.

"Yep. I'll pitch it to the *Times* when I get back to New York. Back to the case at hand. Are you going to pursue the people who did this to Olivia?" Ryan asked.

"I'm thinking about it," said Miles, brimming with anger and resolve. "These people should be punished. If I go to the cops with what I have now and they start nosing around, it could backfire and expose Olivia's participation to the criminals who might then carry out their threat of silencing her. If I can get absolute proof, then I'll go to the cops who can arrest these people and, if need be, protect Olivia."

"You mean the witness protection program?"

"Probably not. The best outcome would be to expose their crimes *en masse*. If we can find evidence implicating them in a large number of cases, they would be charged with a widespread criminal enterprise and not look to Olivia specifically as having exposed them."

"That's going to be quite an undertaking. Going against a criminal organization is dangerous business. I'll gladly volunteer to help out," Ryan offered.

"You're hired! Besides, my other case has resolved itself, so I have the time. For now, however, I'm going back to bed. I'm useless on only two hours sleep." With that, Miles headed upstairs to bed.

Ryan wanted to continue his research but soon his eyes started to cross. He decided to lay down on the couch for a few minutes. He was awakened by Molly licking his face. After pushing her away, he looked at his watch. He'd been asleep for more than four hours. The sound of Miles opening his bedroom door from upstairs got Molly's attention. She bounded up the stairs, allowing Ryan some time to fully shake out the cobwebs.

A few minutes later, Miles came down the stairs with a look of panic on his face. "Just got a text from Jim. When he got back to Mrs. Sims's house, Olivia's condition had gotten worse. He's called an ambulance to take her to Memorial Hospital. I think we should go and see if we can help Mrs. Sims."

Ryan nodded. "Let's go, but we should only stay if she wants us there."

"Of course."

The emergency room at Memorial Hospital was a hive of activity when they arrived. They immediately spotted Mrs. Sims sitting nervously in a corner of the waiting room and staring at the floor. At first she didn't even notice their presence.

"Hi," Miles said softly. "We thought you might like some company."

"Thank you. You're most kind. Can't believe that I finally got her back and now . . ." Her voice trailed off without finishing her thought.

Miles sat down next to her and took her hand. "She's strong and will get wonderful care here."

Just then, Jim emerged from the treatment area and went straight to Mrs. Sims. "A team of doctors are with her. They're working to stabilize her condition with IV medications and fluids. So far she's holding her own. They're going to transfer her to a bed in the ICU shortly."

"When will I be able to see her?" she asked.

"I assume once they've settled her in a room, they'll let you see her. It might be a couple of hours before that happens. Why don't the three of you go to the cafeteria and have something to eat and drink? I'll stay here, and should they decide to move her, I'll let you know immediately."

Jim was being a real mensch, Miles thought.

Reluctantly, Mrs. Sims agreed to go with them to the cafeteria. It had been many hours since they'd eaten, so even the hospital food looked good to Miles. He and Ryan ate while Mrs. Sims only had an iced tea. The two men tried to distract her with a detailed account of their recent fishing excursion on Lake Michigan with George.

She smiled wistfully. "My husband, Louis, loved to fish."

"On Lake Michigan?" Ryan asked.

"Sometimes. Mostly on the smaller lakes, though. He had a little boat he'd tow with his car. He really enjoyed being on the water, just himself and the fish." There was an unmistakable loneliness in her voice. She obviously missed him even more now, given their daughter's condition.

Once they finished their food, Miles placed the tray of empty dishes on the conveyer belt leading into the kitchen and returned to the table with refills on their beverages. Ten minutes later, Jim joined them.

He spoke directly to Mrs. Sims. "They're in the process of moving her to the ICU. I suspect it will be at least another hour until you'll be allowed to see her. There's nothing more I can do here for the moment, so I'm going to head home."

Mrs. Sims stood and hugged Jim without saying a word. He smiled and promised to look in on Olivia tomorrow. He had been a huge help, particularly since this wasn't his area of medicine.

Miles walked him out to his car. "Jim, I can't thank you enough. This was out of your comfort zone, I know, but I suspect she wouldn't have made it this far if you hadn't agreed to help."

"Glad I could contribute in some way. Let's hope she makes a full recovery."

The two men shook hands and Jim left. On the way back to the cafeteria, Miles began beating himself up for not bringing Olivia straight to the hospital the night before. His plan to protect her from possible harm at the hands of the criminals who did this could end up costing her everything.

After escorting Mrs. Sims to the ICU waiting room, the two men headed home, but not before promising to check on Olivia's condition first thing in the morning.

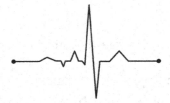

CHAPTER 14

After a good night's sleep and resumption of a normal meal schedule, Miles was primed and ready to begin his workweek with a search for the criminals trafficking in human organs. If he could provide the authorities with a provable case, it would not only protect Olivia but undoubtedly save others from a similar fate.

Shortly after he arrived at the office, he received a text from Jim.

"Saw Olivia. Her condition has improved some. Her mom was there, and her condition seems to have improved as well."

He immediately called Ryan to update him.

"That's good news, Miles," Ryan said. "Or at least better news. I've been researching the whole business of illegal loans. The sheer volume of it is staggering, and it's not simply the old-fashioned neighborhood-loan-shark type of thing. One current practice, which may be relevant to Olivia's case, is loan companies denying loans and then supplying criminals the names of possible targets for various schemes."

"You mean schemes like buying kidneys?" Miles said.

"Yes, and prostitution, or other forms of labor, with most or all of the 'wages' going to pay off the loans."

"So . . . slavery?" Miles wasn't really asking a question. He already knew the answer.

"Believe it or not, yes," Ryan lamented. "Loans backed by human collateral, you might say."

Picking up on referrals from a legitimate loan company to a

criminal one was an angle worth pursuing. Miles would see if Janine could shed any light on how Olivia got started with all of this.

Even though they'd received Jim's text, Ryan volunteered to call Mrs. Sims to touch base while Miles dialed up Janine to enlist her help.

"Hi, Mr. Darien," she answered. "How's Olivia doing?"

"She's under doctor's care and so far, so good," Miles replied.

"Is there anything I can do to help her?" Janine offered.

"Yes, there are three things you can help with. First, check Olivia's mail. If there is anything other than junk mail, send it to the address on the card I gave you. I'll reimburse you for the shipping cost, of course. The second thing is to immediately let me know if someone contacts you looking for Olivia. That's extremely important. Finally, can you give me any additional information about how Olivia got mixed up with the illegal loan people?"

"No problem sending the mail, and I'll certainly let you know if anyone comes looking for her. As for where Olivia got the loan, I know Olivia had applied to a ton of places and told me she'd been turned down by all of them. Then, all of a sudden, Olivia was all excited and relieved because she'd received a call from one place offering her a loan."

Holding back his excitement over this development, Miles thanked Janine for her help and promised to give Olivia a hug on her behalf.

Any phone contacts between Olivia and the illegal loan people would be listed in her phone records. This could lead them straight to the source of Olivia's misery. He knew Olivia had her phone when they packed up her things to bring her home. If Ryan hadn't already spoken to Mrs. Sims at this point, he would take over the questioning and specifically inquire about the whereabouts of Olivia's phone. As he left the office, he called Ryan and updated him on what Janine had told him about the call Olivia had received from a loan company.

"Did you get through to Mrs. Sims?" Miles asked.

"Sorry, not yet. Just got back from taking Molly for a walk."

"No problem. I need to talk with Mrs. Sims now anyway."

When Miles called Mrs. Sims, her phone went right to voicemail. He chose not to leave a message or call the nurse's station. Instead, he decided to go to the hospital to check on how things were going and to inquire about the phone. On the way, he stopped by his house to see if Ryan wanted to tag along. He did.

Typical for Monday morning, the hospital corridors were buzzing with activity when they arrived.

"What a change from Saturday," Ryan commented.

"Staffing costs and insurance company limits on hospital stays incentivize both groups to send as many patients home as possible on weekends."

"You have to wonder how much those cost reduction measures affect care."

Ryan's speculation went without a response as they reached the ICU nurses station.

"Can I help you?" the nurse behind the desk asked.

"We're looking for the mother of Olivia Sims."

"She's in the room with her daughter. We only allow patients one visitor at a time, and they have to be on a list."

"I understand," Miles conceded. "My name is Miles and this is Ryan. Would it be possible to see if Mrs. Sims would meet us in the waiting room?"

"I'll ask her."

With that, the nurse disappeared into the ward. Miles and

Ryan adjourned to the vacant waiting room. The TV was on but the sound was off, so the room was quiet. A couple of minutes later, they were joined by Mrs. Sims and a nurse. Both men began to rise but the nurse motioned for them to stay seated.

Miles assumed the description of Olivia's condition hadn't changed much since Jim's visit earlier that morning, but he asked anyway.

"The doctors say she's improving," said the nurse. "She sleeps most of the time, so I really don't know how she's feeling."

"How are you holding up?" Ryan asked Mrs. Sims.

"I'm fine. Just worried about my baby."

"We wanted you to know that we're trying to find the people who did this to Olivia," said Miles.

"Olivia's back with me now. Why stir up trouble? Besides, I can't afford to pay you for all that."

"First of all, what we do from here on out is not at your expense. These people need to be stopped, and we may be able to give the authorities what they need to make that happen. Besides, they owe Olivia money. We believe the $2,500 they gave her was just a down payment. If we can recover any more of what she's owed, it will help offset some of Olivia's medical expenses."

Mrs. Sims took a moment to collect her thoughts. "You two are so kind and you're right, these people should be punished, but no further harm must come to my daughter."

Miles nodded.

"Actually, catching these people will go a long way toward preventing that," said Ryan.

"You must promise me you'll not stress that child out with a lot of questions. She's in a very fragile state," Mrs. Sims pleaded with them.

"We'll keep the questions to a minimum until she regains her strength," Miles said. "We do need to have a look at Olivia's phone, which I assume is back at your house. It may hold the key to tracking down the people who may try to harm her again."

"Sure. All of her things are in her room in the same bag she came home with. Here's my key. Just leave it on the table with mail when you leave. I'll use the spare I have hidden in the backyard."

They thanked her and set off to retrieve the phone and computer. Ryan checked his phone on the way to Mrs. Sims's house. He saw one missed text from Ted:

"When will you be back? I'd really like to nail down your next piece."

The man is relentless, Ryan thought. He responded, "I'm not sure exactly when I'll be back. As soon as I have that nailed down, I'll give you call."

Ryan hoped that would keep Ted at bay, at least for a little while.

They arrived at Mrs. Sims's house just as he hit Send on his reply. Once inside, they headed to Olivia's room and quickly found her laptop and phone. They would likely need Olivia to give them her log-ins for both when she regained consciousness, even though they promised her mother they wouldn't disturb her. To be sure, Miles tried the phone. Surprisingly, it was not password protected, but the laptop was. They'd focus on the information on the phone and ask for the laptop log-in once Olivia was feeling better.

They started to open the front door to leave when they heard a loud, authoritative voice.

"Drop everything and come out slowly with your hands in the air!"

Assuming the command came from law enforcement, they immediately obeyed. When they emerged from the house, there were two cops awaiting them with guns drawn.

Unfazed, Miles addressed the policeman simply as one law enforcement professional to another. "Officer, I'm Miles Darien, a licensed private investigator and I can explain our presence here."

"Okay," the first officer said. "Explain yourself."

Just as Miles was about to offer an explanation, the second officer started laughing and lowered his gun. "How are you, Miles?"

It was Joe Svenson, someone he had worked with a couple of times when he was in the department.

"I'm fine, Joe. Listen, we're just here to help out a friend who lives here. She asked us to fetch a couple of her daughter's things and bring them to the hospital where her daughter is being cared for." Miles had lied a little, as they were not actually taking the items to the hospital. "By the way, why are you here in the first place?"

Joe shrugged. "Neighbor called. People around here look out for one another, you know."

"I do know, and it's one of the reasons I love living here."

Joe gave Miles a quick wave as the officers returned to their squad car. Miles was headed to his car with the laptop and phone when he saw Ryan still standing on the porch as if frozen. Seeing Ryan was in some distress, Miles did an about-face and joined him on the porch. "Are you all right?" he asked.

"Never had a gun pointed at me before," Ryan stuttered.

"Well, now you have. Let's go." He gave Ryan, still dazed, a little push to get him moving in the direction of the car.

By the time they arrived at Miles's office, Ryan had calmed down a little. Miles began the examination of the phone first, leaving the laptop alone until he got the log-in information from Olivia. Before using his investigative training to trace the accounts linked to the phone numbers on the cell phone, he searched the device for other bits of information. First, he downloaded her contacts and her call history into spreadsheets and uploaded them to his computer. There were no significant saved voicemail messages or texts. Since the phone information he needed was now on his computer, he let Ryan have the phone to comb through the emails using the app that was linked to her email account.

Then Miles traced the phone numbers from her contacts and recent-call list, looking for a connection to the culprit or any other calls that might produce a lead. He assumed they'd be at it quite a while, so he paused to order lunch to be delivered from the sandwich shop down the street. He wasn't sure if Ryan had calmed down enough to actually eat his sandwich, but he ordered him one anyway.

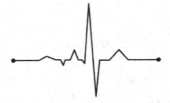

CHAPTER 15

T he hunt for leads on Olivia's phone had consumed the entire afternoon through the evening, and still bore no fruit. Miles realized the best source for leads lay in a bed at Memorial Hospital, so first thing the next morning, he called Mrs. Sims to see if Olivia was well enough to talk to him.

"Good morning, Miles," she answered in a muffled tone.

"Hi, Mrs. Sims. How's Olivia doing?"

He heard her step out of the room so she could talk. "She's doing a little better but she's sleeping now. They're going to move her out of Intensive Care later this morning."

"That's good news. Would it be okay if we stopped by this afternoon for a visit?" Miles had his fingers crossed that Mrs. Sims would allow it. What Olivia could tell them was vital.

Mrs. Sims paused for a moment before answering. "Why don't you call me after lunch, and we'll see."

Miles sensed the reluctance in her voice. Undoubtedly, she was concerned about how the pursuit of those responsible for her condition might upset Olivia. The fear of reprisal is what kept her from seeking medical help in the first place, and that threat was most certainly still out there. He agreed to call after lunch and told her that they'd like to stop by just to say hi. If Olivia chose to talk about what happened to her, fine. If not, that would be fine too.

Mrs. Sims acknowledged she was being overprotective, but given Olivia was still in real danger—and not just from her medical condition—protection was foremost on her mind.

Even though Miles knew Olivia's safety ultimately depend-
ed on bringing those responsible to justice, he decided this was
not the time to push his luck. He told her he understood and
promised to tread lightly.

She thanked him and ended the call.

When Miles headed downstairs to refill his coffee cup, he
found Ryan at the kitchen table, his eyes glued to his laptop
screen. Molly was lying quietly under the table, keeping him
company.

"Good morning," Miles said. "Nice to see you and your faith-
ful companion have begun the workday." He looked over Ryan's
shoulder at the laptop. "Uncovering anything interesting?"

Ryan turned toward Miles and showed him his notes.
"Miles, I've been looking for arrest records on cases of illegal
human organ sales. It seems that this is a relatively new phen-
omenon here in the US. There are numerous cases in Asia,
particularly China, but virtually none here. Seeing that Olivia
lived and worked in Chinatown, do you think there could be a
connection?"

"That's certainly a possibility. Due to the complexity of the
crime, it definitely requires an extensive organization of some
type. I'll check for criminal organizations known to be operating
in that part of Chicago and what, if any, specific activities they're
known to be involved in. After I have a little something to eat
I'm going to call a guy I know at the Wisconsin DOJ to see if
he can be of any help. I trust he can at least steer us in the right
direction."

Miles turned his attention to fixing a bowl of cereal while
Ryan returned to his research. After finishing off the last of the
Cheerios, he called his contact at the Wisconsin DOJ.

"Agent Harris."

"Hi, David. It's Miles Darien. How are you?"

"I'm fine, thanks. Don't tell me we're involved in another case with you."

"No. I'm actually calling to see if you can shed some light on something I'm looking into." Miles proceeded to fill him in on what had happened to Olivia and what they'd uncovered so far.

It turned out they hadn't had any cases of organ trafficking referred to their office. He would know, as his department would handle such a case if there was one. David did add that he thought they were on the right track by looking into some syndicate facilitating this type of operation. His counterpart in the Illinois DOJ might be able to provide some guidance in their jurisdiction and offered to send over her contact information. He told Miles to use his name as a reference, then added, "You're smart enough to know this, but I'll say it anyway. If you detect any lack of interest or stonewalling, it's likely there's already something on their radar related to what you're after."

"Wouldn't they be interested in what our client has to say?"

"If it's a state investigation, they would. If the case has been moved to the Feds, they'll back off. I know it sounds weird, but once they've been told to stand down they'll do just that. She might pass your name along, but that would be the extent of it."

Miles thanked David for the guidance and the Illinois DOJ contact that would follow. He turned to Ryan, who hadn't really been tuned in to Miles's conversation, and shared what he had learned. Ryan's face clearly showed his confusion.

"I don't get it. Why wouldn't they work in concert on something like this?"

"Some of it is competitiveness or maybe even a lack of respect," Miles told him. "I prefer to think it's efficiency. Keeping the investigation compartmentalized eliminates mistakes and assures control. Also, if they're looking at this as a violation of federal law, the FBI would handle it in accordance with federal statutes and guidelines."

"I get all that, but wouldn't they at least pass information along?" Ryan still wasn't buying it.

"You'd think so, but based on what David said, it's typically hands-off. Back to our investigation. We should both go to see Olivia this afternoon if Mrs. Sims allows us to visit. It should be a social call. If the opportunity to approach Olivia about what we're doing comes up, I'll handle that."

Miles already had a strategy in mind for a gentle interrogation.

With Miles busy handling household chores, Ryan decided to take a mid-morning break from his research to catch up on the news from New York, so he went to the *Times*'s online site. As he scrolled through the headlines, one immediately caught his eye: "New Network Drama to Focus on a Latina Run Clinic in NYC". Ryan knew immediately it was Rebecca's show. The article focused on the story line: "Latina doctor returns to her NYC roots to provide much needed healthcare to an underserved community." It was also very complimentary of Rebecca's previous work and included a few quotes from her and the show's producer. All in all, very good publicity. It also provided him with the perfect opportunity to call her. Not unexpectedly, he got her voicemail.

"Hi there. Just saw the article in the *Times*. They really shined a bright light on the show and its star. Congratulations! Anyway, if you get a chance and are in the mood, give me a buzz back. Bye."

Ryan was coming to the realization that his feelings for Rebecca had changed. It was no longer an occasional night of revelry for him. When they last spoke she admitted to missing him. He wondered if it meant she also felt things were changing between the two of them. His thoughts were interrupted by Miles coming down the stairs, vacuum cleaner in hand.

"Be sure to dress warm when we leave the house later," Miles advised. "It's overcast and damp. The wind's off the lake so it hardly feels like spring."

"I know, the 'cooler near the lake' thing. Thanks for the weather report. What time are you calling Mrs. Sims?"

"In about an hour. Gives me time to vacuum up Molly's furry contributions to the floor and furniture." Miles didn't seem too happy to have assigned himself that task.

"I'll do it," Ryan offered. "I need to 'sing for my supper,' so to speak."

He got no argument from Miles, who then decided to turn his attention to the contact at the Illinois DOJ.

"Beverly Stillman," answered the Illinois DOJ agent.

"Agent Stillman, my name is Miles Darien. I am a licensed private investigator from Lakeville, Wisconsin. I've been referred to you by David Harris, your counterpart at the Wisconsin DOJ."

"What can I do for you?" she asked curtly.

"My client is a young woman who appears to be a victim of an illegal loan-sharking operation. One that allows its customers to sell their body parts to repay their loans. I believe my client is in imminent danger from these people, as they've threatened to take all necessary measures to keep her from exposing their activities."

"Why do you say 'appears to be a victim'?"

"Unfortunately, my client is in the hospital unable to speak at the moment. We have quite a bit of evidence linking her missing kidney as payment to an illegal loan outfit. If you're investigating similar crimes, she may be able to assist you once she's well enough to share what she knows."

"In exchange for what?"

"Safety. Either by seeing these people brought to justice or some form of protection from them. Without some assurances that she'd be protected, her agreement to share what she knows would put her in further danger."

"I understand. Since we don't have any current investigation of this type underway, there's not much I can offer in the way of assistance."

"Do you know if the federal authorities are looking into this in Illinois?" Miles thought her use of "current investigation" might indicate exactly what David Harris meant by stonewalling.

"I can't comment directly on that, but I can refer you to a contact at the Chicago FBI office." It was evident in her voice that she was helping in the only way she was permitted to.

"That would be great, thank you."

She gave Miles the contact information for FBI Agent Jeremy Wright and ended the call with, "I hope you're successful in keeping your client safe. I wish I could do more."

His call with FBI Agent Wright was short and unproductive. The agent didn't give Miles any indication there was an investigation underway, which either meant there wasn't one or he wasn't about to share if there was. The agent took Miles's name and number and said he'd be in touch should they have a reason to interview his client. Miles was able to withhold Olivia's identity to keep the FBI at arm's length, ensuring they would be able to discuss protection ahead of any testimony. It was curious, he thought, that there was so little interest in Olivia's situation. If there was an investigation underway, she could very likely supply valuable information. If there wasn't anything in process, why weren't the Illinois DOJ or the FBI interested in looking into the matter as evidence of new criminal activity? At the very least, it appeared David Harris was right about the stonewalling he might encounter. He suspected something was very likely going on, but for the moment he needed to focus on Olivia.

His next call was to Mrs. Sims, who reluctantly agreed to let him and Ryan come to the hospital for a visit. Miles again promised to keep the conversation light and avoid any mention of the circumstances that led to her predicament.

When they arrived at Olivia's hospital room, she was alone and sitting up in bed. Mrs. Sims had apparently stepped out for the moment. Olivia greeted them with a smile.

"Thank you for saving my life."

"We're so glad you're doing better," Miles replied. "You had us all very worried."

"I know."

Miles couldn't help but notice how much she now looked like the beautiful young woman in the picture her mother had given them, a welcome change from her distressed appearance just a couple of days before.

Mrs. Sims, who had gone to the gift shop, returned to the room with a bouquet of flowers. "Just needed to get something to brighten up this room."

"Thanks, Mom. I was just thanking these two for saving my life."

Mrs. Sims only nodded. Miles could see she was trying as best she could to keep her emotions in check. As promised, the brief conversation that followed was light and stayed away from the circumstances that landed Olivia in the hospital. As Miles and Ryan got up to leave, they promised to see her again very soon. Miles motioned for Mrs. Sims to join them in the hallway.

"It's so nice to see how much better your daughter is doing," he told her. "Now we have to focus on keeping her safe."

"I know you need to talk to her about all that's happened, but I'm afraid that if you stir things up, it'll put her in danger." Her motherly protective instincts were showing again.

"If we don't get to the bottom of things, there's no way we can keep her safe. The only way I know of to eliminate the danger is to eliminate those who might threaten that safety." Miles's appeal seemed to be getting through.

"The doctors say she is still not totally out of the woods. Let's see how she is tomorrow," Mrs. Sims conceded.

Miles nodded and held out his hand. She gently pushed his hand away and gave him a big hug instead of a handshake. She added one for Ryan as well.

As they walked across the parking lot to Miles's car, Ryan asked the obvious question. "What do we do next?"

"Go home, have a drink, and decide on dinner."

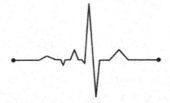

CHAPTER 16

When they arrived back at the house, Miles retrieved the mail while Ryan surveyed the dinner options in the kitchen.

"Looks like we can build a meal around the beautiful salmon filet George prepared for us," Ryan offered.

"That'll work. We received a large envelope from Janine."

It was Olivia's mail. Inside were a few bills and a plain envelope without a return address. Ryan reached for it and was about to open it when Miles grabbed his hand.

"Let's leave that one unopened. In case it's a payment from the people who bought her kidney, we need to preserve the contents so it can be properly examined."

"You're a forensic scientist. Why don't you 'properly examine' it?"

"I could, of course, but the authorities will want it as untouched as possible. That is, if we can interest them in the case." Miles was frustrated. He decided to try Agent Wright at the FBI one more time.

"Agent Wright."

"Hi. This is Miles Darien. We spoke earlier about a case I'm working on involving trafficking in human organs."

"Yes, I remember. Thought I told you I'd be in touch if we needed anything from your client."

"I have important evidence that could lead you to the perpetrators."

"Hold the line a moment." His response was a sure sign Miles was on to something. After being on hold for almost five minutes, his call was picked up again.

"Hello, Mr. Darien. This is Agent Audrey Drummond. Agent Wright has given me some background on your inquiry. What can you tell me about the evidence you'd like to provide?"

So, Miles was right. There was an ongoing investigation. Miles decided to provide complete details on everything that had happened to Olivia, including what he and Ryan had uncovered thus far. He punctuated it with the latest addition, the envelope.

"That's all very interesting. Explain to me why you think the unopened envelope is from the people involved."

"The envelope is a plain #10 envelope, hand-addressed with a Chicago postmark. The only person in Chicago who my client could possibly receive a personal letter from is the person who forwarded the letter to me. I haven't opened the envelope to ensure preservation of any fingerprints or DNA evidence that might be inside. Now I've told you what I know, please be forthcoming with what you know."

"Okay. I can tell you this. We are looking into dubious loan practices including those involving illegal methods of payment. It appears that your client may well be a victim of a crime of that type. My apologies for what may have appeared to be indifference on our part, but the confidential nature of what we're after needs to be safeguarded. Agent Wright did take your inquiry seriously, we just hadn't gotten around to circling back to you. By the way, based on your understanding of evidence preservation, you seem unlike most private investigators we come across. What's your story?"

Miles proceeded to walk her through his background in

forensic science, experience with the Lakeville Police Department, and his private investigator practice.

"Very impressive and explains a lot. We'd like to interview your client and retrieve the envelope as soon as possible."

Miles explained that Olivia was still in a very fragile state, so he recommended they wait a few days on the interview. As for the envelope, he offered to place it in an evidence bag and send it to her by bonded courier.

She went one better by arranging to have an agent pick up the evidence the following day. As for the interview, she agreed to wait a few days, offering Monday as the date for the interview.

"Should work," Miles said. "As you well know, these people can play rough. It's imperative that my client be kept safe at all times."

"Understood. We're pretty good at that," she with a slightly sarcastic twist.

"What's the best number to reach you to confirm that Monday will work?"

She gave him her phone number, verified she had his and closed with a promise he'd hear from her office first thing in the morning about the evidence pickup.

While Miles was talking to the FBI, Ryan had been exchanging texts with Rebecca.

"Got your voicemail," she texted. "In non-stop rehearsals. Thanks for the kind words about the article. Hope you're enjoying your vacation but hurry back."

"Supposed to be back this Sunday but may stay a couple extra days to help Miles out with a project. I'll fill you in when we talk," Ryan replied.

He loved the "hurry back" part of her text. She was obviously very busy, so he'd wait to hear back from her to continue the conversation.

Over dinner, Miles filled Ryan in on the details of his conversation with Agent Drummond. They also discussed the need to interview Olivia first so they knew what she would be telling the FBI. It was imperative that Olivia be seen by the authorities as a victim, not as someone who committed a crime. Miles knew that once the authorities got involved, his access would very likely be limited. While he was confident the FBI would ultimately apprehend and punish those responsible for Olivia's plight, her safety might ultimately depend on his continued diligence. Ryan would be heading back to New York soon, so Miles would then be on his own.

"You know, don't you, how imperative it is that you keep her out of that article you're planning," Miles said.

"Of course, I do. If I use her story it will be anonymous, and I will not use it at all until we know she's safe. What about the financial aspects of all this? She still has all the bills that got her into this predicament in the first place. Add her medical bills to that and she's got really serious money problems."

"Agreed. First off, I won't be charging them for anything beyond what Mrs. Sims has already paid me. Hopefully, the FBI will eventually let her cash the check if there is one in the envelope. She'll likely have to move home for a while to minimize her monthly expenses. I trust the hospital will accept some sort of payment plan for her medical expenses."

"Maybe I can help in another way," Ryan offered.

"Explain."

"Well, I have a couple of ideas. Let me develop them a little more before I bring you up to speed."

"Okay. But time is of the essence." Miles wondered what Ryan could possibly have up his sleeve.

Ryan changed subjects before Miles could probe further. He was supposed to leave on Sunday but thought maybe he should stay a few extra days to help out with the investigation. He was concerned that Olivia and Mrs. Sims may need more protection than they could expect the FBI and Miles alone to provide.

Miles agreed. "As it relates to the investigation, there's not much more for us to investigate. The FBI now knows what we know. They have infinitely more wherewithal than we do. They'll add in the missing pieces and hopefully find the people responsible. As for security, unless you have some newly acquired self-defense and weapons expertise, you'll be unlikely to offer the Simses any additional protection." Sensing Ryan might be feeling under-appreciated, Miles added, "Don't get me wrong. You've been an enormous help in finding out what we know so far, and you've been particularly great with Olivia and her mom. Now it's just time to turn things over to the proper authorities."

"Are you planning to stay on the case?"

"Of course. Once we hear what Olivia has to say, I'll decide what leads I'll pursue, if any. At this point, my focus is simply to keep them safe."

Ryan conceded less than enthusiastically he'd be leaving on Sunday as planned.

Miles was quick to let Ryan know he was welcome to stay as long as he liked. He just wanted him to understand what was needed as it related to the case.

Ryan conceded that while he was totally invested in this

thing, he understood that all he could provide was moral support. Miles reminded him about his next essay exposing the breadth of this problem. The sooner he started on it, the sooner it could bring the issue out into the open.

"Ryan, the best way for you to help Olivia and others like her is to expose the criminals who are victimizing these people."

Ryan nodded. Now that the date of his return to New York had been decided upon, Ryan texted Rebecca: "I'll be home Sunday as planned. Looking forward to seeing you soon!"

She responded immediately: "How about Sunday night?"

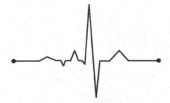

CHAPTER 17

When they got to the hospital on Friday morning, Olivia was, much to their surprise, dressed and ready to leave. Mrs. Sims was packing up Olivia's personal items.

"So, they're you letting out." Miles tried not to sound concerned that she was being discharged so soon.

Mrs. Sims finished packing up Olivia's belongings. "Yes, the doctor was in this morning and said she could go. I'm taking her to my place for a while."

"Mama knows best," Ryan added.

Miles changed the subject. "The FBI wants to meet with Olivia to learn all about her dealings with the loan-sharking operation. I've pushed them off until Monday, giving us time to go over what things she's going to tell them. Olivia, it'll be helpful for you to know the types of questions they'll be asking and, since I won't be with you during the interview, it's important to be prepared. Also, the FBI will be instrumental in protecting you once they've established the danger you're in from the criminals responsible."

"Okay. How about getting together on Sunday?" Olivia offered.

"Perfect, I have to drop Ryan off at the Milwaukee airport at nine a.m. How about I bring over lunch and we'll talk?" Miles always thought having serious discussions over a meal made things seem less serious.

"Lunch is fine," Mrs. Sims chimed in. Then she added, "But I'm supplying the lunch. We'll miss you, Ryan."

"I'll miss you as well," Ryan admitted.

An orderly arrived a couple of minutes later, pushing a wheelchair for Olivia. Once she was on board, they walked to the parking lot together. After hugs were exchanged all around, the women left for home. Miles and Ryan went back to the office to put together their list of questions and to wait for the FBI representative to retrieve the envelope in the evidence bag.

Not particularly surprising, an FBI agent was waiting for them when they arrived at Miles's office. After Miles was satisfied with the agent's identification, he handed over the evidence and the agent was on his way.

"Any chance it was a mistake, handing over the evidence?" Ryan asked.

"Not really," Miles replied. "They'll extract more information from it than I would. More importantly, it will help get them engaged in Olivia's situation as an integral part of their investigation. We need to focus on Olivia, not single-handedly go up against some organized crime syndicate."

They spent the next couple of hours coming up with questions for Miles's Sunday discussion with Olivia. It would be important to find out not only what had happened to her, but on a more human level, where she would go from here. Just as Miles had finished making his notes, his cell phone rang. It was George.

"Hi, George. What's up?"

"Would you and Ryan, if he's still town, like to go fishing tomorrow? I've had a cancelation."

Miles deliberated for a moment about whether it was a good idea to head out fishing in the middle of their investigation. After sensing that an opportunity to take a breather from the case would be therapeutic, he relayed George's offer to Ryan, who enthusiastically gave two thumbs up.

"We're in. Same time?"

"Yep. Your turn to pack a lunch. See you bright and early."

Ryan gave another thumbs-up. Miles was ecstatic that Ryan had come to love the whole fishing thing. It would be a welcome change of pace from what they'd been doing the last few days. He was sorry Ryan had to leave Lakeville, both because of the new friends they'd made but also the time they spent solving crime as a team.

On the way home from the office, they stopped at the store to pick up supplies for that evening's dinner and tomorrow's lunch out on the lake. The conversation for the rest of the ride home shifted to unrelated topics, including the upcoming elections and the New York sports scene. Once back at the house, Ryan made notes for his new essay series while Miles prepared a few sandwiches for the boat trip and then labored over a very challenging crossword puzzle for an hour. They both turned in early knowing their alarms were set for 4:45 a.m.

Jake's Jazz Bar was abuzz with live music and a boisterous Friday night crowd. Janine was serving drinks as fast as she could pour them. Out of the corner of her eye she saw a familiar face. Not one she cared to ever have to see again. It was the man who dropped Olivia off at her place after the surgery. His greased-back hair, three-day-old beard, and dark eyes made him look every bit the criminal he was.

He waved for her to come over. Reluctantly, she moved down to his end of the bar.

"What can I get you?" she asked, trying her best to be nonchalant.

"Hi, I'll have a Bud and some information."

She handed him the bottle of beer and asked, "A glass?"

"No glass. Just tell me, have you seen Olivia?"

Miles had coached her on what to say if she encountered any of the people who had been involved in Olivia's "loan." "Not since she left my place a week or so ago."

"Any idea where I can find her? We have some unfinished business with her." He emphasized the word "unfinished." Apparently trying to avoid any alarm, he added, "We'd like to know how she's doing."

Janine knew Olivia's well-being was the furthest thing from this guy's mind. She did her best to hide her contempt for him. "Don't know where she is at the moment. She said she was feeling well enough to go back to her apartment and would be in touch. I assumed she just wanted to continue recovering at her own home. "

He finished his beer in one giant swig and then leaned in toward her. "When you hear from her, please tell her to contact William, okay?" It wasn't actually a question.

"Sure," Janine answered, doing her best to keep her cool.

William turned and walked out without another word. Janine knew he meant business, and not the good kind. After she stopped trembling, she texted Miles.

Miles didn't see Janine's text until he awoke the next morning. Since she had likely worked until well after midnight, he'd wait a couple of hours before calling her. After they let Molly out, they packed up the lunch provisions and headed to the pier. Once they had loaded the car, Miles asked Ryan to drive so he could call Janine. She related details of the encounter she'd had with William. Miles asked her to keep him appraised of any additional contacts with William or any of his associates.

He decided not to mention the FBI's involvement to her just yet.

"Why are they looking for her?" Ryan asked.

As he spoke, Miles's eyes shifted back and forth from the road ahead to Ryan and then back again. "It's likely they want to be sure she's recovered from the surgery. If she seeks additional medical attention, the missing kidney could raise questions that could somehow be traced back to them and their illegal activities. They'd also like to be sure she kept her mouth shut."

"Is she in danger?" The expression on Ryan's face was one of deep concern.

"Not immediate danger. I suspect if they don't find her soon they will likely become suspicious and put on a full-court press to find her. If they're openly searching for her they might expose themselves to the FBI, which would be a break."

"What do we do now?"

"We go fishing," Miles replied calmly.

The puzzled look on Ryan's face asked its own question.

Miles smiled at him. "Try to relax. I'll get in touch with Agent Drummond as soon as we return to the dock. She's calling the shots now, so we'll take our directions from her. If the bad guys didn't know where Olivia was late last night, they don't know where she is now."

At that point, they had reached the dock. George was waiting there, holding a tackle box in one hand and the handle of his beer-ladened cooler in the other.

"Good morning, gentlemen. The fish await."

They stowed the gear on board and were quickly underway. Once past the breakwater, George opened up the throttle and soon there was no land in sight. After heading northeast for another fifteen minutes he slowed the boat to a full stop. Ryan was again blown away by the multicolored sunrise over the lake and how the total stillness of the water had calmed him as well. They soon had all their lines in the water and waited for the fish to initiate some action.

For the first three hours, they had nothing to show for their efforts. Then all hell broke loose with all three poles spewing their lines. Each man grabbed a pole and began their individual battles. Ryan was first to bring his catch aboard. It was a small brown trout that fortunately allowed him to bring it on board without assistance as his companions were in no position to help. George was next to bring his catch alongside the boat. He coached Ryan on how to scoop up the fish with the net while he maneuvered it into position. This fish was also a brown trout but much larger.

Miles continued to wrestle with his fish while George and Ryan cheered him on. Once Miles finally had his fish positioned alongside the boat, George adeptly brought it on board. The twenty-and-a-half-pound coho salmon turned out to be the catch of the day.

George clapped a hand on Miles's shoulder. "Quite a nice fish there, Miles. You're gettin' real good at this."

"Thanks, George. You and Ryan snagged a couple of nice ones too."

"Of course mine was the small one," Ryan lamented.

"Not bad for a beginner though." George said. Miles smiled, knowing George had comforted many novice fishermen in the same manner. It was good practice for stimulating return business.

George reached for a celebratory beer, and this time his mates joined him.

They returned to the dock a couple of hours later having only caught one more fish, a small lake perch. George offered to have them over in a couple of days to enjoy the fruits of their labor, but sadly Ryan had to decline because he was going home. Miles also requested a raincheck due to his likely unpredictable schedule. They each thanked George profusely and promised to join him again soon.

When they arrived at Miles's house, he and Ryan each had some calls to make. Miles needed to relay Janine's information to the FBI while Ryan decided to call both Ted and Rebecca. Ryan waited for Miles to finish his call with the FBI before making his own calls, as the results might impact what he would say to Ted.

"My call with the FBI was short and to the point," Miles explained. "Agent Drummond was very interested in the visit William had made to Janine. She also confirmed that they would be in Lakeville Monday morning to interview Olivia. I shared Mrs. Sims's address, which I assume they obviously already had. They are the FBI, after all."

Ryan called Ted with the news he was on to something that could be a series. He would fill him in when they met. Ted protested, saying he wanted some idea of what the series was all about. Ryan told him to hang on until Monday so he could flesh out his premise more fully before going into detail about it. They confirmed a ten a.m. meeting at Ted's office. Ryan's next call was to Rebecca.

"Per your request," he told her, "I'll be home tomorrow afternoon."

"Didn't know I had that much influence over you," she teased. "I'll have to use it more often."

"How about dinner tomorrow night?"

"Love to. Can I call you after we finish rehearsing? Should be no later than seven thirty."

"Of course. By the way, how's the show coming along?"

"We've made remarkable progress. We should start filming in about a week. I've already got opening-night jitters." There was genuine pride in her voice. This show could very well turn out to be her long-overdue *tour de force.*

Ryan could barely contain his excitement over what had transpired while he was away. His voice had a slight quiver as he responded. "See you tomorrow night. Can't wait to hear all about it."

"Safe travels," Rebecca answered.

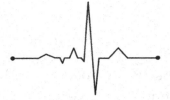

CHAPTER 18

As they pulled up to the airport, Miles suggested that Ryan check his airline app one last time. Happily, it showed his flight was still listed as "on-time." After a hearty handshake, Miles said goodbye to Ryan, who then disappeared through the door marked "Departures".

It was still barely mid-morning, so Miles would have no problem arriving at Mrs. Sims's house well before lunchtime. Once there, his first order of business would be to find out all he could from Olivia about how she ended up in this predicament. He also wanted to be sure she knew how to tell her story to the FBI, as it was imperative they understood the danger she felt from the people she had gotten involved with. It was so important that they understood she was a victim of an unscrupulous mob, not a willing participant in a crime.

"Good morning, Miles." Mrs. Sims greeted him with a huge smile as she opened her front door. Having Olivia back home was obviously therapeutic for both of them.

"Hi. I know we said lunchtime, so I hope I'm not too early."

"Not at all. We're just sitting around catching up."

Miles walked into the living room and took a seat across the coffee table from Olivia. "How are you doing?" Olivia's condition had obviously improved dramatically. The ashen look on her face had been replaced by a much more natural one. "Better, thanks. Did Ryan get off okay?"

"His plane was on schedule when I dropped him off at the

airport. He asked me to say goodbye and to convey his best wishes for your continuing recovery."

Olivia smiled. "Much appreciated."

"Olivia, let me begin by reminding you that the FBI's goal is to stop crime. The people who took your kidney committed a crime. You did not. It is important that you let them know you didn't know what they were doing was illegal. Isn't that, in fact, the truth?" Olivia straightened up in her chair before responding. "I knew people donate kidneys all the time, so while I thought it was unusual to use it as loan collateral, at the time I didn't think it was illegal."

"Good. Now tell me, how did all of this come about?"

Olivia gave a long sigh. "I was just telling my mom about my plan to enroll in art school. That's what started all of this. That, and after the money my dad left me ran out, I was getting a little over my head in credit card debt. First, I went to my bank, which turned me down for a loan. So did half a dozen other loan companies. They all said I needed collateral, which I didn't have. I figured my dream was dead and I'd have to ask Mom to bail me out. Then I got a call. It was from a man, William, who said he represented a company called LoanTime. He told me he got my name from one of the companies I had applied to who had turned me down."

"What was the name of the company that referred you to him?"

"You're going to think I'm really stupid, but I never bothered to ask. I guess I was just so happy to have someone interested in giving me a loan that it never crossed my mind."

"Go on."

"We arranged to meet the next day at the Starbucks near my apartment. He said it was on his way to the office and he'd spare me the inconvenience of driving all the way to the company's office in Oak Lawn. So, like I said, we met at Starbucks. He asked me a bunch of questions like where I worked, did I own a home, all the usual stuff. When he finished, he told me he thought he could help me and would be in touch."

Miles was curious why, since they had spoken in the phone, William's number hadn't shown up on her call list.

But she showed him William's number was, in fact, in her call list. It was just as Miles had suspected. It was the number of a prepaid phone from Walgreens, one Miles could not possibly trace. The FBI could conceivably connect the purchase back to a credit card, but that was likely a dead end. These guys knew how to cover their tracks.

"What happened next?"

"He said he had an offer for me and asked to meet me the next morning at the same Starbucks. The offer was for a ninety-day loan of up to $5,000 at 15 percent interest. I thanked him but said I couldn't do that. No way could I repay the loan in ninety days. Then he told me he had an alternative. He said his firm handled the financing for a medical clinic that was in desperate need of kidneys for their African-American clients. They would pay $2,500 upfront and $12,500 after the surgery."

"So, $15,000 in total. Did you say yes at that point?"

"I told him I'd think about it. It sounds silly, I know, but after giving it some thought it seemed like a good solution. I would be able to pay off my debts and have enough for a year's tuition. I'd already been accepted at two art schools for the fall, so this would make it happen."

Mrs. Sims, who had been silent up to this point, interrupted. "Why didn't you just ask me for help?"

Olivia turned to her mother tiredly. "You were going to help. My plan was to move home with you and enroll at MIAD to study graphic design."

"MIAD?" Miles asked.

"Milwaukee Institute of Art and Design. I'd commute three days a week for in-person classes and study online the rest of the time."

Out of the corner of his eye, Miles could see Mrs. Sims fidgeting in her chair. She was apparently having a difficult time keeping it together. On the one hand, she was likely elated that Olivia would be moving home. On the other, it must have been eating her up inside over what Olivia had gone through to get there.

Continuing her story, Olivia explained how she signed the documents the next day. After signing, William took her to a doctor's office where they gave her a brief examination and a prescription for some tests to be taken at a local clinic. If the results of the tests were satisfactory, they would proceed with the loan arrangements.

"Two questions," Miles said. "Do you have copies of the documents you signed, and do you know the name and address of the doctor's office?"

Olivia shook her head no and explained that after having the prescribed tests at the clinic, Olivia was told to go to a storefront in a strip mall on Halsted for the surgeon to examine her. She complied, and after seeing the surgeon, William gave her the check for $2,500; and then she took a cab to her bank, deposited the check, and went home. Then Olivia called Janine to tell her she was going to have surgery and might need some help for a few days. Janine offered to have her come to her place after it was over so she could help her with the recovery. The next morning, William picked her up and took her back to the doctor's office for the surgery. He promised to give her an envelope with the loan documents and medical paperwork after the operation.

"Next thing I know, he's dropping me at Janine's," Olivia recounted.

"No paperwork, I assume."

"You assume right."

Miles placed his palms on the table and laid it out for her. "Tell the FBI your story just the way you told it to me. Just as I thought, you were victimized by con men. They'll see that right away. They'll also see why they need to ensure your safety." What Miles didn't say was that the FBI needed to protect her not only because she was entitled as a citizen, but because she was also a witness whom they'd need to testify in order to bring those responsible to justice.

At that point lunch was ready, so they adjourned to the kitchen. Mrs. Sims made a beautiful dish of barbecued shrimp served over rice. Quite elaborate for a midday meal, he thought. The conversation turned to Olivia's goal of becoming a graphic artist, followed by Miles extolling the virtues of fishing on Lake Michigan. Mrs. Sims just kept smiling.

"Will they let me keep the money?" Olivia asked.

"Assuming the envelope did actually contain a check, I would think they'd eventually let you have the funds. Be sure to ask the FBI agent about it tomorrow. It's unlikely to be top of mind for them unless you bring it up."

"I really hope so. The $2,500 I already received will only cover a portion of my bills, and then the hospital . . ." Her voice trailed off without finishing her thought.

"Don't worry about that now. We'll figure it out," Mrs. Sims said, trying her best to be comforting.

"When you get the hospital bill, call their finance office and ask them for a payment plan," said Miles. "They are usually very good about spreading out payments." He planned to look for other ways to assist them, but that would have to come later.

After they finished lunch, Miles said his goodbyes and added, "Please call me as soon as the FBI interview is over."

Olivia nodded just before he opened the door to leave.

On his way home, Miles reflected on all that had transpired in the last few days. Finding Olivia and now being in hot pursuit of the people responsible for her predicament had his forensic-trained mind fully engaged. Miles had no sooner pulled into his driveway than his phone rang. It was Ryan.

"How was your flight?" Miles asked.

"Perfect. Even arrived a couple of minutes early. How did your chat with Olivia go?"

Miles filled him in on the details of Olivia's account of what had happened, including her worry about the hospital bill.

"I intend to help with that. Since she's the inspiration for the series of essays I intend to write on modern-day loan-sharking, I'm going to have the paper send her some of my advance. Should be at least $10,000 for her."

"Ryan, that's incredibly nice of you. She'll be thrilled." Once again, Ryan had proven what a great person he was.

"Happy to do it. One question from her account of the events. It doesn't seem logical that the criminals have a full-blown surgical center set up in a strip mall storefront."

"Obviously not. My theory is, they gave her some sedation there and then transported her somewhere else for the surgery. It was likely a small hospital or other medical facility of questionable character. Maybe even a dentist's office or vet clinic. That way they can move their storefront office whenever they feel they might be detected while keeping their operating room as is. "

"Jesus!"

"Yeah, I know. I'll give you a buzz after I get a read on the FBI interview from Olivia."

"Good. Thanks."

CHAPTER 19

After dropping off his bags at his apartment, Ryan headed off to buy a few groceries and a bottle of the nice Prosecco he knew Rebecca liked. He texted her that he was home and would wait for her call to discuss plans for the evening.

He then sat down to prepare his outline for tomorrow morning's discussion with Ted. Ryan knew he was on to something, and it was imperative that he convince Ted to buy in, particularly since he had some of the advance already spent.

After working on his outline for two hours, he closed his notebook and decided he should try a nap so he could be wide awake for his date with Rebecca. Thirty minutes into his nap, the phone rang. Unfortunately, it was Ted and not Rebecca.

"Are you back in town?" Ted asked.

"I am."

"Good. Then we're on for ten a.m. as planned."

"Yes, we are. I think you'll be very interested in what I have in mind."

"Care to offer a preview?"

"See you tomorrow morning, Ted. Bye."

He tried to resume his nap but soon realized Ted had spoiled that possibility. He turned his attention to the mail that had accumulated while he was away. It took him all of five minutes to separate the junk mail from the important stuff, which consisted of two bills and his new American Express card. All in all, nothing requiring any additional effort.

His phone rang again. This time it was Rebecca.

"Glad to be home?" she asked.

"Now I am. How is your rehearsal going?"

"Looks like we'll be finished soon. They just finished reviewing the video of today's work. If they're satisfied, we're done for the day. Should we make a plan?"

"I have a bottle of the Prosecco you like. You can just stop over once you're finished there, and then we can decide on a meal, and whatever, when you get here." As soon as he said it, he realized how obvious "whatever" must have sounded.

"A meal and whatever both sound good." She had let him off the hook. "See you soon, then."

"See you soon." Ryan felt like a schoolboy who had just secured a date to the big dance. He also wondered if getting more involved might ruin the arrangement they both enjoyed so much. He decided, *que sera sera.*

Ryan spent the next hour unpacking his bags and washing up. He was placing two wine glasses on his coffee table when the intercom bell rang. Rebecca had arrived. He buzzed her in and opened his door, not waiting for her to knock even though he knew it showed how overanxious he was.

"Welcome home!" she said, wrapping her arms around him. She punctuated the hug with a short but tender kiss.

"Nice to be home. Nicer that you're here." He wasn't doing a very good job with hiding his feelings. "Glass of wine?" he asked, momentarily shifting the conversation.

"I'd love one," she answered as she sat down on the couch next to the glass-topped coffee table with the wine glasses.

Ryan returned with the Prosecco, poured a glass for each of them, and sat down next to her on the couch. "Tell me what's going on with your show."

Rebecca described the roles of each of the recurring cast members in great detail, finishing with her own. "She's an incredibly competent and empathetic physician who believes in treating the whole person, which includes assisting with their nonmedical problems."

"I like the concept. It's not just the disease-of-the-week type thing."

"Exactly. It takes the show into the community, and because of the many problems people might have, it allows us to bring in guest stars playing those who have the problems, those who help solve the problems, as well as those who create them." It was obvious how entirely invested in the premise she had become.

"When do you start filming?"

"Hopefully by the end of the week. They have some logistics to work out with locations and such. We're hoping to be on camera by Thursday or Friday."

Ryan held up his glass and offered a toast. "Here's to the success of *Compassion Clinic* and its star!"

After downing their first glass of wine and then a refill, they settled on sushi for something to eat. The very traditional sushi bar Ryan loved was just a few blocks away. It was a beautiful evening, so they decided to walk. Along the way, Ryan told her the story of Olivia's plight.

"I can tell you're already starting to write your essay," she remarked.

"How so?"

"Just the way you've laid it all out. You've definitely begun organizing your words and putting a form to the piece. Unfortunately, it's a sad story both for Olivia and any other people who have been victimized in that way. Hopefully Olivia's story will have a happy ending."

Ryan explained that Olivia had big-time money problems to start with, and now adding her medical bills to that, those problems become almost insurmountable. So, he had decided to contribute some of his advance from the series to help alleviate a portion of her financial burden. His declaration inspired a squeeze of his arm and a kiss on his cheek.

As they walked into the restaurant, the sushi chefs greeted them in unison with the traditional, *"Irasshai!"*

They sat at a small table in the corner and ordered the combination sushi platter. Ryan then shifted the travelogue to tales of his fishing expeditions and golf outing. But he mostly talked about all the warm, down-to-earth people he'd met.

"Certainly not the pace or excitement of our city, but wonderful in its own right."

She winked. "You'll have to take me with you next time."

"I'd love to." Ryan was sure Rebecca would get along famously with Miles, not to mention Molly.

They finished their sushi and a carafe of saké before going back to Ryan's. She took his hand and held it the entire way back. Things had clearly escalated between them, and Ryan was totally on board with the new paradigm.

They had barely made it into the apartment before their holding hands shifted to kissing, then removing their clothes. What ensued was way beyond mere sex. It was genuine lovemaking with each one fully tuned in to what would express their innermost feelings, not just their passion.

Afterward was different, too. Instead of the usual quick cuddle and one of them leaving for home, they lay in bed just holding one another. He felt totally in touch with Rebecca both physically and emotionally and didn't want to let go. They talked for about an hour and then slowly drifted off to sleep. Tomorrow would definitely be different, Ryan thought as he closed his eyes.

Ryan arrived at the New York Times office right at ten a.m. As he approached Ted's corner office, he saw him standing in his doorway as if expecting a special delivery. It always amused Ryan that in this age of technology, Ted's desk was completely blanketed by large piles of paper.

"Welcome back to civilization," was Ted's sarcastic greeting.

"Actually, I'm returning *from* civilization," Ryan said, not at all sarcastically.

"Okay, I get it. Sit down and fill me in."

Ryan began by relating the story of how he and Miles had become involved in saving Olivia, both by getting her the medical attention she so desperately needed and then discovering how she came to be in such trouble in the first place. He then went on to explain what he had learned about this new form of loan-sharking.

"These criminals employ several methods to use people's financial desperation for profit. Besides trafficking in human organs, they coerce women into prostitution to make their payments, or they offer people the chance to pay off their debts doing manual labor like farmwork. In both of those cases, since their "customers" need some money along the way to live on, the victims never quite manage to pay off their debts. You get the picture. It's a form of slavery."

"How do you plan to structure the series?" Ted was obviously already on board.

Ryan laid out his vision to open with an overview of the issue in the first installment. It would discuss the reality people with financial problems face when their debts far exceed their income, and they have no real assets to speak of. How they literally have no legitimate way out. Their only hope is an illegitimate way out, which, unfortunately, isn't a way out at all. From there, he would shift to an installment on each of the ways these people become entrapped. The final installment would address the law enforcement efforts that are underway and what legitimate alternatives, if any, these people have to alleviate their financial burden.

Ted rose from his chair, wide-eyed, and paced furiously.

"Wow. This is explosive. Obviously, we're onboard. A couple of questions. First, how are you going to find concrete examples of each of the other methods of illegal loan-sharking?"

"Obviously, that'll take some digging and possibly some fieldwork, which you'll have to fund. There are, however, quite a number of cases on file which we may be able to follow back to the source. Second question?"

"Time frame. How long before you can have something ready to publish?" Ted asked.

"Not quite sure. The first two installments could be ready in a couple of weeks. The rest could take a couple of months, or maybe even longer."

"This is Sunday feature stuff. I can wait a month or so to start, then each installment would follow in consecutive weeks. Can you make that happen?"

"Here's what I propose. I will turn in the first installment when I'm sure the others can follow, one per week. Fair enough?"

"What choice do I have?"

Ryan knew Ted had almost zero leverage.

"As for the financial arrangement, I can offer you $20,000 per installment with the first one upfront," Ted continued. "Expenses need to be approved by me in advance. You good with that?"

"More than fair. I do have a small request. I want half of the advance to go to Olivia Sims. It's something I can do to fight against this problem beyond simply exposing it to the light of day."

"I can certainly make that happen." Ted shook his hand. "You're a good man, Ryan Duffy. Not a bad journalist, either."

"Thanks, Ted. Coming from you, that's quite a compliment."

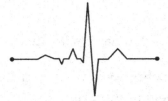

CHAPTER 20

I t had been a quiet Monday morning for Miles. He was on hold until after Olivia's FBI interview, so he did some repair work on a broken shelving unit in the kitchen. Around eleven a.m., his phone rang. It was Janine.

"Mr. Darien, something terrible has happened." She sounded beyond upset.

"Tell me."

After taking a few seconds, she continued. "Mrs. Winters has been killed."

"What?" he exclaimed.

"I went to Olivia's apartment to see if there was any new mail and to pick up a few things to send to her mom's house. When I got there, it was covered in police tape and a couple of cops were standing outside talking to some of Olivia's neighbors. One of the neighbors recognized me and came over to fill me in on what had gone down." Her voice had begun to quiver so she paused for a couple of seconds to compose herself. "Apparently, Mrs. Winters had confronted a man who had broken into the building. The neighbors heard them arguing in the hallway in front of Olivia's apartment door. They could hear Mrs. Winters threatening to call the police, and then a scream and a loud crash. They opened their door only to find Mrs. Winters unconscious. Her assailant had vanished. They called 911 but when they arrived, Mrs. Winters had died." Janine's voice tailed off to a whisper as she finished her story.

"How horrible! Have you told Olivia about this?"

"No, I called you first. What should I do now? I'm really scared." Her voice began quivering again.

"Do not go home until you hear back from me. Stay as far away from there as possible. Do you have someplace safe you can go?"

"I guess I could go to my sister's place in Rockford," she offered.

"Perfect. Go there immediately and wait to hear from me. Janine, stay calm and we'll all get through this." Miles tried his best to be reassuring.

"Okay."

As soon as he hung up, he called Agent Drummond, who was on her way to the interview with Olivia. He brought her up to speed on what had happened to Mrs. Winters and its obvious implications to Olivia's case.

"This creates a whole new level of danger. We need to get both Ms. Sims and her mother to a safer location. Immediately." Agent Drummond's voice rose a couple of octaves as she spoke.

"How about my place?" Miles offered. "I have plenty of room and a security system."

"And a gun?"

"Yes."

"All right. We're almost at their place. We can handle the interview at your house if that's okay with you."

"Of course." Miles was relieved both to have the two women at his place for their safety and the opportunity for him to now be present for their interview. "When you arrive pull all the way into the driveway and park in front of the garage. You can enter the house through the back door. I also suggest you leave both of their cars at the house to give the appearance they haven't left."

"You should be in law enforcement."

"I was. Taught me a lot. Please reassure my clients that this is purely precautionary."

"Of course I will. My time in law enforcement has taught me a lot as well," she said lightheartedly.

Immediately after hanging up, Miles headed upstairs to prepare for his guests. He straightened both guest rooms, thankful he had changed the bed linens after both Bobbie's and Ryan's departures. He added another set of towels in the guest bathroom and then returned down the steps to set up the living room for the interview.

Shortly thereafter, Miles heard a knock on his back door. His guests had arrived. The fearful look on both Olivia's and her mother's faces spoke volumes. Agent Drummond and her associate from the local FBI office followed them into the house carrying both women's suitcases. Miles showed them all into the living room and invited them to make themselves comfortable while he took the luggage upstairs.

When Miles returned to the living room they had all found seats. A recording device had been placed on the coffee table, as had a legal pad filled with notes. Miles grabbed a chair from the dining room and, for moral support, positioned himself where Olivia could easily see him.

It was obvious that Agent Drummond had filled them in on what Miles had heard from Janine. She had also explained why they would be staying with Miles. He added the part about Janine leaving town to stay with her sister. Olivia started to cry.

"I can't believe I've caused so much trouble for everyone. Mrs. Winters was murdered because of me. Now Janine has to go into hiding."

Her mother, who was seated next to her, handed Olivia a Kleenex and gave her hand a squeeze.

"Olivia, your friend Janine has stepped up like true friends do," said Miles. "She's safe and glad she's been able to help you. These people are also on your side." He gestured to the agents. "They'll get to the bottom of this and see that the people responsible are prosecuted."

After thanking Miles, Agent Drummond began the interview by asking Olivia to tell her story from the beginning, which she did in great detail. Along the way the agent asked a number of questions, mostly relating to how the original connection with the loan people was made. The interview took a little over an hour, after which Agent Drummond asked Olivia for a key to her apartment so they could search it for any additional clues they might be able to uncover.

The FBI agents got up to leave immediately after the interview. Before walking out they promised to stay in close contact with Olivia to update her on any new developments. Miles walked the agents out to their car and asked, "What will you be doing to protect her?"

"Two things," Agent Drummond replied. "First, we'll be providing surveillance of your house to safeguard the three of you. Second, we're going to find, arrest, and prosecute the individuals responsible for this."

"Exactly what I'd hoped you'd say. Thanks." Miles offered his hand to Agent Drummond, who obliged with a handshake and a nod as she got into the car.

After they left, Miles went back into the house and climbed the stairs to check on his guests. He found Olivia on her bed with Molly curled up next to her. It was amazing how dogs instinctively respond to those in need, Miles thought. Mrs. Sims had chosen to keep busy by unpacking her things.

Seeing that all was calm on the second floor, Miles went downstairs to the kitchen to lay out some food in case either of his guests were hungry. He also put on a pot of tea. Before it could come to a boil, Ryan called.

"What's the latest?" he asked.

Miles filled him in on what he had learned from Janine's call and what had transpired since. Ryan was shocked and dismayed about Mrs. Winters being killed.

"She certainly didn't deserve this. All the more reason to see these people behind bars," he lamented angrily.

Changing subjects, Ryan explained his deal with the *Times*.

"Once again, that's incredibly generous of you," said Miles. "Do you want to tell Olivia about it? I can put her on the phone."

"Not now. I think she's had more than enough to digest for one day. Are you comfortable with being primarily responsible for her safety and her mom's?"

"Comfortable, no. Confident, yes. Hopefully, the bad guys will never even suspect they're here but if they do, the FBI and I have the wherewithal to keep them safe." Miles sounded positive, although deep down he had his doubts.

Satisfied for the moment with Miles's explanation, Ryan switched the topic to his rapidly evolving relationship with Rebecca. As close as he and Miles had been since childhood, Ryan had always withheld his innermost feelings, particularly about the women in his life. That is, until now.

"Sometimes all I see are the roadblocks," Ryan explained. "Our jobs, our lifestyles, our history."

"Do you love her?"

"I do, but that doesn't necessarily define a clear path forward."

Miles could sense the conflict in his friend's voice. "There is never a clear path forward, buddy boy. You simply buy a ticket and get on for the ride," he advised.

"You're right, I guess. It's simply a matter of this being new territory for me. I'll keep you posted as things progress with Rebecca. Please continue to keep me up to date on Olivia's case as well. I'm just as invested in her future emotionally as I intend to be financially."

"Absolutely. I'll call or text with any new information. I'm going to let you break the news of your contribution to Olivia. She should hear it from you. Gotta go. Kettle's boiling."

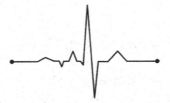

CHAPTER 21

When Agent Drummond returned to her office the next day, there was a forensic report on her desk detailing the evidence found in the envelope and on the check Olivia had received in the mail. They were a positive ID match from their database. The prints and DNA belonged to Alexander William Stratford, also known as William Ford, very likely the "William" whom Olivia and Janine had dealt with. Turned out he had a long record of violent criminal activity including several assault convictions.

She instructed her assistant to call their contact at the Chicago Police Department to ask to review any evidence recovered from the scene of Mrs. Winters's murder. It was a good bet the murder was at the hands of one Alexander William Stratford. Since Mrs. Winters's assailant hadn't broken into Olivia's apartment, it was unlikely the police had searched it. After confirming that with their CPD contact, a forensic field agent was dispatched to Olivia's apartment to search for additional clues.

Agent Drummond's staff of investigators then set about to research any of Stratford's past known associates, particularly ones who might be involved in loan-sharking schemes. While the arduous process of connecting the dots had just begun, they now had some solid leads to go on.

___

After a quiet morning Miles realized he, Olivia, and Mrs. Sims needed some type of activity as a distraction from simply sitting around and worrying. He had an idea that might be fun and would also be safe. He placed a call to George that immediately went to voicemail.

While he waited for George to call back, he joined the two women in the living room. Olivia was on her laptop and her mother was reading a book she'd found in Miles's bookcase. It was the classic, *To Kill a Mockingbird* by Harper Lee.

"I remember seeing the movie decades ago," she remarked when she saw Miles enter the room.

"A great movie," he said. "The book's even better. Listen, I'm working on an outing for this afternoon. It would be nice to get some fresh air and a change of scenery."

Olivia looked up from her laptop. "Can we do something like that and stay safe?"

"I'm working on something that should fit the bill perfectly."

As if on cue, his phone rang. It was George. Miles asked him if he had any plans for the afternoon. Turned out George had none.

Relieved, Miles asked if George would take him and a couple of friends out on the lake. "It's a beautiful day and I thought it would be the perfect way to spend the afternoon. We'll pay you the usual charter fee, of course."

George was agreeable and suggested they meet at the pier at one p.m. He added that he'd have fishing gear ready to go if anyone wanted to fish.

"Just a pleasure trip. What can I bring?" Miles asked, already knowing the answer.

"Refreshments for the three of you."

Knowing his friend as he did, Miles added, "And certainly a six-pack for you."

"Read my mind. See you at one p.m."

Miles turned to his guests, who seemed puzzled by the portion of the phone conversation they'd overheard.

"We're going for a boat ride. It a lovely day and a perfect opportunity to enjoy a cruise on Lake Michigan."

The concept brought big smiles from both women. They would be outside on a beautiful day, and being out on the lake couldn't be beat for a safe environment. Miles told them they'd each need to bring a jacket along in case it got cool on their cruise.

Before leaving, they had some lunch and packed a few soft drinks in Miles's cooler. After a brief stop at the Beer Barrel to pick up George's six-pack, they were on their way to the pier. Their assigned agent followed closely behind.

George was already on the boat when they arrived. He helped Miles hoist the beverage cooler onto the deck. After brief introductions, they set out onto the lake, leaving the agent in the marina parking lot to stand guard. George set the boat in a northerly route following the shoreline towards Milwaukee. Along the way, they passed a succession of beautiful homes, then a college campus and a state park, each situated on the picturesque tree-lined bluffs overlooking the water. A light warming breeze from the west allowed them to stash away the outerwear they'd brought along.

Besides a jacket, Olivia had brought along her sketch pad and was busy capturing the scenes they passed along the way. George asked Miles to assume the role of captain while he put out one of the fishing poles. Miles was a little puzzled until he saw George explaining the angler's art to Mrs. Sims in great detail. It was clear George's interests went beyond a lesson in catching fish. Miles hoped she was interested as well. A friendship between them could help them both fill the holes in their hearts from losing their spouses. He laughed at himself for ascribing so much significance to a fishing lesson. Nonetheless, if something developed he was confident it would prove to be good for both of them. Olivia noticed them too. She looked up from her sketch book and caught Miles's eye. She silently mouthed the words, "So cute!" and then returned to her drawing.

The afternoon on the water finished up two hours later. After tying up the boat, they unloaded the cooler and said their goodbyes. When they returned to the car, Mrs. Sims was the first to speak.

"Thank you so much for arranging this. It was so beautiful on the lake and George was a terrific host."

"So glad you enjoyed yourself," Miles replied. "Hopefully, you'll get more chances to experience it."

"I'm sure George would be on board with that," Olivia teased.

"Well, he did ask for my number," Mrs. Sims confessed. With that, they all broke out in uncontrollable laughter.

Back at the FBI office, the field agent had returned with his findings from Olivia's apartment. It appeared that Mrs. Winters's assailant had not been able to break into the apartment prior to the altercation. His search of the apartment, including Olivia's latest mail, provided no additional clues.

Shortly after debriefing the field agent, Agent Drummond's assistant, Roger, arrived at her desk. He was a very large man with a quiet voice that belied his stature.

"CPD just called. Turns out they had taken in Mrs. Winters's phone as evidence after the incident. Apparently, the assailant had tried to grab it during the struggle but left it behind when the neighbors showed up. Guess what they found," Roger asked quietly.

"Stratford's fingerprints, I assume," said Agent Drummond.

"Correct, so now they're preparing a warrant for his arrest."

"If they can find and arrest him, it will certainly help us get to the bottom of the whole loan-sharking operation. If they do capture him, hopefully we can get the Chicago DA to work with us on a plea deal. If we can flip him, it could bust this thing wide open," Agent Drummond surmised. "Let's not forget he's the tip of the iceberg. Anything on the storefront they used as a doctor's office?"

"It's owned and managed by the people who own the entire strip mall. It appears they lease that space for a variety of short-term rentals, like political campaigns or seasonal tax preparers. The current lessees, our suspects, paid upfront for a three-month rental with a cashier's check."

"See if you can backtrack the bank that issued the check. Any leads on the place where the surgery took place?"

"No leads so far. I've checked with CPD and they say they have no reports of anything similar."

"Thanks, Roger. Keep working on the bank information and the surgical location. Update me on any developments immediately."

Agent Drummond turned her attention to the other files on her desk. Unfortunately, the number of federal crimes currently being investigated seemed almost limitless. This case was, however, top-of-mind for her. She prioritized this case with her staff because it crossed so many lines of criminality. Most egregious was a calloused disregard for human life. She vowed to herself to use all of the resources she had at her disposal to bring these perpetrators to justice.

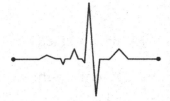

CHAPTER 22

Miles received a call from Ryan, who was checking in to see how Olivia and her mom were doing. He went into another room so they could speak candidly.

"Nothing new yet from the FBI," Miles said. "Olivia and her mom are doing as well as could be expected under the circumstances. On the plus side, we did have a great afternoon yesterday out on George's boat."

"Catch any fish?"

"No, but George may have snagged a new girlfriend."

"Olivia?" Ryan asked in disbelief.

Miles corrected him with a laugh. "Of course not. It's Mrs. Sims."

"Wow, good for them. A ray of sunshine, so to speak. Listen, I've just completed a draft of the first installment of my exposé. I'd like you to review it before it's finalized."

"Happy to. Send it over. What's happening with you and Rebecca?" Miles asked, feeling himself being nosy.

"It's kind of strange," Ryan admitted. "We're acting like things have escalated into some form of committed relationship but we've not actually acknowledged it out loud."

"What are you waiting for?" Miles said in a disapproving tone.

"Fear of rejection, I guess."

"Or maybe fear of acceptance?"

"Probably a bit of both, I suppose."

"Go out on a limb, buddy boy. That's where the fruit is!"

Miles hoped his encouragement might spur Ryan into openly expressing his feelings to Rebecca.

"I'll try. Give my best to Olivia and Mrs. Sims."

After hanging up with Ryan, Miles went back into the living room to rejoin his houseguests. When he got to the room Mrs. Sims waved him over with a huge smile on her face.

"Olivia has a gift for you," she declared.

It was the drawing she had begun on the boat, a beautiful view of the homes along the shoreline as seen over the shoulder of the boat's captain, Miles. He was genuinely touched and gave Olivia a huge hug without squeezing too tight, given her body was still tender from what she had recently endured.

"This is so amazing. I can't wait to get it framed. Speaking of amazing, you are truly talented. Art school is definitely the place for you."

He immediately took the drawing down to his workshop in the basement where he had stored some old pictures from his apartment. With a little luck, one of the frames could be better utilized showcasing Olivia's artwork. After finding a suitable candidate, he quickly exchanged the old picture of a New York street scene with his new acquisition.

Before heading upstairs to show off his handiwork, Miles called Agent Drummond to check on any new developments she might have. She brought him up to speed on the warrant for Stratford's arrest and her team's efforts to find the rest of the people involved. She also told him the local authorities had been briefed and would be patrolling both his and Mrs. Sims's neighborhoods with increased regularity.

"I'm sure Stratford has been assigned the task of getting rid of Olivia," Miles said.

"I agree. She's a major threat to expose their illegal enterprise.

He was likely given the edict to stop at nothing to eliminate that threat. That edict has already cost Mrs. Winters her life."

Ryan had decided to take Miles's advice. He and Rebecca had plans to go out for dinner that night to celebrate her first day of actual filming. The timing was perfect, as she expected it would be a short day since they were scheduled to only shoot a single scene on location in the Bronx. His afternoon would be occupied reediting the first installment of his series of essays. He'd send Miles a copy of what he had at the end of the day. Hopefully, Miles would be back shortly thereafter with his input.

He noticed a notification on his phone. An email from Ted. It was, as expected, a request for an update on the progress of the first installment. With the deadline for this Sunday's edition just twenty-four hours away, he replied that it wouldn't be ready for Sunday but promised, without fail, it would be submitted in time for next week's edition.

No sooner had he finished the email than he was surprised by the unexpected ring of his doorbell. He pushed the Talk button on the intercom and asked, "Who's there?"

Turned out, it was a delivery from the wine store. He went downstairs to retrieve his package. It contained a bottle of very expensive champagne and a note which read: *This is for our celebration. The rest of the night is your responsibility. Love, R.*

It quickly dawned on him that she, too, wanted to celebrate more than just her first day of filming. He had previously made a reservation at a fancy seafood restaurant in Midtown but decided to change it. There was this very cozy little French bistro on West 69th Street, near Central Park, which he decided would be a much more romantic destination.

After a slow start, Rebecca thought the first day of the show's filming went smoothly. The challenge of location work is almost always getting things set up. After they finally had all of the equipment in place and the actors made up, they could begin. Getting all of the angles figured out for both the long shots and the close-ups while assuring that all the props were placed properly was the most challenging part of the process. Once that was complete, they finally began actually rolling the cameras. Thankfully, it only took a few takes before they had what they needed. Once excused, Rebecca quickly removed her costume and makeup before making her way to the car assigned to her. The driver had already plotted the route back to her apartment and she was there in less than thirty minutes, giving her plenty of time for a quick nap before she had to begin prepping for her date.

She was awakened from her nap by the ding of a text alert. It was from Ryan: "Got the lovely bottle of champagne. For before or after?"

"After!" was all she texted back.

He picked her up promptly at seven fifteen p.m. as originally planned. She was waiting for him in the lobby. After a big hug and kiss, they jumped into the cab and were at the restaurant fifteen minutes later. They ordered a cocktail and started recounting the day's events.

"I assume by your mood and punctuality that things went well today," said Ryan.

The drinks arrived and she took a sip of her martini before answering. "They did. Very well. You never really know until you see the finished product. But so far, so good. Our director is meticulous, and it shows in how organized everything is. It also helps working with actors who are real pros. So, how was your day?"

"Productive. I finished a draft of the first installment and sent a copy to Miles for his critique. He'll be great at spotting any errors in the criminal investigation part of the essay. Ted's been pressing me for a time commitment, so I promised it for next week." Ryan still seemed concerned.

"If you've finished a draft, that shouldn't be a problem. Should it?" she asked.

"The first installment is basically done. So, no big deal getting that part to him in time. The additional installments are supposed to follow, one per week, until the series is complete. That's where the real time pressure comes in."

Rebecca sensed Ryan was feeling the pressure of his assignment. "You'll do fine. Have you told Olivia about your gift?"

"Not yet. I wanted to first talk to Ted and find out when I'll have the money in hand. Then I'll surprise her with it. Speaking of surprises, I need to change the subject before I explode."

"Please don't explode. What's on your mind?"

"Throwing caution to the wind, I have to tell you my feelings about us have changed." She was stricken. Before she could speak he added, "Turns out I'm in love with you."

Her fear was replaced by a gigantic smile and a steady flow of tears. Unable to speak at first, she held out both arms, demanding an embrace. Ryan quickly obliged while she whispered, "I love you too!"

The rest of the evening was a bit of a blur. A couple of drinks and dinner quickly faded into a long night in bed partaking of the champagne and each other. No plans were made before they parted the next morning. There'd be plenty of time for that in the days to come.

CHAPTER 23

Miles got up early, made enough coffee for the three of them, put his in a travel mug, and left for the office. It had been several days since he'd been there, so he expected plenty of mail to have been put through the slot in the door. Most of it turned out to be junk mail. Turning to his email, which was littered with junk as well, he did, however, spot one that caught his attention. It was from Richie at the Lakeville Police department.

Richie's email had a coroner's report from Gary, Indiana attached. "This came in today as a result of the inquiry you initiated. Thought it might be of interest if you're still looking for Olivia Sims. Sorry it took so long to get it. Guess the Gary Coroner's office has been busy."

It was of interest. The report provided clinical details about a Jane Doe whose description closely matched Olivia's. She had died from a heroin overdose complicated by a severe infection. The autopsy report included, among other details, a notation about a recent surgical scar on the left side of her abdomen from a nephrectomy, the removal of a kidney. Miles was floored by the parallels. This was very likely the work of the same people who were responsible for what happened to Olivia. If that were, in fact, the case, their activities had now crossed state lines. Because that expansion involved Indiana, it also meant these people could face the death penalty there if apprehended and convicted of murder.

Miles immediately called Agent Drummond and filled her

in on what he'd just learned. They both recognized this was a very significant development which might well lead the FBI closer to the source of the criminal organization. The sooner they found these people, the sooner Olivia and others like her would be safe. Agent Drummond thanked Miles and asked him to forward Richie's email with the attachment to her, which he did immediately.

A few minutes later he heard his phone buzzing and had to search through the pile of papers on his desk to find it. It was Bobbie.

"Hello, counselor," he answered. "Did I forget to mail the rent check?"

"Hi. No, you're all paid up. In fact, I'd like to send some money your way," she offered.

"You have my complete attention," he responded anxiously.

"My new client is a company that is being sued by their competitor, who claims my client may have unlawfully obtained some of their competitor's proprietary software. I need concrete evidence proving otherwise in order to defend the lawsuit. Interested?"

"You bet. Fill me in." Miles jumped at the chance to investigate some big-time corporate espionage.

"I'll email you a zip file containing a series of related documents as well as notes from my meeting with the client. After you've had a chance to look over everything, we can talk. Monday, early afternoon work for you?"

"How about I call you around two p.m.?"

"Fine. I'll send the file over before the end of the day. Oh, and say hi to Ryan for me."

"He's back in New York. I'm probably speaking out of school, but I believe he's just professed his love to this woman he's been seeing."

"Good for him." Bobbie's attempt at a congratulatory response did little to mask her disappointment.

Miles was elated about the prospects of this new case. It would certainly provide a substantial number of billable hours which he could really use given all the pro bono work he'd been doing on Olivia's behalf. He spent the next couple of hours doing busy work around the office, even wiping down the furniture with a dust rag. Anything to provide a distraction from what he anticipated to be an ever-increasing drama surrounding Olivia and her antagonists.

Before leaving the office he decided to call Mrs. Sims to see if she needed him to pick up anything on his way home.

"Miles," she said, "I hope you don't mind, but I've decided to cook dinner for all of us tonight."

"That would be great. Do you want to give me a shopping list?"

"Actually, I took the liberty of inviting George to join us. I've given him the shopping list. Hope that's okay."

"Of course it's okay. Sounds like fun," Miles acknowledged.

Miles wasn't sure which one of them had escalated the relationship, but he was happy for them both. Two wonderful people who had hopefully now found a cure for the emptiness in their lives. So far, the events of the day had provided a huge lift to his spirits. Mrs. Sims's cooking would likely continue that pattern.

Before leaving for the day, he decided to check in with Ryan to get the latest details on his romance.

"You disappoint me," Ryan said, opening the conversation.

"How so?" said Miles.

"I expected a call from you at the break of dawn."

"I would have, but I didn't want to interrupt any morning calisthenics." His joke only brought a groan.

quered

"All right. Here's what you want to know in a nutshell. I told her I loved her. She told me she loved me too. Nothing else was decided."

"Congratulations. I trust that, despite your rather cold description, you're way beyond excited."

"As far beyond as one could imagine. The thing is, I'm not sure what we do next." Ryan's puzzlement was understandable, particularly given this was new territory for him.

"Welcome to the world of relationships, my friend. Just be straight with one another and you'll figure out how to handle whatever comes next." Miles even surprised himself with the quality of that advice.

"Guess you're right. What's happening there?"

Miles proceeded to bring Ryan up-to-date on current events including the investigation, Olivia's improving condition, the coroner's report from Indiana, the infatuation of George and Mrs. Sims that began on the boat ride, and his new case assignment. He decided not to complicate things by mentioning Bobbie asking about him. They concluded their call by agreeing to keep updating one another on all new developments. Once the call was over, Miles closed up shop and drove home to what he hoped would be a very low-key evening.

After receiving his customary squealing greeting from Molly, he followed the scent of something delicious into the kitchen. There were Mrs. Sims and George, each clad in an apron, knee-deep in dinner preparations.

"George, you look very dapper in that apron," Miles declared.

"Cora's teaching me how to make risotto," George replied with pride.

"Just keep stirring!" she demanded playfully.

"What else is on the menu?" Miles asked. He was struck by

how much George and Mrs. Sims already seemed like a couple, given the short amount of time they'd known one another. A sharp contrast to the lengthy process Ryan and Rebecca had been going through.

"Chicken piccata and haricot verts," she responded, waving a lightly floured chicken breast over the frying pan.

"Anything I can do?" Miles asked.

"Open a bottle of red wine, if you have any."

"I do and I will," Miles said as he headed to the basement to retrieve a couple bottles of Chianti from his makeshift wine cellar.

The dinner was wonderful. The food, the wine, and the four of them enjoying each other's company was just like what a dinner with friends was supposed to be, Miles thought. He decided not to spoil the evening with talk about the autopsy report he'd received that afternoon. After they finished eating, Miles retired to his room to finish writing up his notes on Ryan's essay. He needed to get that done so he could shift his focus to Bobbie's case.

Ryan and Rebecca were having a late dinner as her second day of shooting had been a much more lengthy one. Since her arrival had been uncertain, they had agreed to order a pizza once she was on the way to Ryan's. They sat on opposite sides of the dining room table and, over beer and pizza, they began the "what comes next" discussion.

"Having said we love each other creates so many questions, don't you think?" Ryan asked.

"Boy, does it. But hopefully they're delightful questions. Want to start?"

Ryan could see she was all in. "Okay. Here's a big one. Do

you think we should live together, and if yes, now or at some time later on?"

"That is a big one. I definitely want us to live together, but the where and when part is challenging."

They began with the "where." They agreed that neither Ryan's nor Rebecca's current place was adequate for two. Naturally, that would dictate the 'when,' as Ryan's apartment would have to be sublet, Rebecca's condo would have to be sold, and they'd have to find a new place suitable for the two of them. They agreed that starting to look for a place was their first step. They also agreed it was enough of a start for now as it was getting late. Before going to bed, Ryan saw Miles had emailed him his thoughts on the essay. It would keep until tomorrow, he thought. Hopefully, it would help him finish the first installment and get a head start on the next one.

CHAPTER 24

The previous night had been a wonderful, albeit brief, return to normalcy. Unfortunately, the wonderful night was only a momentary respite from the danger that had Olivia and her mom in hiding. As much as he wanted to be proactive in resolving their case, Miles knew he'd have to wait for the FBI to uncover some new information before he'd be able to provide any meaningful assistance. He decided to turn his attention to the new case Bobbie had provided, so he headed to his office to begin unpacking the contents of the digital files she'd emailed him.

The case centered around a lawsuit brought against Bobbie's client, Jefferson/Shaw LLC, for allegedly using proprietary software that belonged to their competitor, AccuTest, Inc. Both companies specialized in product design. The software in question provided the opportunity to digitally perform tests on products by simulating the actual conditions those products would encounter in the real world. The example cited in Bobbie's notes detailed simulated wind-tunnel testing for aircraft parts. These digital simulations would cost a manufacturer a small fraction of what actual live testing would.

Jefferson/Shaw was founded and originally owned by Ralph Jefferson and Richard Shaw. Ralph Jefferson passed away two years ago and his stake in the company had been left to his son, Alan. Jefferson/Shaw's owners were the only people with the encrypted access to their program's code, which would be needed to allow anyone to modify their program to include the allegedly stolen software. They had both vehemently denied any wrongdoing. Bobbie had been hired by them to fight the lawsuit brought by AccuTest. She in turn hired Miles to find the evidence needed to exonerate her clients.

Miles spent the balance of the day developing a list of questions for Bobbie and her client's principals. The answers would be critical in helping him form the strategy for his investigation. Before leaving the office, he emailed Bobbie the list of questions along with an offer to come to Madison to meet with her and the client. On his way home, Ryan called.

"Thanks for your comments on my essay," he told Miles. "They were very helpful."

"Glad to help. Are you finished with it now?"

"Yes. On to installment two." Ryan sounded genuinely relieved.

From there the conversation shifted to current events. Ryan's blossoming love affair with Rebecca, George's new relationship with Mrs. Sims, Olivia's health continuing to improve, and the case Bobbie had given him.

"Looks like we both have our hands full," said Ryan. "Are you expecting something to break in Olivia's case soon?"

"I sure hope so. We're all living in an alternate reality until this thing gets resolved," Miles lamented.

"With the FBI's involvement, I'm optimistic things will come to head quickly now."

"I suspect that will be the case. The question now is only, 'How soon?' Speaking of how soon, any discussion of the M-word between the two of you?" Miles prodded.

"Jeez, we've just begun discussing living together. Who knows, we may never cross that bridge." Ryan was notably unnerved by the question.

"I wasn't suggesting you should, just curious if it had come up," Miles said apologetically.

"Sorry, this is new territory for me. For both of us, actually. The commitment to each other is certainly there in full. Anything ceremonial is, at least for the moment, not on our radar."

"I'm really happy for you. Can't wait to meet her." Miles was really curious what the woman who had captured Ryan's heart was like.

"Well, come to New York for a visit." Ryan offered.

"I'd like that."

When Miles returned home, he again saw George's SUV in the driveway. The three of them and Molly were in the living room, apparently awaiting his arrival.

"Are we preparing for a repeat of last night's festivities?" he asked.

"Please come sit down. We have an idea to run past you," Mrs. Sims said, motioning for him to take a seat on the couch next to Olivia.

"Okay, I'm all ears." Somewhat perplexed, Miles took a seat on the couch as instructed.

George took the floor. "My family has a small cottage on Rock Lake. My brothers and I share it. I thought it might be fun for Cora, Olivia, and me to escape there for a long weekend. It will relieve you of watching over them for a little while and give you time to get some work done. There's no way any of the people who might be looking for Olivia would know where we are. What d'ya think?"

"I guess I have no major objections," said Miles, "but we need to run it by the FBI first. I'll call Agent Drummond to see if she's okay with it."

Miles called her right then and briefed her on the proposal. Her response was very short and to the point. He relayed it to the others.

"She said it's okay, but you must be extremely careful. No going into town for Olivia and no phone calls to anyone except me. And use George's phone for all communications. Okay?"

They nodded in unison.

"So, when will you be leaving?"

Mrs. Sims got up from her seat and smiled at Miles. "We're all packed and ready to go. Just wanted your approval before taking off."

"Miles, don't worry. I will see to it that they're safe at all times," George promised.

As much as he worried about giving up his role as protector, Miles knew George would do everything possible to keep them safe. Their remote location, as George noted, would be almost untraceable. Before they left, Miles pulled George aside.

"Do you have a gun, just in case?" he asked quietly.

George simply gave him a reassuring wink.

The threesome arrived at the cottage less than two hours later. They unpacked the car and started getting acclimated. George suggested he go to the store to pick up some groceries.

"Here's $40 for the groceries," Mrs. Sims said, stuffing two twenties into the breast pocket of George's shirt. He tried to return the money, but she wouldn't have it. He smiled dutifully and took off for the store.

"You two act like an old married couple," Olivia observed.

"Funny you should mention that," said Mrs. Sims sheepishly. "How would you feel if I shared the big bedroom with George? The other one is quite small for two."

After thinking about it for a moment, Oliva responded, "Only if you promise not to be groaning all night."

Obviously a little flustered by Olivia's joke, Mrs. Sims shot back, "Be careful, child. I can still wash your mouth out with soap."

With that, they both broke out laughing. It seemed that this was the happiest either of them had been in quite a while.

George returned less than an hour later. After stowing away the groceries, he took them for a ride on the small boat he and his brothers owned. It was an old Boston Whaler with seating for four. After a couple of presses on the starter button, the motor kicked in and they were off.

With everyone gone, Miles decided to spend the weekend cleaning the house and playing with Molly. On Sunday morning he was able to see Ryan's article in print. He assumed now that it was printed, Ryan would let Olivia know about his gift to her. Now if only they could end the threat from the loan-sharking criminals, things would finally be back in full working order.

CHAPTER 25

Being summoned to the boss's high-rise apartment on Wacker Drive was seldom a positive development. Stratford entered the building at nine a.m. Monday morning as instructed. The doorman allowed his entry after confirmation from the owner of the penthouse, Jonathan Reese. Mr. Reese was not your typical businessman.

The elevator delivered Stratford to the forty-third floor. The door to Mr. Reese's unit was already open when he arrived. He walked in and found his boss staring out at the expansive Chicago skyline along Michigan Avenue. Jonathan Reese was a tall, dapper man in his early fifties whose wide-ranging business enterprises included both the criminal, like loan-sharking and protections schemes, to the legitimate, like Oak Lawn Property Management and a chain of laundromats.

Without turning around, Reese motioned for Stratford to be seated in a chair next to the window.

"This scene never gets old," Reese said. "I do some of my best thinking while taking in the view. My sources tell me the authorities are looking into our activities, so I've decided to suspend our loan operations for a while. I've already instructed your coworkers to shut things down at the sites involved."

"What do you want me to do?"

Reese turned around and focused his steel-blue eyes on Stratford. "Our clients, with one notable exception, have all recovered. They have no reason to betray us by going to the authorities because they know full well doing so would put them in legal jeopardy. I'm told the other one is missing and is likely suffering from the after effects of her surgery. She is now the only one who is a liability. She's one of yours, so you are to focus on finding and eliminating that threat once and for all."

Reese had issued Stratford's marching orders and pointed toward the door, which was Stratford's cue to leave. Stratford hurried to get out of Reese's apartment. He was not the type to be afraid of anyone, but his boss had him scared. On the elevator ride down, Stratford realized he first had to find Janine if he was going to locate Olivia. Janine was very likely in contact with her friend and would know where she was hiding out. Once he had what he needed from Janine, she would have to be eliminated as well. To find her, he would first stake out Jake's Jazz Bar for a night or two. If he found her there, he'd force her to divulge Olivia's whereabouts. Stopping by her apartment would be his fallback plan. It would be far riskier, as the neighbors might see or hear him. Also, confronting her in the apartment would make getting rid of her far more complicated.

Stratford decided to handle this job on his own. He'd only enlist some of his comrades if his search for Janine came up empty.

At the FBI office, Agent Drummond was reviewing the Gary police report on the Jane Doe. The fact that she was a Jane Doe in the first place was puzzling given her heroin overdose as a cause of death. Most addicts have a history of arrests which would put their fingerprints into the database. Even more puzzling was the lack of a coroner's note regarding additional "tracks" on her body from previous injections. The facts led her to conclude the victim was not a local or an addict, just a victim who had simply been drugged and dumped there.

There was a whole lot of information missing, including a motive. She'd have her staff research missing-person reports and contact area hospitals to see if this Jane Doe might have legitimately donated a kidney. Even if they concluded she was somehow connected to loan-sharking activities, they were nowhere near finding a connection beyond the missing kidney.

It was eleven a.m. and time for her staff meeting. When she entered the conference room, all seven agents who had been busily engaged with their laptops turned their attention to her. After a few updates on other pending cases, the discussion shifted to the loan-sharking operation.

"Do we have anything new on this one?" she asked.

Agent Stevens stood, taking on the role of spokesperson for the group. "We have uncovered three other Chicago-area storefronts that had been rented in a similar manner to this last one. Also, the MO of using a cashier's check to pay three months' rent in advance is the same as used by the man who the landlords dealt with. It matches our Mr. Stratford."

"Have we uncovered any other possible customers of the loan sharks?" Agent Drummond asked.

"Just the one possibility in Gary."

"How about any connections Stratford had to other known criminals or organized crime?"

"We're looking into the people with whom he'd been arrested and served time with. It's quite a list, but we're working through it. So far nothing stands out."

"Thanks. Please keep me updated on any new developments. I sense this one is going to escalate very soon. If there is nothing else, meeting's adjourned."

A small pile of mail from Saturday was waiting for Miles

when he arrived at his office on Monday. He found an email from Bobbie at the top of his Outlook inbox which contained a number of answers to the questions he had sent her regarding the Jefferson/Shaw case. She noted the other answers would follow as soon as possible and then asked if he could meet with the client at her office in Madison on Wednesday at ten a.m. He responded by thanking her for the answers she provided and accepting the meeting invitation.

It occurred to him he would pass by the exit for Rock Lake on his way to Madison. If his friends were still going to be there, he'd stop by to see them on his way back to Lakeville. This would be a perfect opportunity for Ryan to call Olivia with the news about his gift. It gave him another reason to check in.

"Morning, Miles," Ryan answered. "I assume you saw the article."

"I did. It was extremely well done. What's the reaction been?"

"Too soon to tell. It'll take a couple of days for the number of online downloads and shares to be measured. The *Times* folks have been very positive about the piece. Let's hope the public feels the same way. Regardless, I'm well into the second installment."

"Listen, George has taken the women to his cottage for a few days. I have a meeting in Madison and will likely join them Wednesday afternoon. Would you like me to call you when we're all together so you can tell Olivia about your gift?"

"Good idea. I'll be here typing away, so call whenever you're ready."

"Will do." As soon as Miles ended the call, he texted George to see if they'd be there on Wednesday afternoon. While waiting for an answer, he returned to his review of the information in Bobbie's email.

Those answers spelled out who the owners had allowed within their organization to work on software modification, the company's past dealings with the competitor who was suing them, and the relationship between the partners. What was missing were the details he requested regarding Jefferson/Shaw's financial history, any clients the two competitors may have had in common or had as targets for new contracts, and any employees, past or present, who may have worked for both firms.

Nothing in the answers provided immediately stood out as a link to the alleged software pirating. He'd have to take an in-depth look into the employees listed in the email who had worked on the software to see if he could uncover any connections to the rival firm. He'd need to send Bobbie a return email asking for more information on those individuals.

Bobbie's email went on to say there were no known conflicts between the competing companies, but he'd need to dig deeper into that angle to be sure. The current partners appeared to get along fine except for the understandable suspicion this whole mess had created. What wasn't mentioned was the relationship issues between the founders, Ralph Jefferson and Richard Shaw, before Mr. Jefferson passed away. He would definitely add that question to the others he'd take with him to the meeting on Wednesday.

The growl in his stomach told him it was time for a lunch break. He'd brought along some leftovers from the meal Mrs. Sims had made, which far surpassed his usual luncheon fare. Between bites he checked his phone and saw a return text from George confirming they'd still be at the cottage on Wednesday, and he provided the address along with detailed directions. George went on to explain the need for those directions because some of the access roads would not appear on the GPS on Miles's phone.

After lunch, Miles returned to the Jefferson/Shaw case. He spent the next two hours making a list of additional questions and copies of documents he needed for the meeting in Madison with their executives.

CHAPTER 26

In his effort to find Janine, Stratford staked out Jake's Jazz Bar on Monday night without even catching a glimpse of her. It would be unusual, he figured, that a bartender would miss out on two consecutive nights of work, so there would be a very good chance she'd be at the bar on Tuesday. He was wrong. There was no sign of her the next night either, so he decided to inquire with the bartender on duty.

"What can I get you?" the bartender asked.

"I'm looking for my friend Janine," Stratford answered.

"She's on vacation."

"Any idea when she'll be back?"

"Nope. Didn't say where she was going or when she'd be back."

That sealed the deal. He'd have to go over to her apartment right away to see what he could find out. It was after one a.m. when he arrived at her place in Cicero. There were no lights on or sounds coming from her apartment. Because her unit was on the first floor he was able to pry open her bedroom window and enter without detection. Once inside, it was obvious she wasn't there, and the spoiled milk in the refrigerator was a sure sign she hadn't been there for a while. It was also apparent she had left in a hurry, planning to be gone for an extended period of time. All of her toiletries were gone, and her closet and drawers were half empty and left askew. He did find something he deemed to be significant: a business card of someone by the name of Miles

Darien. Stratford assumed there was a good chance this guy, Miles Darien, knew where to find Olivia.

To avoid being seen, he left the apartment the same way he had gotten in.

The report from the Cicero Police Department detailing the early morning break-in at Janine Banner's apartment was on Agent Drummond's desk when she arrived on Wednesday morning. Modern police technology had identified Ms. Banner as a person of interest for the Chicago office of the FBI and had forwarded the report over immediately. The report read:

"A neighbor who was walking his dog along East Avenue saw an unidentified man crawl out of the window and jump into his car. After the intruder had driven off, the neighbor called 911. A squad car with two Cicero officers (Officers Rodriguez and Hazleton) arrived less than five minutes after the call. The neighbor described the man to Officer Rodriguez as tall and Caucasian. Unfortunately, it was so dark he couldn't be sure of the man's age range, or the make and model of the vehicle or the license plate number. Officer Hazleton inspected the break-in. It appeared nothing other than women's clothing had been taken, and there was no sign of a struggle. After finishing their assessment at the scene, both officers returned to the station to check their database to confirm the identity of the apartment's rightful occupant as Janine Banner."

Based on the information in the report, it was apparent to Agent Drummond that the break-in meant the loan shark's henchmen were likely hunting down Janine in hopes of locating Olivia. Miles had shared Janine's current whereabouts with the FBI. Even though it was unlikely she'd be found, the police in Rockford were alerted to be on the lookout for any suspicious activity near Janine's sister's home. Next she placed a call to Miles to alert him of the latest developments.

"Olivia and her mom are not in Lakeville with me," he informed her. "They're still in hiding at the place I told you about, which is fifty miles from here."

"Good," she said. "I needn't tell you how resourceful these guys can be, and they play rough. If they somehow make a connection between you and Olivia Sims, they will certainly pay you a visit. Please stay diligent."

"I understand. Thank you for the warning. What's being done to protect Janine, given the likelihood they're looking for her?"

"We're taking every precaution to protect everyone in-volved," Agent Drummond assured him. "I'll keep you updated on any new developments, and I need you to do the same."

"Of course," he promised.

After finishing his call with Agent Drummond, Miles breathed a sigh of relief knowing all of the people in Olivia's circle were safely out of sight and in hiding. His trip to Madison couldn't have been more opportune. He'd be on his way in half an hour. Molly loved car rides, so he decided to take her along. It also alleviated the need to rush home after meeting up with the group at Rock Lake.

The ride to Madison was uneventful. Molly slept the entire way, soothed by the jazz music on the satellite radio. Miles arrived in town on schedule, and after a brief search found a parking lot a couple of blocks from Bobbie's office. The short walk to the office building was refreshing and gave Molly a chance to pee. As he approached the building it occurred to him that Molly might not be welcome there. Too late now, he thought.

Undaunted, the two of them marched into Bobbie's office suite like they owned the place. Thankfully, the receptionist was a dog lover who promised to look after Molly while he went into the meeting. She informed Miles he was the first to arrive.

Bobbie was waiting for him in the conference room. It was spacious, with beautiful views of Lake Monona and downtown Madison with the State Capitol as its centerpiece. Miles grabbed one of the bottles of water on the credenza and joined Bobbie at the table.

"How was the ride?" she asked.

"Relaxing. Molly loved it."

"She's here? Where?"

"Your receptionist has graciously offered to watch her. How are you?"

"Well, this case has me a little stressed. I hate not having anything concrete to base a defense on. What's your take?"

Miles sat down and pulled out his notebook. "Given the high degree of likelihood that the software theft would be detected, it seems unlikely to me that either of the owners were involved. At least not knowingly. I'm expecting to find someone else who's responsible. Likely a current or previous employee who found a way to gain access to the source code of both organizations. That employee could attempt to claim that the stolen code was actually something they created and, if it went undetected by AccuTest, garner all the benefits from Jefferson/Shaw, such an accomplishment would deliver. Also, I think it's a possibility that AccuTest may have planted the code so they could use its detection to destroy Jefferson/Shaw."

"Really. That's quite a leap."

"Not really. Think about it. If their involvement went undetected, they'd be able to put their main competitor in terrible legal jeopardy."

"Holy shit. If that's what happened, this goes way beyond a simple theft of some trade secrets."

Before she could continue, there was a knock on the door. The Jefferson/Shaw people had arrived. She gave Miles a look that clearly said, *Please keep your theories to yourself for now.* He nodded.

For the next hour and a half, Miles asked questions of the two men. They were very forthcoming with information and offered Miles access to any data he needed, even inviting him to visit their operation in the neighboring town of Sun Prairie.

Once the meeting concluded, Bobbie and Miles debriefed.

"They were sure forthcoming with information," said Miles. "My gut tells me they are not the bad guys in this situation. I'm going to focus on who else might have done this, why they did it, and who helped them. Are you good with that approach?"

She shrugged amicably. "You're the investigator. Do your thing. Would you and Molly like to stay and have an early dinner?"

"Can we have a rain check? I have a stop to make on the way home."

"Sure," Bobbie said, wiping a fake tear from her eye. She walked him out to the lobby, gave Molly a belly rub, and reminded Miles to apprise her of any developments.

The ride to George's place on Rock Lake took less than an hour. Miles was glad he hadn't been left to use his GPS to find the cottage. After traversing several back roads that seemed more like footpaths, he arrived safely. Once everyone exchanged hellos, they sat down in the yard and made small talk, a welcome change for the group who had spent so much time in recent days discussing Olivia's predicament. After a few minutes of casual chatter, Miles brought up Ryan's article, which they had all read online.

"A well-written article, for sure. Important, too," Mrs. Sims commented.

"It sure made me realize how easily people like me who are in trouble can get sucked in," said Olivia. "I can't thank Ryan enough for including elements of my story. I hope it makes it real for anyone thinking about doing such a stupid thing."

"How about thanking him now?" Miles offered.

Olivia nodded, so he dialed Ryan and put the call on speaker phone.

"Hey, Ryan. I'm here with Olivia, her mom, and George. They'd like to offer their comments on your article."

"Hi, everybody. Comment away."

Olivia spoke first. "Ryan, I'm honored that my situation helped you write your story. I can only hope it helps some unsuspecting people avoid a tragedy."

"Well, Olivia, I hope so too. Thank you for inspiring me to write this essay and the others to come in the series. As a special thank you, I'd like to give you a gift. My editor gave me $20,000 for this first installment. I'm going to split it with you, fifty-fifty. Hopefully, it will help you with your medical expenses and art school tuition."

Olivia and her mom both started to cry, so Miles spoke up first.

"There are some happy people here, buddy boy. Give them a moment to collect themselves before they speak. How is essay number two coming along?"

"I've made significant progress on it. You'll definitely see it on Sunday."

Olivia had composed herself and leaned in towards the phone. "Ryan, you are my guardian angel. I don't know how I'm ever going to thank you."

"Simple." He replied. "Graduate from art school and pursue your career."

"I will. Mom's a little overwhelmed, so she'll have to thank you later."

"Sounds good. Bye, everyone." The call ended and Miles allowed the group, still quite stunned, to sit quietly for a few moments before saying anything.

George broke the silence. "Ryan's a gem. Particularly since I taught him how to fish."

Everyone's tearful smiles broke into laughter.

"You knew about this all along, didn't you?" Mrs. Sims accused Miles.

"Yep. It was a well-kept conspiracy. Now on to some other important business. I'm hungry. How about an early dinner so Molly and I can get back to Lakeville before it gets late? I'm working on a new case and need to begin on it early tomorrow."

Mrs. Sims jumped into action, setting off for the kitchen to turn the groceries George had brought from the store into a meal. Over dinner they talked a lot about how Olivia's future had brightened. Miles suggested that they continue to lay low just to err on the side of caution. He also reminded George to keep his gun handy at all times.

Immediately after finishing their meal, Miles and Molly left for home. On the way, Miles's thoughts turned back to the daunting task of assuring Olivia's safety.

CHAPTER 27

A s Miles approached the front of his house, he noticed a
large black Chevy Suburban parked several houses down
from his. He knew all of the neighbors' cars, and this was
definitely not one of them. It could be someone visiting one of
those neighbors, but maybe it was something more sinister.
He decided to park down the block in the opposite direction
and leave Molly in the car. He also removed his handgun from
underneath the driver's seat and tucked it into his belt.

He approached his house through the backyard of the house
next door. Circling around his garage, he was able to advance
to his back door undetected. The kitchen light was on, and he
knew he didn't leave it on when he left. He was very particular
about such things. There was a conversation going on in the
kitchen, which he assumed was likely Stratford and his men.
Then he heard a familiar voice. It was Agent Drummond.
Relieved, he entered the back door and yelled, "Hello!"

"Hi, Mr. Darien." She looked down at his gun. "Sorry if my
agents and I frightened you in some way. We tried to call you
to bring you up to speed, but our calls went to voicemail." She
went on to introduce Miles to Agents Stevens and Maye.

Miles took out his phone and, sure enough, it was off. He
must have unintentionally shut it off when he hung up from
the call with Ryan.

"Sorry about that. Why are you here?" Miles asked.

"We've been watching your office and home as well as the
Sims's house ever since Janine Banner's apartment was broken

into. We didn't know for sure if Stratford would come looking for you until we saw evidence that he'd been to your office."

"What evidence?" Miles asked.

"Like I said, our agents have been periodically checking on your office to watch for any suspicious activity," Agent Drummond explained, somewhat annoyed at being pressed. "This morning one of our agents saw someone fitting Stratford's description leave your office building in quite a hurry. Possibly to look for you here. It is our opinion that he will try again, as you are his best chance to find Ms. Sims. When we couldn't reach you, I decided to position ourselves here just in case he decided to break in under the cover of darkness. We also have agents patrolling the street where Mrs. Sims lives, and we're continuing to watch your office."

"So, now we wait?" Miles asked even though he knew the answer.

"Now we wait," she confirmed.

"One suggestion. Move that big SUV away from here. It's a dead giveaway," Miles recommended.

"We will," Agent Drummond said, giving Agent Maye a scowl. Then she said to Miles, "And you need to bring your car into the driveway."

Miles and the agent slipped out the back door. Each one headed in a different direction using backyards for cover. Once Agent Maye was in the yard corresponding to the SUV, he nonchalantly walked out to it, got into the SUV, and drove off to find a parking space out of sight of the house. Miles used a similar tactic, but instead of driving off he pulled into his driveway. He and Molly walked in through the front door this time. Molly immediately went to greet the agents. She'd never met a stranger she didn't like.

After Agent Maye left in the SUV, only Agent Drummond and Agent Stevens remained with Miles.

"Here's how I'd like to proceed," said Agent Drummond. "We'll stay the night. Tomorrow, I'd like you to go to work like you would normally do. Once you've left the house, we'll wait a few minutes and then leave as well. Our agents will be watching your office. If Stratford shows up, they'll arrest him."

"That's all fine and dandy, but what if he doesn't show up? Will we be going through this same ballet indefinitely?"

"No, but for the time being it is imperative that you keep Olivia Sims out of Lakeville. She's the real target, and we need to keep her out of harm's way."

Miles immediately texted George to keep his companions away from Lakeville until he directed them otherwise. He then offered his empty bedrooms to the agents, but they declined, deciding instead to camp out in the living room. None of them actually slept.

The next morning, Miles skipped his usual breakfast routine and left immediately after getting dressed. He left for his office around nine o'clock as he had been instructed. On the way, he stopped for gas and a cup of coffee. He wasn't too happy about the lack of artificial sweetener, but it wouldn't ruin his day. When he got into his car, he tried to get his drink situated for driving when the passenger door opened. A man in a hooded sweatshirt jumped into the passenger seat and drew a gun on him.

"Start the car. Don't say a word."

Miles froze.

"Start the car," the man demanded.

Miles fiddled nervously with the keys and finally started the engine. The gun pointed at his head was making him sweat. The man in the hoody kept his eyes focused on Miles.

"Drive out of this lot, turn right at the corner, and park a block down."

Miles knew there was no way he could get his gun from under the seat before his passenger would shoot him, so he obeyed. Once he parked the car, another car pulled up behind his. A man got out, walked to Miles's car, and got into the back seat. Miles assumed it was Stratford.

"Mr. Darien, I assume you know why we're here," Stratford told him.

"Haven't the slightest," Miles replied.

Stratford leaned forward and pressed the barrel of his gun to the back of Miles's head. "Where's Olivia Sims? Before you answer, be aware if you really don't know or pretend not to know, there's no reason for me to keep you alive."

Miles knew he had to escape. He had seen the faces of both of his two unwelcome passengers and could now identify them. Miles knew he had to do something bold. Since the car was still running, he slammed it into gear and stomped on the gas pedal. Neither man had fastened their seat belt, so the car lurching forward knocked each of them out of their seats and sent the gun to the floor. Miles seized the opportunity to open his door and roll out onto the street. The car continued careening down the street with the two thugs aboard and smashed into a concrete light post at the end of the block. Miles was able to quickly gather himself and run in the opposite direction toward the main thoroughfare where the gas station was. Stratford and his accomplice got out of Miles's mangled car and hurried back to theirs. Apparently deciding that chasing Miles onto a busy street was unwise, they sped off.

As soon as he caught his breath, Miles called Agent Drummond to come and get him.

"I just left your house and will be there in two minutes," she told him.

While he waited, he called AAA to retrieve what was left of his car. Agent Drummond picked him up in her black SUV five minutes later and left Agent Stevens behind to wait for the tow truck.

"You all right?" she asked as Miles reached into his now-crippled car to retrieve his briefcase and his gun.

"Well, let me see. My life has been threatened at gun point, my clothes are ruined, my left arm is ripped open from the elbow down, and my trusty Toyota is wrapped around a light post. Would you consider that all right?" he growled.

"Of course not. But you're alive. Let's get you to a doctor so we can have your arm looked after."

On the way to get medical assistance, she handed him a picture of Stratford, whom he immediately identified as the man he had seen in his rearview mirror holding a gun to his head.

"What now?" Miles asked.

"Hard to say, but I think you're still their immediate target. They need to find Olivia, and unless she turns up on her own, you're all they've got."

"Well, that's reassuring," Miles deadpanned.

"We're going to look after you," she assured him.

"Like you were when that guy just put a gun to my head?"

"We won't let that happen again."

After a brief stop at Memorial's walk-in clinic, Agent Drummond dropped off Miles back at home where two agents were waiting. They would be his bodyguards until this case was closed.

Before departing, Agent Drummond pulled Miles aside. "I'm heading back to the Chicago office. None of you will be safe until we first apprehend one Alexander William Stratford. Once he's in custody and confronted with life in prison, or quite possibly the death penalty, he'll sing like a bird. He possesses all the leverage required to secure a lenient sentence for himself by simply providing us with the mountain of evidence he surely has about his bosses' criminal activities. It's time to pull out all the stops to affect his capture and break the case wide open."

They shook hands and off she went.

Alone with the agents, they all settled into the living room. Miles then remembered he still had work to attend to. Since he'd promised to get moving on Bobbie's case right away, he went upstairs to his bedroom to get started on his investigation of the software theft. There was a deadline looming, and Bobbie would need time to prepare her defense. The thing was, he couldn't stop his hands from shaking.

Just then Miles's phone rang. The caller ID said it was Ryan. He decided to let it go to voicemail. No sense ruining his day, too.

CHAPTER 28

O n Friday morning, Ryan handed in the second installment of his series to Ted at the *Times*, as promised. He decided to take the rest of the day off from work and do a little house hunting. If he came across anything interesting, he'd try to take Rebecca to see it over the weekend. They each loved living on the Upper West Side. Their wanting to stay in that part of town greatly narrowed his search.

He studied all of the current online listings which matched their wish list of layout, amenities, price, and location. There were several condos that seemed to be worthy of a visit. One on West 58th near West End Avenue seemed ideal, so he contacted the realtor online, who immediately responded by phone.

The realtor, who introduced herself as Lisa Reynolds, offered Ryan a walk-through the next day at two o'clock.

Ryan confirmed the time would work for them. She told him to meet her in the lobby of the building and added that it was a new listing, and it would likely be gone in short order. Ms. Reynolds was already pushing for a close.

Ryan said goodbye, purposely without acknowledging her none-too-subtle pressure tactics.

He texted Rebecca and asked her to give him a call when she had finished filming. They planned to spend the weekend together at her place, and he wanted to head over there as soon as she was on her way. There was a bottle of Barolo in his wine rack, which would be a perfect accompaniment to the pasta

Bolognese they had discussed ordering. He put it on the table next to his front door so he wouldn't forget it.

Rebecca called shortly after five o'clock and invited him over around six thirty. In an intriguing voice, she mentioned having something important to share with him. Ironically, he had something important to share with her as well.

He buzzed the intercom promptly at six thirty. Ryan was being his usual unfashionable self by arriving exactly at the appointed hour. It was why she hadn't given him a key.

"There was no telling what state of disarray you might find me in if you could enter unannounced," she once told him.

After a big "hello" hug and kiss they made their way to the couch.

"I thought this wine would go well with dinner," he said, setting the bottle on the coffee table.

"2007 Barolo, huh? You really know how to impress a girl."

"Is it working?"

"Guess you could say in this instance it's overkill. You impressed me a long time ago," she whispered in her most flirtatious actress voice.

"So, what is it you wanted to discuss?" he said, shifting the subject.

"Here it is. The producer and I were talking about this season's remaining episodes. He said they were all in development except for the finale. I asked him if I, meaning you and me, could submit a script. He agreed, provided we have a storyline to him within a couple of weeks." She paused, hoping for a sign of enthusiasm from Ryan.

"I'd love to work on something with you, but we don't even have a premise at this point and I'm still in the middle of my loan-sharking exposé."

"Turns out your exposé is where my idea for the premise comes from. I see a young woman coming into the clinic with a high fever from an infection. In the course of treating her, they discover she is missing a kidney, and from there we go on to the loan sharks' angle where the bad guys get brought to justice. A fictional version of Olivia's story would make for a really dramatic episode, don't you think?" Her enthusiasm was bubbling over.

"It's actually a really good concept. It will take a lot of work to turn it into a finished story but it's doable, I think. Since it's at the end of your season and would follow after my articles have all been published, the timing would work. Could be the perfect way to shed further light on the problem."

"So, you're onboard?"

He nodded. That being settled, they ordered dinner for delivery from their favorite Italian restaurant. They continued their discussion of the script concept over pasta and wine. After they cleaned up the dishes, Ryan gave her the lowdown on the condo he'd uncovered. He took out his phone and showed her the pictures and diagrams of the unit on the real estate company's website.

"Looks promising," she said. "It's unlikely we'll find 'our place' first time out, but we have to start somewhere."

"I'll start anywhere with you," he said, giving her a huge smile.

Miles was tending to his wounds when the phone rang.

"Hey, Miles. It's George."

"Hi, George. How are things at Rock Lake?"

"We're all fine here, but I have a problem. Actually, three

problems. I've booked three charters coming up starting Monday. I really need to honor those bookings, and I can't just up and leave Cora and Olivia here."

"Not to worry, my friend. I had a little run-in yesterday with the guys chasing Olivia. Luckily, I got away from them and the FBI has now stepped in full force. They've not only escalated their pursuit of these creeps, but they've provided agents to guard me and the house. Bring the ladies back to me in Lakeville and they'll be properly safeguarded."

"That'll be a load off my mind. Will you be home tomorrow afternoon?"

Miles promised him he would be there from noon on.

———

Stratford and his cronies made their way back to Chicago to regroup, realizing they had to solve the "Olivia Sims problem" before the weekend was over. Mr. Reese had them on the clock, and they'd better deliver or they would become the prey.

Stratford decided to make a bold move by posing as one of Janine's coworkers who was trying to arrange a meeting with Miles. Using one of his unlisted drugstore phones, he texted Miles.

"I got your name from Sammy at Jake's. We work together and he gave me your number. I have some information about the guys chasing Olivia. Text me back if you're interested. Do not call."

Miles immediately responded: "I'm interested."

"Meet me at Jake's tomorrow night at ten p.m. and bring $5,000 in cash. I know who you are and will approach you. No cops!"

Stratford was really desperate to have tried to bate him into such an obvious trap. It was clearly an attempt to lure him away from Lakeville, leaving Olivia and her mother vulnerable to attack. Stratford suspected the Chicago Police were after him, but his assignment made him press on anyway.

Immediately after the text exchange with Stratford, Miles called Agent Drummond to bring her up to speed and discuss the next steps.

"Someone texted me offering information about Olivia's case. I'm sure it's Stratford." He then read her the text exchange.

"It sure does sound fishy," she said. "Seems odd that he would try something so risky."

"Well, I suppose he's under immense pressure from his organization to eliminate any threat to their loan operation," he hypothesized. "Assuming he is actually the one responsible for the texts, he's either trying to lure me to Chicago so he can force me to reveal Olivia's whereabouts, or to get me out of Lakeville so he could look for Olivia at my house or her mom's."

"Or he could just want to eliminate a roadblock by killing you. Doing it in Chicago wouldn't sound an immediate alarm in Lakeville when he returns there searching for Olivia. First thing I want you to do is confirm the meeting. Then you go to Chicago. We'll have agents positioned to cover you every step of the way, both while traveling and in Chicago. If he tries anything we'll get him. We'll also have agents positioned at your house and at Mrs. Sims's. Actually, it would be best if they weren't at either location. Any thoughts?"

Miles suggested George's place as a viable alternative, and she approved the idea. Miles first sent a return text agreeing to the meeting at Jake's, and then called George to lay out the plan.

"So, I'm taking them to my house instead of yours?" George asked.

"Yes, there will be FBI agents there waiting for you," Miles confirmed.

"Okay, we should be there by four o'clock."

Miles phoned Agent Drummond again to let her know George would bring Olivia and her mother to his house that afternoon. She affirmed there would be agents stationed at the house waiting for them.

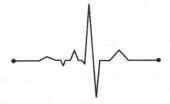

CHAPTER 29

I t dawned on Miles that he had no car to take to his rendezvous in Chicago. He called the dealership where his mangled
wreck had been towed and was told that the insurance
adjuster hadn't been there yet, but it appeared the car was
very likely totaled. Miles asked to be transferred to the sales
department.

The salesperson checked their inventory and described two
possible candidates. She offered to come pick him up and bring
him to the dealership's used car lot. He agreed, and she pulled
up in front of his house twenty minutes later. The two options
were both 2015-model Camrys. He chose the silver one, which
had the lowest mileage. Negotiating the deal took less than
half an hour. He drove out of the lot less than two hours after
initially calling the dealership. Hopefully, the rest of his day's
adventures would be equally painless.

When Ryan and Rebecca's cab pulled up in front of the building for their two p.m. appointment, they could see the Hudson
River to the west. They hoped the condo, being on the 33rd
floor, would have an even better view of it. As they entered the
building, Lisa Reynolds was waiting for them dutifully in the
spacious, well-appointed lobby. She opened the door for them
and, after brief introductions, they took the elevator up to the
33rd floor.

The online pictures of the unit didn't do the place justice. It was spacious, tastefully updated, and fully equipped. The view did not disappoint, either. Standing on the balcony, looking west, they could see the river and New Jersey across the way. Looking east, they had a partial view of Central Park. As they went back inside, Rebecca gave him a raised eyebrow and approving smile. She was very impressed. The tour of the rest of the unit checked all the boxes. Besides being very large with an *en suite* bathroom, the main bedroom also had a beautiful view. The second bedroom, dining area, and kitchen were all top-notch. Ryan could definitely imagine them sharing this place. They spent a few more minutes looking around before Lisa began her sales pitch in earnest.

"Well, what do you think?" she asked.

Rebecca replied first. "It's beautiful. All we could ask for."

"Are you considering making an offer?" Lisa's question had a hopeful tone to it.

This time, Ryan spoke up. "It's worthy of consideration, but we've just begun our search. We'll let you know once we've made a decision."

"I totally understand," Lisa said, moderating her sales pitch. "If this place is gone before you decide, I'd be happy to show you some other properties."

They thanked her and promised to let her know immediately if they wanted to make an offer or look further. As the two of them took the elevator down, Ryan could see Rebecca was hooked.

"So much for the first-one-we-see disclaimer," he teased.

She laughed and, ever the actor, gave him the "Can we? Can we?" pleading pout. When they arrived in the lobby, Ryan called Lisa and asked if they could come back upstairs.

To pass the time before he needed to leave for Chicago, Miles ordered some lab equipment online and took Molly out for a long walk. Around eight p.m., the FBI agents who would be following him to Chicago told him it was time to go. Miles settled into his new ride, keeping the car driven by the two agents in his rearview mirror the entire way.

The closer he got to Chicago, the more hopeful he got that tonight they would end this saga once and for all. The two cars arrived at the parking lot near Jake's Jazz Bar around nine thirty. The plan was for Miles to go to Jake's first with the agents close behind. Another agent would already be stationed in the club keeping an eye out for Stratford.

When he got to Jake's, the place was jumping with the usually raucous Saturday-night crowd and the jazz trio on stage. Miles took a place at the bar and ordered a beer. After downing half of his beer, he checked his watch. It was 10:05 p.m. and no sign of Stratford. Either he was late or, as they thought might happen, had just intended to lure Miles far enough out of Lakeville to be of no help to Olivia. Another thirty minutes passed without any contact, so they initiated their Plan B. Agent Stevens left first, followed by Miles a couple of minutes later. Agent Maye followed Miles shortly after that. The third agent, who Miles didn't know, stayed behind just in case Stratford eventually showed up.

As Miles was halfway back down the dark street to the parking lot, a shot rang out. The bullet narrowly missed Miles but broke the window of a storefront a few feet in front of him, spraying glass in every direction. He dove behind a garbage can for cover. Agent Stevens, who had been in front of him rushed to his side. With one hand on Miles's back to hold him down, and the other on his gun, the agent scanned the perimeter looking for the shooter. A second shot rang out, but it sounded as if this one came from a different direction.

"Suspect down," yelled Agent Maye, who had followed Miles out of the bar. He had been the one who'd fired the second shot.

"Stay here!" Agent Stevens, who had been holding Miles down, demanded before taking a defensive posture between Miles and the gunman.

Miles peeked around the garbage can and saw Agent Maye slowly cross the street with his gun drawn to assess the state of the shooter, who lay face down and motionless on the pavement. The two shots also brought out the third agent from the club followed by a group of onlookers. He called for backup.

"No need for medical assistance," the agent reported. "Everyone is okay except for the gunman, who is deceased."

Miles could see the gunman wasn't Stratford. The agents searched the man for some form of identity. All they found on the body was some cash and a picture of Miles. It was apparent to Miles the shooter was merely a hired gun.

While the agent from the bar remained at the scene to interface with the local authorities, Miles, Agent Stevens, and Agent Maye headed back to Lakeville in Miles's car.

"You're going to have to drive back to Lakeville. My hands won't stop shaking," Miles admitted.

"No problem. By the way, you have a hole in your pant leg with some blood dripping out. Looks like it's just a scratch. Here's my handkerchief. Hold it on the wound."

Miles did as he was told. The handkerchief was soon bloodied but effectively stemming the flow from his wound.

"Thanks. I didn't even feel it until you pointed it out. Guess I'm still in shock over what just happened. My heart rate is just starting to return to normal. Stratford trying to have me eliminated was one of the scenarios I discussed with your boss, but I thought it was the least likely one."

"Apparently Stratford has decided you weren't going to lead him to Olivia Sims, so he decided it was best to remove you from his path. One good thing: it seems unlikely Stratford is aware of our involvement." As soon as they hit the highway, Agent Maye dialed Agent Drummond, setting the phone on the dash in the hands-free speaker mode.

"I just hung up with your partner who updated me on the shooting. Is Mr. Darien okay?" she asked.

"I'm fine," replied Miles. "A little shaken up, once again, but fine."

"Good. I have alerted the team in Lakeville to stay vigilant at all three locations. Rest assured if they try anything we'll stop them. Please check with me as soon as you get back to Lakeville."

"Will do," Agent Maye responded and hung up.

Miles glanced at his phone and saw he had a missed call and a voicemail from Ryan who said, "Just called to catch up. Give me a ring back when you have time. Lots to tell you!" Miles decided his call back could wait until morning.

It was just after midnight when Miles and the agent pulled into his driveway. While the agent checked back with Agent Drummond as ordered, Miles let Molly out into the backyard rather than take her for a walk. Being out on the streets after midnight, even accompanied by an FBI agent, was more than he could deal with at that moment. He went to bed shortly thereafter, even though he knew sleeping wasn't likely, given his apprehension over what Stratford might try next.

CHAPTER 30

After a fitful night of sleep, Miles dragged himself out of bed just before eight a.m. Once downstairs he found Agents Stevens and Maye in the kitchen with Molly. The agents had apparently been up early. Coffee had been brewed, fresh-baked goods had been set out, and Molly had been out for her morning walk.

"Thanks, guys. I really needed this," Miles said as he lifted the coffee cup to his mouth.

Both agents smiled, grabbed their cups in unison, and walked to their respective posts, one in the living room with a full view of the front of the house, the other in the dining room with a similar view of the driveway and backyard.

After downing his initial cup of coffee and a piece of cheese Danish, Miles was ready to face the world. The first order of business was calling Ryan back.

"Sorry I didn't get back to you right away. I was busy being shot at," Miles said matter-of-factly.

"What? You were shot at? Are you okay?" Ryan was under-standably shocked.

Miles told him that, other than being traumatized, he was fine. He went on to explain why he had gone to Chicago and what had transpired outside the jazz club.

"Holy shit!" said Ryan. "I can't even imagine how shaken up you must have been. I assume you're going to lay low now so Stratford and his goons can't get at you," he pleaded.

"Don't worry. I'm well-guarded, and so are Olivia and her

mom. Let's talk about something else. You said you had lots to tell me. Please proceed." Miles needed to shift the conversation, hopefully to something more positive.

"First, and most important, Rebecca and I are now in a committed relationship. In fact, we've decided to buy a place and move in together," Ryan explained.

"Wow. When you say you're buying a place, does that mean you've decided on one?"

"Yes. Believe it or not, it was the first one we looked at. I'll send you a link to the description on the real estate company's website. From the walk-through to making an offer, it all happened in the matter of a few hours. After some back and forth, they accepted the deal last night." Ryan sounded both excited and scared at the same time.

Miles, ever the pragmatist, wanted to make sure his friend's interests were protected given the newness of this relationship. "I assume you'll be sharing the purchase price and subsequent expenses equally."

"Fifty-fifty all the way. I have my portion of the down payment in my investment account. Rebecca will do the same with hers until her condo sells. The monthly nut is roughly the same as we're paying individually, so it works."

A huge smile came across Miles's face. "I'm so happy for you. Both for the condo and, more importantly, your rapidly expanding relationship. Any talk of marriage, now?"

"This thing has moved at breakneck speed already. I think we're going to have to settle into it for a little while before approaching any further escalation. On another subject, you'll be interested to know we're going to submit a script concept for the season finale of Rebecca's show. Olivia's story is the inspiration. It will deal with a woman in a predicament similar to what she's been dealing with. It will also be another way to expose the problem I've written about in my series for the *Times*. As it turns out, we do want your help in writing the part of the script that deals with the investigation. You'll get on-screen credit and a nice little payday to boot."

"Absolutely, count me in. Looking forward to it. I can't tell you how much your news has cheered me up, buddy boy. Keep me posted on all future developments." Miles's voice was particularly upbeat as he gave Ryan his full-throated endorsement.

Over the length of the conversation, Miles's outlook had turned one hundred and eighty degrees. He even allowed himself to wonder what it would be like if he were in a committed relationship like Ryan's. It had been a couple of years since he and Robert had broken things off. Thankfully, he was now able to look back on it without that empty feeling in the pit of his stomach. Still, he was lonely. Lonely in a way that could only be cured by a loving relationship.

Once the conversation ended, Miles had to return to his current reality. There were some bad people out there who had tried to kill him and would likely try again. Even though he was being well protected, he vowed he'd be ready to return fire if they tried again. To do the only thing he could think of to be prepared for that possibility, he went to the basement and cleaned his handgun.

Janine's phone rang from a number she didn't recognize, so she let it go to voicemail. Then she played the message.

"Ms. Banner, this is Detective Phillips from the Chicago Police Department. Please return my call as soon as possible. We need to speak to you regarding Olivia Sims. Thank you." Janine immediately returned the call.

"Detective Phillips."

"This is Janine Banner returning your call."

"Thank you for your quick response. As you know, we're doing our part in protecting Olivia Sims. We believe the people looking for her have your number and may try to use it to locate you and then somehow coerce you into helping them find Ms. Sims. We certainly don't want them to find you, so we intend to use your phone number's ID to draw them out into the open. In order for that to work, we need you to turn your phone off completely for the next forty-eight hours or so. If you give me your email address or an alternate phone number, we'll notify you once the coast is clear."

"Of course. I'll do anything to help her." She proceeded to give him her sister's cell phone number.

"One more thing," said Detective Phillips. "It would help protect you if you could go somewhere away from your current location just in case they've used your device locator to find you."

"Sure," she replied.

CHAPTER 31

Agent Drummond had given Miles the go-ahead to join his three friends and their FBI bodyguards for dinner at George's house. He put Molly on her leash and grabbed a bottle of wine on his way out the door. Agent Stevens, who had been staying at his house, rode with them.

They walked into quite a scene at George's. Mrs. Sims was in the kitchen stirring one pot while checking on another in the oven below. Olivia was setting the large dining room table for six. George was comically struggling to open a bottle of wine with one hand while sipping a beer with the other. The agents, ever vigilant, were making sure Miles hadn't been followed. Molly went room to room, checking out George's digs.

Less than five minutes after they sat down to eat, Olivia heard her phone ping. It was a text from Janine's phone.

Olivia set the phone on the table and froze. The terrified expression on her face put everyone in the room on edge and brought Mrs. Sims to tears. Miles picked up the phone and read the text:

"We have Janine Banner, and her life depends on you doing as we say. You and Miles Darien must proceed immediately to the Lake Forest Oasis on the Illinois Tollway. You will wait there, in your car, for further instructions. If we see any evidence of police presence, she dies. Do not call back or she will immediately suffer the same fate."

Miles then handed it to Stevens sitting next to him, who immediately called Agent Drummond. After the two agents spoke for a few minutes, Agent Drummond instructed Stevens to put Miles on the phone.

"This is Miles."

"I just tried Ms. Banner's number and it went right to voicemail. We have no choice but to assume they have her. You need to leave immediately. Our agents will follow you at a safe distance."

"I understand the assumption that they have Janine," said Miles, "but why would we agree to what would obviously be a trade of one life for another?"

"Because they're counting on Olivia not wanting to sacrifice her friend to save herself. Regardless of whether it makes sense or not, we will pretend to comply. I'll have an armed female agent who fits Olivia's description meet you at the Russell Road exit at the border. The two of you will proceed to the Oasis. Despite the instructions, I will have several agents positioned in various spots at the Oasis. They will all be in plain clothes and moving about like tourists so they won't attract attention. At the first sign of Janine or the bad actors, we'll take appropriate action. One more thing, be sure to take Olivia's phone with you."

Miles took a sip of water before responding. "Okay. I'll leave right away."

Miles told Olivia he needed to take her phone. She handed it to him, and he headed for the door. As he walked to his car, he double-checked to be sure his handgun was tucked securely into his belt. Stratford's choice of the Oasis was a smart one, as the authorities would definitely be hesitant about opening fire in a crowded public place. The bad guys wouldn't think twice about it. Miles couldn't believe he was being lured into an obvious trap for the second time in two days. Hopefully, he'd be lucky enough to survive this one as well.

The drive to the rendezvous point took less than twenty-five minutes. Olivia's stand-in was waiting in a car at the border exit as planned. She got in and they were on the move.

"Hi. I'm Agent Beth Harmon."

"I'd say nice to meet you, but . . ." He purposely declined to finish the sentence.

She smirked silently. In just over fifteen minutes they pulled into the Oasis parking lot, which was almost at capacity. After briefly navigating the aisles, they found a space. Per their instructions, they stayed in the car and waited for someone to call Olivia's phone.

They sat in silence as thirty minutes passed, and nothing happened. Then suddenly Agent Harmon's phone rang. It was Agent Drummond. She had called off the operation and instructed all of her agents to stand down and return to their original posts. Agent Harmon handed the phone to Miles.

"Mr. Darien, there's been an incident back in Lakeville. I need you to proceed through the Oasis and out to the lot on the opposite side of the building. Agent Tomassini will be waiting for you at the door. He will brief you on what will happen from there. Agent Harmon will see to it your car is returned to Lakeville later this evening."

Without saying a word, Miles handed the phone back to Agent Harmon and entered the building, which spanned the highway and serviced the traffic on both sides headed in opposite directions. He quickly made his way weaving through the crowd of people in line for food or to use the restrooms. His mind was racing as he finally approached the door leading to the lot for the northbound traffic. What had happened in Lakeville? Was anyone hurt or—God forbid—killed? As promised, Agent Tomassini was waiting for him by the exit door. The agent identified himself, showed Miles his badge, and then led him to his car. A moment later, they were racing back to Lakeville.

"What's going on?" Miles demanded frantically.

"What I can tell you is there has been a confrontation in Lakeville where shots have been fired," Agent Tomassini said. "Our personnel and members of the Lakeville PD are on the scene. I have been ordered to take you to your home where agents will be waiting. That's all I know so far."

The forty-minute drive to Lakeville was torturous. None of the scenarios going through Miles's head had positive outcomes. When Miles arrived at his house, the two agents who had been staying with him had been replaced with two new agents decked out in tactical gear. One of them approached Miles while the other kept watch.

"Please tell me what happened!" Miles implored him.

"Here's what I'm authorized to share with you. An incident happened at the home of Mr. George Willis. Two armed men broke into the house and began shooting. Agents on the scene returned fire, killing one of the intruders and wounding the other one. Neither of the agents were hurt. Unfortunately, two of the inhabitants of the house sustained injuries. Agent Drummond is on her way there to take charge of the crime scene. We have instructions to keep you here for the time being."

"I need to hear from her as soon as she arrives," Miles screamed, his face turning beet red. "And I need to know what happened to my friends."

"I'll see what I can do," the agent said sympathetically.

Miles felt like a caged animal. He didn't know what to do with himself while he impatiently waited on news from the scene. The agents who were with him apparently had nothing more to offer about what happened and certainly weren't about to let him leave to go find out. All he could do was wait.

After an agonizing wait of nearly three hours, Agent Drummond showed up at Miles's house. She held up her hand like a traffic cop signaling to Miles to wait while she first talked to her agents. After a quick debrief with the agents, she came over to bring Miles up to date.

"Sorry to have made you wait for information about your friends, but we've had quite an involved crime scene to deal with. Stratford rightly assumed you wouldn't totally comply with his demand and would go to the Oasis without Olivia. Having you out of the way would make it easier for him to get to her. Two masked assailants entered Mr. Willis's home shortly after you left. Our agents exchanged fire with the intruders, killing one and wounding the other. In the melee, Mr. Willis and your dog were injured."

Miles was panic-stricken. "Oh no. How are they?"

"Mr. Willis sustained a gunshot wound to his right shoulder. It appears superficial and non-life-threatening. Your dog was struck by one of the gunmen when she attacked him. She likely saved at least one of your friends' lives by distracting the gunman just long enough for our agent to get off a clean shot killing the man."

"How badly was she hurt?"

"The blow knocked her unconscious. We had her transported to the Emergency Animal Care Center downtown. You are free to go check on her. Since Agent Harmon hasn't yet returned with your car, Agent Nash will drive you."

As Miles headed for the door, he asked, "Have you identified the gunmen?"

"No, but I can confirm neither of them was Stratford."

With that, Miles and Agent Nash left to check on Molly. On the way, he called Olivia.

"Oh Miles, have you heard what happened?" she sobbed.

"I have. How are you and your mom holding up? Are you with George?"

"Mom is really shaken up. George is at the hospital getting his shoulder looked at. I'm doing okay. Poor Molly!" Her voice quivered as she spoke.

"Tell me what happened to her. The agent didn't give me many details."

After taking a couple of deep breaths, she answered. "We were talking in the kitchen. One of the agents was in the living room, the other one was upstairs looking out a bedroom window to get a better view of the street, I guess. All of a sudden we heard a crash. Two men wearing masks broke in through the back door. The first one immediately pointed his gun at me. Before he could pull the trigger, Molly instinctively attacked him. She was amazing. He swatted her away with his gun, knocking her to the ground. I'm so sorry." She paused for a moment, then painfully whispered, "This is all my fault."

"Olivia, you did nothing wrong. We're all going to get through this. What happened after that?"

"The other guy then turned his gun on me, and before he could shoot, the agent came in from the living room and shot him. George had grabbed the first guy who hit Molly, and they wrestled their way out of the kitchen. The gun went off and George went down. The second agent had come downstairs and shot that man as soon as the guy got to his feet."

Miles was amazed she was able to keep it together at all as she revisited the horrible encounter.

"I'm on my way to see Molly at the animal hospital," he said. "Where's George?"

"The paramedics just left with him. He seemed to be doing

okay. They took him to Memorial and let Mom go with him. I'm at his house with a bunch of agents. I hope Molly will be okay. Please let me know what you find out."

"I'll be in touch as soon as I know something."

CHAPTER 32

When Miles arrived at the animal care center, he was told Molly was still unconscious and the doctors were with her. They promised to come talk to him once they had something new to report. He spent the night pacing back and forth in the small, sparsely decorated waiting room while his bodyguard, Agent Nash, waited outside in his car. With Stratford still unaccounted for, everyone was still being guarded.

Just before six a.m., a doctor came out to give him an update.

"She's still not conscious, but the good news is all of her vital signs remain stable. Would you like to see her?"

"Yes, I would," Miles said, doing his best to keep his emotions in check.

They walked down a short hallway lined with pictures of cute cats, dogs, and a host of other creatures. Each one appeared to be smiling. Miles hoped he'd have many more chances to see Molly looking that way.

When they entered the treatment room, she was lying perfectly still on a steel exam table. He grabbed a chair and sat down next to her head.

"Is it okay to pet her?" Miles asked the doctor.

"Absolutely." He smiled and left the room, presumably to attend to another patient.

Miles gently stroked Molly's head until he fell asleep for a few moments in his chair. He was awakened by his companion licking his hand. Molly was awake and trying to stand up on the table. He was able to get her to lie back down by petting her again and giving her a "Good dog," pep talk. One of the staff poked their head in, and seeing Molly was up, went to alert the vet.

"This is good," the doctor said when he entered the room.

After a brief examination, he told Miles it appeared she would make a full recovery, but they would like to keep her there for a few hours to monitor for any post-concussion symptoms that might appear. Miles happily agreed to come back later to pick her up. Now he needed to go check on George, so he had the agent drive him over to Memorial.

When they arrived, Agent Nash accompanied him into the hospital. "In case they give you some HIPPA law crap about visiting your friend, I'll flash my badge at them." The agent finished his sentence with a wink.

Fortunately, they were given his room number, so the badge wasn't needed.

The medicinal smell and the sounds of people suffering always brought back so many unpleasant memories for Miles. I've spent way too much time in this place over the past couple of years, he thought.

As the elevator door opened on the third floor, Miles could hear George's unmistakable laugh. It changed his mood entirely. When he walked into the room, George was sitting up in bed. The ever-vigilant agents stayed in the hallway to stand guard.

As soon as George saw Miles, he stopped laughing. "I'm so worried about Molly. She saved Olivia's life, you know."

"I just returned from seeing her," said Miles. "Turns out she's going to be fine. How are you doing?"

"So glad to hear it. Me? Just a scratch," George said, dismissing Miles's concerns.

"He's a hero too!" Mrs. Sims added proudly.

"So I hear," Miles acknowledged. "What are the doctors saying?"

George pointed to his side. "The bullet passed right through me. Basically just a flesh wound. They want to keep me overnight tonight just to be sure no infection sets in."

"Plenty of flesh to pass through, I'd say. Besides, they don't want you to do anything foolish like go fishing." It was the perfect occasion to tease George.

"You needn't worry about that," Mrs. Sims chimed in. "I'll see to it he stays quiet." She held George's hand in both of hers.

"I have no doubt," Miles replied. He was so happy George was going to be fine and equally happy about the special relationship his two friends had formed. It allowed him to forget, albeit briefly, that Stratford was still out there hell bent on getting rid of Olivia.

After his two successful hospital visits, Miles went home to wash up. As promised, his car was in the driveway waiting for him when he arrived. Also waiting for him was an email from Bobbie.

"How is your investigation coming along? I need your findings soon so I can prepare my defense."

His plan to spend the rest of the day recovering from the chaotic events of the previous day went right out the window. Before locking himself in his room with his computer to work on his investigation, he asked Agent Maye, who had returned to duty at Miles's house, "How did the gunmen find us at George's house in the first place?"

Agent Maye gestured out the window. "My theory is, he was watching your house from afar and followed you there when you left here in your car. Your street is quite long. He could position a car on a side street at each end, out of our sight.

When he or one of his men spotted your car, they followed you to Mr. Willis's house. Old-fashioned but effective."

And you're supposed to be a detective, Miles silently chided himself. "Well, I'm going upstairs to work on an investigation of my own," he said.

"What are you investigating?" Agent Maye asked.

Miles proceeded to tell him the details of the Jefferson/Shaw case.

"I'd start by doing background checks on everyone from both companies who did any work on that software," Agent Maye suggested. "If you can find anyone who may have passed the data from AccuTest and who might have received it on the other end, that should lead you to concluding what actually happened."

"Easier said than done," said Miles. "You folks have far more access to people's backgrounds than I can muster."

Agent Maye shook his head. "Wish I could get you access to our data bank, but I can't. Hopefully, your search using conventional means will uncover the culprits. Good luck!"

Miles retreated to his room and started pouring over the information Bobbie had supplied. His initial review failed to turn up any obvious connections between the personnel from each of the companies. One thing did stand out to him, however. It seemed, based on the timing when AccuTest claimed to have detected the use of their proprietary software, the change in the Jefferson/Shaw's source code was likely made prior to the death of Ralph Jefferson. Was it possible the deceased was somehow involved in the crime? It was definitely a possibility worth pursuing.

Around four p.m. he called it quits for the day. It was time to fetch Molly and bring her home. As expected, an agent rode with him to the animal care center. When he arrived, an attendant brought Molly out of the treatment area. Even though she was still a little unstable from her ordeal, she greeted Miles with her best Golden Retriever smile and tail wag. Once back at the house, she curled up in her favorite spot in the corner of the living room next to the TV and went to sleep.

Agent Drummond and Agent Caldwell, who specialized in interrogation, visited the wounded gunman in the hospital. Lakeville police had officers stationed outside his room, which was in an otherwise unoccupied wing of the hospital. The gunman had been identified, using his fingerprints, as Lyle Underwood. He had served time on multiple occasions, mostly for violent crimes including assault with a deadly weapon.

He had been read his Miranda rights as soon as he regained consciousness following the surgery to remove the bullet from his abdomen. He was wide awake now.

"Mr. Underwood, I'm Agent Drummond with the FBI. This is Agent Caldwell. We're here to ask you a few questions."

"I want to see my attorney," Underwood replied.

"Okay, who's your attorney?" Agent Caldwell said.

"I don't have one at the moment," he shot back.

"Well, we can have one appointed for you, if that's what you'd like."

"No, I want to make a call," Underwood demanded.

"Sure. Here's a phone." Agent Drummond offered him hers.

Underwood must have known he was trapped. "Forget it. I'm not using your phone."

"That's your right. Just be aware that you're likely to be charged with attempted murder, among other crimes. We'll be back to see you tomorrow after those charges have been filed. Given your criminal record, it will be in your best interest to cooperate unless you want to serve some real time. I suggest you reconsider your silence. We'll arrange for a different phone to be brought in so you can make your call."

The two agents left the room and headed to the parking lot knowing Underwood would cooperate eventually. Once this charge was added to his record of previous convictions, he would be looking at serving a life sentence. If he had been involved in the incident in Indiana, he could be looking at the death penalty. Turning over on Stratford and others in the organization would be the only way to avoid either possibility.

CHAPTER 33

Miles wasn't normally an early riser, but Bobbie's case and its deadline had severely limited his ability to sleep. He was determined to find out how AccuTest's code found its way into Jefferson/Shaw's system. After Googling every employee on the list he was given, he turned to social media as his next step. After several unsuccessful searches, one possibility emerged. Timothy Frost's LinkedIn profile showed he had joined Jefferson/Shaw a year before Ralph Jefferson passed away, and he had left the company eighteen months after Jefferson's death. While his work history before and after that showed no other connections, his education did. He had earned a master's degree in computer technology from Syracuse University, a most interesting coincidence since AccuTest happened to be headquartered in Syracuse.

He texted Bobbie. *Do you have access to the personnel records for employee Timothy Frost? If yes, please email them to me.*

A theory began to emerge. What if AccuTest solicited someone who was secretly working for them—say, Timothy Frost—to plant their code into Jefferson/Shaw's software? AccuTest could then detect it's illegal use at a later date, win substantial damages in a lawsuit, and probably put their main competitor out of business in the process. An insidious master plan, to be sure.

His phone rang a few minutes later. Miles assumed it was Bobbie answering his request. Instead, it was Agent Drummond.

"Early this morning, the manager of a motel on the west side of Lakeville reported a dead body. It was Stratford's."

Miles took a moment to digest this revelation. "Well, that certainly complicates things. Do you think his higher-ups decided to change horses, so to speak?"

"It would appear they'd grown tired of his ineffectiveness and the likelihood we were on to him. I have every reason to believe you and Ms. Sims are still in grave danger."

"What do we do now?"

"Guarding all of you in separate places has been difficult logistically. Not to mention, now all of your homes are well-known to your pursuers. We've decided it's in everyone's best interest to move all of you to a safe house we've secured. Please pack your things assuming you'll be away from home for several days. I'll send transportation instructions to the agent who's with you. Your friends will be brought there as well."

Miles agreed and began packing up his clothes, toiletries, and work-related paraphernalia. After he had everything packed, he brought his bags downstairs and then went to the kitchen to grab Molly's dog food and a few chew toys. They packed everything into the car and were quickly on their way.

The safe house, which was just outside of town, turned out to be an old farmhouse with a large 'For Sale' sign out in front. Its drab exterior was framed by a dark, overcast sky. It eerily resembled Dorothy's house from *The Wizard of Oz*. The house was well-positioned as a hideout, as it was surrounded by open, unplanted fields all around, making it extremely difficult for anyone to approach undetected. When Miles got there, Olivia was already unpacking her belongings in the sparsely furnished bedroom she had selected. Miles picked out one for himself and did the same. Molly, who seemed to be her old self again, began sniffing every nook and cranny of the place.

"Where are the other two?" Miles asked Agent Maye, who was keeping watch in the front of the house.

"On their way up the driveway," he noted.

Agents Drummond and Caldwell returned to the hospital. Their interrogation of Underwood had now taken on a whole new meaning. With Stratford's demise, Underwood became their only solid lead to the organization behind the loan-sharking scheme and recent murders. When they arrived, Underwood wasn't alone. The man seated next to him looked every bit the attorney—fancy suit, impeccably groomed hair, and expensive leather briefcase.

"Hello, I'm Attorney Charles McNamara. I represent Mr. Underwood."

"Thank you for coming," said Agent Drummond. "As you may be aware, your client has been charged with first-degree attempted murder. There are also several lesser charges pending, including assault with a deadly weapon, and breaking and entering. I'm sure you've advised your client of the severity of these crimes and the potential penalties, particularly in light of his previous convictions. His cooperation could be instrumental in reducing the charges and penalties."

"We understand. My client will plead not guilty to all charges and has nothing to say at this time," the attorney declared.

"As you wish," said Drummond. "But please be aware, your client's associate, Mr. Alexander William Stratford, was found dead this morning, the victim of a gunshot wound to the head. Your client may well be the target of the same people responsible for that murder. His cooperation will most certainly enhance his chances for survival."

Underwood, who up to this point had kept his cool, showed signs of genuine panic. Beads of sweat had formed on his brow, and he began to fidget in his seat. His attorney picked up on it immediately.

"I'd like to speak to my client in private now," McNamara demanded.

Agent Drummond nodded and motioned to Agent Caldwell to adjourn to the hallway with her.

Once the agents left the room, McNamara turned and spoke quietly to his client.

"Lyle, you need to keep it together. They're just trying to scare you into talking." McNamara was clearly doing damage control.

"Yeah, why should I trust you? You work for the same people who probably killed Stratford."

"All I know is if you talk you'll still be going to prison. Don't make a huge mistake. Follow my directions and you may be able to walk away from this altogether."

"I'm not sure I buy that."

McNamara changed his tone considerably. "You'd better. Don't be an idiot. You just heard what happed to Stratford." The warning definitely hit a nerve.

"You threatening me?" Underwood shouted loudly enough that the agents standing outside his door could hear.

"Please calm down," implored McNamara. "I'm only looking out for your best interests."

"Bullshit. Get out!" Underwood demanded. The attorney grabbed his briefcase and hastily left the room, giving Underwood a look of disgust on his way out the door.

Agent Drummond suddenly realized they had a real chance to turn this guy. "You can come back in now!" Underwood shouted.

When the agents came into the room, Underwood declared, "That guy no longer represents me. I want protective custody."

Drummond pulled up a chair next to Underwood's bed. "That'll depend on whether or not you fully cooperate. We need to know who you're working for and what you know about their operation. Everything!"

"Sure. Sure. Just keep them away from me."

After an hour of preliminary interrogation, Agent Drummond was satisfied that Underwood was going to give them what he had, so she arranged to have him transferred to the Federal Penitentiary in Thomson, Illinois for temporary protective custody and medical care. He would be held there until his cooperation agreement was formally approved and a more permanent placement was decided upon.

Three agents were assigned to keep him company until his transportation arrived. Confident that things were under control, Agent Drummond returned to her office in Chicago armed with the name of Underwood's contact and some valuable details on the loan-sharking operation. Unfortunately, Underwood was a low-level operative, so there was still much work to be done before they could successfully get to the top of the organization and bring it down.

CHAPTER 34

M rs. Sims was able to cobble together breakfast for the group using the limited array of groceries the agents had hastily purchased the day before. It was actually quite amazing how prepared the farmhouse was, given the very short notice the agency had to secure a place and outfit it for seven people.

Miles fiddled with his phone. "There is no Wi-Fi here," he complained to no one in particular.

"I'll be setting up a wireless hotspot after breakfast. It should be adequate, provided you won't be using it for any elaborate video games," Agent Maye teased.

"Great, thanks." Miles was delighted to discover Agent Maye had a sense of humor. He then turned his attention to George, who had retreated to the couch.

"George, how are you feeling?"

"I'm fine. A little sore but none the worse for wear," he said, masking his discomfort to everyone except Mrs. Sims.

"Believe me, he's hurting," she declared.

Olivia stood and started pacing. "We can't stay here indefinitely. It's like we're in prison."

Miles put a hand on her shoulder. "The agents will hopefully get some valuable information from the gunman they have in custody. The criminals know that man has more incriminating evidence on them than you do. It's very likely they'll shift their focus from you and on to him. He can do them a lot more harm than you can."

Miles's wishful thinking seemed to comfort Olivia, at least for the moment.

Shortly after they finished eating, the Wi-Fi was up and running. Miles retreated to his room to get back to work on Bobbie's case. Work was the perfect distraction. After about an hour of trying unsuccessfully to find more information about Timothy Frost, he received an email from Bobbie containing Frost's personnel file. It proved to be very enlightening.

The file showed Frost had been hired to help develop software updates on a top-level development team who reported directly to the late Ralph Jefferson. This made it conceivable that he would have had ample opportunity to introduce the AccuTest code into Jefferson/Shaw's operating system. Proving it would be the real challenge.

Before he could continue his search, Miles noticed he had an unread text on his phone. It was from Agent Drummond asking him to call her. He immediately complied.

"Mr. Darien," she said. "Thanks for getting back to me so quickly. I need to ask for your assistance once again."

Despite Miles's recent experiences, the fact the FBI needed his help again really energized him. "How can I help?"

"The gunman we have in custody has provided us with information, including about his contact within the criminal organization. We need to draw that contact out into the open. It's likely that contact could lead us to the next rung up the ladder toward the top of the loan-sharking operation." She sounded genuinely optimistic, which Miles noted was a real change of pace based on her generally stoic demeanor.

"Of course I will help. But before you brief me on whatever plan you've devised, I could use your assistance with something I'm working on." *Nothing ventured, nothing gained*, he thought.

"If I can, sure. What do you need?"

"I want as much information as possible on a man named Timothy Frost. I need to know where he is, what he's been up to, and any significant changes in his finances over the past three years. I can send you some helpful information on him, like his Social Security number and the like to get things rolling." He hoped Agent Drummond would be more encouraging than the other agent he tried to ask for help.

"If I may ask, what is he involved with?"

Miles explained to her, in some detail, the important elements of the Jefferson/Shaw case and the role Miles theorized Timothy Frost presumably played in the scheme. Being able to get a line on him would be a gigantic leap forward, assuming he was, in fact, a major player in this case. Surprisingly, she took a real interest in it.

"This type of crime, particularly because it includes interstate commerce, is right up the alley of the Department of Justice's Complex Crimes Unit. As the Department's law enforcement arm, we'd be involved at some point investigating such a case. This particular one may or may not be something they would have us pursue, but regardless, I can use the facts you gave me to justify the inquiry."

"So, we have a deal?"

"Yes. I'll have one of the agents who's with you now bring you to my office in Chicago tomorrow morning. We'll discuss the details of what we'd like you to do when you get here. Please bring along enough of your personal belongings to spend a couple of days here, if necessary. I'll try to have the information you asked for on Timothy Frost ready when you arrive."

"Okay, see you tomorrow." Miles was elated. Even though his assignment might very well be dangerous, if it would help put an end to Olivia's nightmare he would gladly take the risk. Besides, he was really excited by the idea of doing some genuine sleuthing for the FBI in a major criminal case. And to top that off, he would be getting the lowdown on Timothy Frost. Tomorrow was shaping up to be a monumental day.

———

Miles and his FBI agent escort had a nice chat on their way to the FBI field office in Chicago. Agent Caldwell was originally from Newburgh, New York just a short sixty-mile train trip from New York City along the Hudson River. Agent Caldwell's dad was a cop and his mom taught drama at Newburgh Free Academy. As a drama teacher, she had access to discounted tickets for Sunday matinees. Her son and daughter would often tag along when she took a group of her drama students to see a play.

As Agent Caldwell described his love of musical theater, Miles realized how unfair his perception was of FBI agents. They were just as diverse a group as any other profession might be. Being a gay man, Miles had been unjustly stereotyped, and now he found himself doing the same to the agent. It was yet another circumstance in a long line of personal growth opportunities that life had presented to him.

When they arrived in Chicago, their first stop was at the Kimpton Gray Hotel. After Miles checked in, he and Agent Caldwell drove to the FBI office a couple of blocks away. Before parting company, Miles thanked him for the chauffeur service and the interesting conversation.

Agent Caldwell was being assigned to another case, so a different agent would be accompanying Miles back to Lakeville once his work in Chicago was completed. After a short wait in the lobby, Miles was escorted down a long hallway lined with glass-walled offices and filled with agents in black suits with matching ties. It reminded him of the headquarters from the *Men in Black* sci-fi movies. At the end of the hallway was the one occupied by Agent Drummond.

"Good morning, Miles." Agent Drummond motioned for him to take a seat in the chair on the opposite side of her desk. "Would you like some coffee or a glass of water?" she asked. She had never called him by his first name before.

Trying not to act surprised, Miles replied, "Good morning, Audrey. No thanks, I'm okay for now," he replied, waiting to see if she'd object to his returning the informal greeting.

"Before I explain our plans for your role in the investigation, I want bring you up to date on your request for information on Timothy Frost. The agent I have assigned to gather information has made significant progress and is hoping to have a dossier ready for you before the day is over. He'll send you an encrypted file via email. To access the file, simply use your mother's maiden name to unlock the file."

"Excellent. I can't thank you enough." Miles was elated to have gotten this level of cooperation.

"Glad to help." She went on to explain his assignment. "Underwood gave us the name of his contact, a man named Harvey Edison. Turns out Mr. Edison works for Oak Lawn Property Management. We found nothing specific on his job title there, which—if he had one—would likely simply be a cover anyway. The interesting thing about the company was its ownership. It's one of many companies owned by a man named Jonathan Reese. Another of Mr. Reese's companies just happened to be Loan2You located on Calumet Avenue, not far from Olivia Sims's apartment. While you were on your way down there, I checked with Olivia and she remembered that company being one of the ones where she applied for a loan and was turned down."

"The plot thickens," Miles interjected.

She nodded. "Your assignment is to march into Oak Lawn Property Management and ask to speak to Harvey Edison. If he's there, introduce yourself and announce that you need to see Mr. Reese. It's likely Edison will play dumb for a while, but you need to press him until Edison asks why you want to talk to Reese. You are then to tell him you know all about the loan-sharking operation and can deliver Olivia to him for a price. Give Edison your phone number and twenty-four hours to respond."

"How do I know about Harvey Edison and where he worked?" Miles wondered aloud.

"Good question. Tell them you were present when we asked Olivia if she knew a Mr. Harvey Edison from Oak Lawn Property Management. Which she said she did not."

"Okay, let's say Edison falls for this and somehow arranges an audience with Reese. Then what?"

"Tell him you're tired of getting shot at and it's time to end this thing. Olivia can't afford to pay you any longer, so you're looking for a financially advantageous solution to finish it. Give him your best impression of a shady private investigator."

"Reese must know the FBI is on the case by now. Underwood's attorney certainly confirmed that. Won't he be on alert for any suspicious actions directed at him and his criminal enterprise?"

"Of course. But he needs to end all threats from people who can expose him or testify against him. You will tell him you have the location where Olivia is hiding out and add a kicker. You overheard the agents talking about where Underwood has been taken."

Miles was impressed with how detailed the plan was.

"Provided he doesn't have me killed on the spot, he could

either negotiate to pay me or throw me out. If he throws me out, then what?"

"Either scenario works, provided you get him to engage in a conversation where he expresses interest in what you have to deliver, or questions your knowledge of his whole operation. All we're after is some confirmation of his involvement. You'll be wearing an electronic device which will send us your entire conversation."

"You know that'll be the first thing they check me for," Miles pointed out.

She assured him these devices have come a long way since the old days of "wearing a wire." He'd also be carrying a gun, which they'd obviously take from him, which would help shift their attention away from searching for an electronic device. Hopefully, her assumption would prove to be correct. If not, he would certainly be done for.

"Assuming this all goes according to plan, and you get the acknowledgement you need and I escape with my life. Where do you go from there?"

"It goes back to why you're doing this in the first place. We only have hearsay and circumstantial evidence at this point. The FBI can't go marching into a well-connected businessman's place and demand information without a warrant. You are our conduit to getting one, assuming you can secure some form of real evidence showing his involvement, which a judge or grand jury could use as grounds to issue a warrant."

"Why don't you simply use one of your agents to pull this off?"

"The bad guys know who you are and what your involvement in all of this has been. You'll have instant credibility and therefore are the obvious candidate.

"I see. When do we begin?" Miles said, accepting his role as the bait.

"Be here at eight a.m. tomorrow morning."

"Good, that gives me time to draw up my will."

CHAPTER 35

With only sixty days left before closing on their new condo, Ryan and Rebecca had a mountain of preparatory work to do. Each of them had to distill their belongings down to the things they really loved. Even then there would need to be compromises, as their new place would only accommodate so much stuff. The good news was that there was plenty of closet space. The long hallway leading to the bedrooms was lined with closets. Rebecca kiddingly told Ryan he could have one of them.

The real issue would be furniture and the decorative things they would showcase on it. Ryan's style was modern minimalist. Rebecca's was French Provincial. After several attempts working together to pick what gets moved and what does not, it became apparent to Ryan that it would be best to simply let Rebecca decide. He did, however, draw the line at his books. They were all coming, even if he had to use his one closet for them.

Ryan's apartment would be easy to sublet. His landlord was even considering just canceling the remainder of his lease given the enticing prospect of a new tenant at a higher monthly rent. Once on the market, Rebecca's condo would likely sell quickly but they had to be sure the timing of the closing worked well with the closing on their new place. All in all, they were very excited about the move, in part because of the beautiful condo they would be living in, but mostly because they would be living there together. Ever since Ryan had returned from Lakeville, they had mostly been staying together at Rebecca's, but that wasn't the same as having "our own place."

Unusual for a Wednesday evening, the weekly installment of his series for the *Times* was finished. Rebecca also had a short week due to a labor dispute between the show and one of the crafts unions. They decided to have a night without discussing work or the move.

"Any ideas for dinner tonight?" she asked while pouring each of them a vodka on the rocks.

"Let's go to Little Italy and eat outside at one of those places on Mulberry Street," Ryan offered. "Pretend we're tourists."

"Sounds like fun."

They finished their drinks and headed downstairs to catch a cab. Miles called just as Ryan gave the cab driver their destination.

"Hey, there. What are you two up to?" Miles asked.

"We're in a cab headed to Little Italy for dinner. And you?"

"Well, I called because after tomorrow you might be reading my obituary," Miles deadpanned. His morbid sense of humor was on full display.

"What? Are you sick?" The alarm in Ryan's voice frightened Rebecca as well.

"Put him on speaker phone!" she demanded.

"No, I'm fine," Miles said. "It's just, the FBI has me entering the lion's den tomorrow."

He filled them in on all that had happened since they last spoke, as well as his assignment for tomorrow.

"That's crazy, Miles. There must be a safer way to get what they need."

"It appears I'm their best option at this point. We need to end the threat to Olivia, and this seems to be the most expedient way to affect that outcome."

"Miles, this is Rebecca," Rebecca said, leaning toward the phone in Ryan's hand. "Please be careful."

"Nice to meet you, Rebecca. Don't worry, I'm a professional. Besides, I intend to come to New York and steal you from that guy next to you." Miles was doing his best to deflect their concern.

"We both know you don't stand a chance," Ryan replied, trying not to laugh.

"There's more to a relationship than sex, my friend," Miles said, returning fire.

"Not for me!" Rebecca interjected, causing both men to burst into laughter.

"Take care of that one, buddy boy. She's obviously a keeper. Enjoy your dinner. I'll update you after my adventure concludes."

"You'd better!" Ryan implored.

The dossier on Timothy Frost showed up in Miles's inbox just before seven p.m. as promised. It was incredibly detailed, which wasn't all that surprising, given it was prepared by the FBI. Frost had no employment record after Jefferson/Shaw. Three months after leaving the company, he traveled to the small South Pacific island country of Vanuatu. The report explained Vanuatu offered citizenship to persons willing to make a substantial investment in the country's economy. It was also on the list of countries that do not extradite criminals wanted in the United States.

Within a month of his arrival there, he opened a dive shop which serviced tourists who came to explore the country's incredible coral reefs. The outlay was sufficient for him to gain citizenship and represented only a small portion of his wealth, considering he had wire transferred $1.8M to a Vanuatu bank just before he arrived there. It was also interesting where the $1.8M had come from. Just over $100,000 of it was from liquidating his brokerage account. Approximately $200,000 represented the proceeds from the sale of his house. The balance of $1.5M had been electronically transferred into his account a week before he left the United States. The transfer emanated from a bank in Delaware. While AccuTest was headquartered in Syracuse, it was incorporated in Delaware, as many companies are for tax purposes. The FBI's search was able to trace the transfer directly back to AccuTest's Delaware holding company.

Miles was elated. He immediately called Bobbie, who answered on the first ring.

"I hope you're calling with some good news," she said without a greeting.

"Hello to you too," he teased.

"Sorry. Hello, Miles. How is your day going?"

"Funny. Listen, I not only have evidence that will exonerate your clients of any wrongdoing, but I have proof AccuTest staged the whole thing. Your countersuit will be worth its weight in gold."

"Wow. Fill me in immediately." Bobbie was usually a real cool customer, but her excitement was palpable.

Miles detailed the facts he had acquired, which pointed directly to the plot orchestrated by Timothy Frost and AccuTest. Not surprisingly, she only took a moment to digest the implications of what he told her before responding.

"Holy shit! This is astonishing. How in the world did you come up with all of this?"

"Incredible investigative skills, of course. And let's just say I also called in a couple of favors along the way." He decided not to divulge the source of the favors just yet.

"Please get me your written report right away. I need to meet with my clients as soon as possible to lay out our strategy."

"Sure. What strategies are you considering?"

"We will either seek criminal charges and sue for damages, or quietly negotiate a massive settlement. Either way, my client will be greatly enriched."

"As will you," Miles pointed out.

"We both will, Miles. I can't thank you enough. Your work on this has been stellar. By the way, don't forget the rent's due on the first."

They both enjoyed a chuckle as they finished the call.

The wheels in Miles's mind were turning full speed now in anticipation of tomorrow's caper, playing out every scenario he could think of so he could practice his responses. Out of nervousness, he checked his gun three times to be sure it was in proper working order. Then, just before turning in, he decided to call George.

"Hi, Miles. How are things in Chicago?" George asked.

"Fine. I'm back in my room and wanted to see how you and the girls are doing."

"We're all fine. It's kind of nice having federal agents taking care of us. They even went out and picked up barbecue for dinner."

"That'll get old fast. I'm sure once we wrap this mess up, it'll be nice to resume normal life again. By the way, sorry you lost your charters this week."

"It's all right. I may have lost some revenue, but I've gained something too." No doubt George was referring to his newfound relationship with Cora.

"I'm happy for you and pleased all is well there. If things here go as planned, I'll see you very soon." Miles hung up and tried to get some sleep. He was not successful.

CHAPTER 36

Miles arrived at the FBI office promptly at eight a.m. the next morning. As instructed, he was dressed in khaki slacks and a light blue button-down shirt. He smiled as he slid on an impeccably fitted navy blazer. Of course, the FBI had him perfectly measured. An agent spent the next twenty minutes fiddling with the electronically enhanced top button on the front of the blazer. Once the agent was satisfied it was in proper working order, Miles was asked to walk around the office hallways while whispering to himself. He was amused that no one he passed along the way thought his whispering parade was the least bit odd. After making a full tour and returning, the agent signaled to Agent Drummond that the listening device was fully functional.

"Any questions?" she asked.

"Just one. How do you want me to get to Oak Lawn's office?"

"We have a car downstairs waiting to take you. It's disguised as an Uber, windshield sign and all."

"I wouldn't have expected any less. I guess I'm off then." Miles's voice was anything but enthusiastic.

Agent Drummond escorted Miles down the elevator to the first floor and through the back exit of the building. The mock-Uber car was waiting when he arrived. Trying his best to look professional, he climbed unceremoniously into the back seat without saying a word to her or the driver. The ride to Oak Lawn Property Management took just fifteen minutes.

The office was in an unassuming single-story red-brick

building. The front door was locked so he pressed the doorbell. He immediately heard footsteps coming his way. A tall man in a dark suit opened the door a crack and asked, "What can I do for you?"

"I'm looking for Harvey Edison."

"And who might you be?" the man asked quizzically.

"My name is Miles Darien, and I need to talk to Mr. Edison about a matter concerning his boss." Miles used his most authoritative voice.

"I'm Harvey Edison. Come in," he said, turning aside to let Miles enter.

Edison led Miles through a large open room filled with empty desks. If ever a place looked like a "front," it was this place. Edison then directed him through a doorway and into a small office. Edison sat down behind his desk and offered Miles a seat. Now that he had a clear view of Edison, Miles was surprised at how unimposing he was. Slight of build and with a receding hairline, he looked more like an accountant than a lieutenant in a criminal enterprise.

"So, what's on your mind?" Edison asked.

Miles did his best to sound sinister. "I'll cut to the chase. I have information on the whereabouts of two people you and Mr. Jonathan Reese are interested in locating. I want to meet with Mr. Reese to determine the value of that information."

"What makes you think I can get you an audience with this Mr. Reese?"

Miles pulled his chair closer to the desk and said calmly, "Because Lyle Underwood inadvertently told me you could."

Edison didn't flinch at the mention of Underwood's name. But Miles was certain Edison knew he wasn't playing games and likely had something his boss would find valuable.

"It seems strange that Lyle would suggest anything of the

sort. He's merely a part-time employee we use to help with property maintenance," Edison said calmly.

"He was pretty pissed off when I spoke to him. Said he fired the lawyer you sent to bail him out."

"He called me asking for help. I called our lawyer, Charles McNamara, to see if he could do anything to help Lyle out. Apparently, that did not go well."

Miles realized his assignment was going to be a lot tougher than he had originally thought. He decided to push a little harder. He stood up, put two hands on Edison's desk, and menacingly leaned forward.

"Regardless, it got me to you. Now I'd like you to get me to Mr. Reese. You can continue to play dumb about this, but I'm telling you I know the whereabouts of the two people he needs to find."

"I have no idea what two people you're talking about," Edison said.

"Sure you do. At least one of them, Lyle Underwood." Miles was baiting the hook.

"Why would Mr. Reese be looking for Lyle?" Edison was very good at playing dumb.

"Because he can implicate Mr. Reese in a whole host of crimes," Miles shot back.

"I'm afraid you're barking up the wrong tree, Mr. Darien. Sorry, I can't help you. Now I have a meeting to go to, so I'll have to say goodbye." Edison finished by motioning to the door, signaling Miles to leave.

Miles stood, reached into his pocket, and placed his business card on Edison's desk. "When Mr. Reese is ready to talk, give me a call."

Even though he hadn't secured a meeting with Jonathan Reese as planned, Miles was confident he had given Edison enough information to motivate him to set up a meeting. As Agent Drummond instructed, once he left the building he called the number of the agent who had brought him to Edison's office in the mock-Uber. On the way back to the FBI office, he checked his messages. The only significant one was from Bobbie. He decided to wait until after the finished his debriefing at the FBI office to return her call.

"What was his body language like?" Agent Drummond asked.

Miles told her how Edison played it cool, keeping his cards close to the vest. The detailed information Miles had given him was surely enough to tantalize Reese into a meeting. Edison now had Miles's number and would likely be calling before long.

Agent Drummond agreed that Miles would very likely get a call within the next day or so. She instructed him to stay nearby and, should he choose to venture out, her agents would be watching him from a safe distance.

"Thanks," said Miles. "Maybe the agents would enjoy riding the Ferris wheel at Navy Pier."

"Very funny. I highly recommend more low-key activities. Please be sure to leave your blazer here before you leave. We'll need to recharge the listening device before you need it again. Let me know as soon as you hear from Edison or anyone else in Reese's inner circle."

"Will do."

With that, Miles decided to go back to the hotel and relax. He hadn't slept much the night before, so a short nap was definitely in order. First he needed to respond to Bobbie, so he placed a call to her office. Her assistant answered and put him right through.

"Hi, Miles. How are you doing?"

"I'm fine. Just chasing gangsters."

"Hope you catch them before they catch you. Listen, I have some really good news to share. Thanks to the information you uncovered, we've been able to flip the script on AccuTest. Their Executive VP, who they discovered had orchestrated the plot, has been forced to step down. Now we're in the middle of negotiating a substantial settlement. We've offered not to pursue criminal charges if they offer an agreement, which is to my client's liking. We're talking somewhere in the low eight figures and a licensing agreement to use the software." Bobbie's voice couldn't mask her excitement.

"That's great. Your clients deserve every penny they get."

"Speaking of pennies, they've approved a nice addition to your normal fee. How does fifty thousand sound?"

"Looks like I'll be able to make my next rent payment." After a brief pause for comedic effect, he added, "All kidding aside, that's extremely generous."

"Well deserved. I need to make a trip to Lakeville soon so I can deliver the check in person. There are a couple of family photos I'd like to dig out of the basement."

"Anytime. See you soon, then."

After the call, he lay down on the bed to try napping. Replaying Bobbie saying "a fifty thousand bonus" made for a wonderful lullaby.

About an hour after he fell asleep, his phone rang. It was Edison.

"Mr. Reese would like to meet with you. I need you to be back here right away."

Miles knew he had to accept. "I'll be right there."

He called Agent Drummond immediately. "They want me back at Oak Lawn ASAP and I don't have the blazer."

"That's not a problem. We just delivered the blazer, fully charged, to the agents in the room adjoining yours. Just knock on the door and let them know you're leaving and need the jacket. Take a cab this time. We want to be sure they didn't take notice of your ride when you left earlier."

"You do think of everything."

"That's my job. Now get going."

Miles had his marching orders, which set the butterflies in his stomach in motion as well. After washing the sleep out of his eyes, he knocked on the door to the adjoining room and retrieved the recharged jacket. He made one last check of his sidearm and headed out of the hotel to catch a cab back to the Oak Lawn building.

When he arrived at the door of Oak Lawn, Edison was waiting for him. Without saying a word, Edison led him back to his office and motioned for him to sit and wait there. Miles did as instructed. Obviously, he had struck the right nerve and now things were moving in the intended direction. After several minutes, Edison returned with another man who must have been waiting somewhere else in the building. This man was huge and looked as if he had been in more than his share of physical confrontations and won them all. Miles decided immediately he would do as he was told.

"Stand up," Edison demanded.

When Miles complied, the huge man patted him down and, in the process, found his gun, which the man removed from his shoulder holster. Edison then motioned for Miles to follow him into another section of the building. The huge man brought up the rear. They walked through what appeared to be a warehouse, as it was filled with all sorts of boxes and crates of various sizes and shapes. Finally, they got to a doorway leading to an empty parking lot behind the building. A large black Mercedes sedan with a third man behind the wheel was waiting there with the motor running. Miles and his two companions got in with Miles positioned in the back seat on the passenger side next to the huge man. Edison hopped into the front passenger seat and away they went.

They rode in silence until they pulled up in front of a high-rise on Wacker Drive. Edison got out first, followed by Miles and then the huge man. They walked quickly through the lobby and boarded an elevator headed for the penthouse.

Miles knew the FBI had three agents positioned in a maintenance room three floors below. They had surveillance monitoring equipment set up to receive the blazer's transmission of any verbal evidence Miles might be able to coax out of Jonathan Reese. They were also heavily armed in case the assignment turned into a rescue operation.

When Miles and his escorts arrived at the door to the penthouse, two more of Reese's men were there waiting. One of them patted him down again and then led him down a short hallway and into a room that appeared, based on its furnishings, to be an office. He was told to sit in a chair at a small round table positioned in the center of the room. Everything in the room looked expensive, particularly the solid wood table and desk. After a short wait, a tall and dapper-looking man who appeared to be in his early fifties entered. He took the seat across from Miles and, without saying a word, studied him as if they were opponents in a poker game. Miles just sat there, trying his best to look unfazed.

"Mr. Edison here says you have some information you want to share with me," Reese said, breaking the silence.

"'Share' would be a generous interpretation," Miles calmly replied.

"So, you think you have something to sell, I take it."

"I do. The whereabouts of two people who can help expose your less-than-Kosher operation." Miles decided the best defense was a good offense tactic.

"Why are you making this offer?" Reese inquired, his steely eyes focused intently on Miles.

"First of all, because I'm sick and tired of being shot at. Secondly, the client who hired me can no longer afford to pay me. I want out of this mess with my body intact and my bank account enhanced."

"Let's say I would agree to such a bargain. What kind of money are you looking for?"

"One hundred thousand dollars," Miles demanded without blinking an eye.

"That's a lot of money for simply supplying the location of two individuals, wouldn't you say?" Reese was only gently pushing back.

"I'd estimate that's about as much as you sold Olivia Sims's kidney for. Seems to me breakeven is a good deal for both of us."

"I would need more from you for that price." Reese relaxed a bit and sat back in his chair. He was definitely buying what Miles was selling.

"What do you mean by 'more'?" Miles asked.

"If you want a big payday, you'll need to eliminate the threats yourself."

"You want me to kill Olivia Sims and Lyle Underwood?" Miles had to have him actually say it if he were to get the confession the FBI would need to secure warrants and ultimately indictments.

"You catch on quickly. Do we have a deal?" Reese asked.

"We're close. I need some assurance that I'll actually get paid."

"Get rid of Olivia Sims and you'll get the first half. You'll get the second half when you've handled both assignments."

"I need some of it up front. How about twenty-five grand up front, twenty-five after the first job is complete, the balance when I'm done?"

"Fine. Come back to Mr. Edison's office tomorrow and he'll have your earnest money. This meeting's over. Everyone out."

Miles couldn't get out of there fast enough. Edison led him out of the penthouse with the huge man following as before. On the way down in the elevator, Miles got his sidearm back sans its ammunition.

When they got to the lobby, Edison said, "Two p.m. tomorrow." Then, much to Miles relief, they parted company. He hailed a cab to go directly to the FBI office.

Until he had a couple of minutes in the cab to gather himself, he wasn't aware that his shirt was soaked through with sweat. The electronic surveillance better have worked. He wasn't about to do a repeat performance. When he walked into Agent Drummond's office, he got the confirmation he'd hoped for. Agent Drummond was on her feet and applauding.

"Nice work, Miles. Not bad for a first-timer. Not bad at all."

"So, you got what you need?" he said, hoping for an affirmative reply.

"Almost."

"Almost? What else do you need?" Miles immediately regretted the question.

"We need you to go pick up that money tomorrow."

CHAPTER 37

Secure in the knowledge that his previous pursuers would be leaving him alone, at least for the time being, Miles decided to take a walk down Rush Street. It seemed to him it was very much like New York but without the same level of hyperactivity. He wandered past an eclectic mix of high-end stores, hip-looking nightclubs, posh hotels, and chic restaurants. Eventually, he decided to go into an upscale men's shop. As he began looking through a rack of shirts, there was a tap on his shoulder.

"Small world, isn't it?"

Miles turned to see Agent Caldwell.

"Are you tailing me?" Miles asked in mock anger.

"No, just out shopping. See the bag with the slacks inside? We do real stuff like that from time to time." Agent Caldwell laughed as he said it, showing Miles he was just giving him some shit.

"Of course you do. It's just that I've gotten so used to being accompanied or followed by you or one of your associates that I simply made an assumption. What do you think of this one?" Miles asked, holding up a light gray button-down shirt with thin navy stripes.

"Nice, but a little too conservative for my taste."

"Not for Lakeville," Miles pointed out. "By the way, I never asked your first name."

"It's Ken."

"Nice to meet you, Ken. It was great running into you in the real world."

"Likewise. Enjoy the rest of your day," Ken said as he turned toward the door to leave.

Miles immediately began speculating if this really nice man might possibly be gay. When his professional dealings with the FBI were over, he would do his best to find out.

Once back at the hotel, he decided to first call Ryan and then follow with dinner at some elegant bistro worthy of his new shirt. He had Bobbie to thank for both the dinner and the shirt.

"Hey, Miles. Apparently you've survived the lion's den. Hopefully your undercover work is now complete."

"Not totally, I'm afraid. One more foray into the breach tomorrow. Bring me up to date on your series, your new home, and the love of your life." Miles was intent on changing the subject.

"The series is almost complete. I have a draft of the next installment, which I'm in the process of editing. The one after that will be the last one, and I'm hoping to get your help with part of it. I'd like to include a little something about the resolution of the case you're working on. No names, of course."

"It's certainly okay to use Olivia's case as long as you use it in a nonspecific way. I'm sure we can make that work, assuming we actually have resolution of the case."

"Good. The new-home planning is definitely a work in progress, but we are slowly making some headway. The give-and-take we're going through is really helping Rebecca and I get to know one another on a very fundamental level. Fortunately, the more I know about her, the more I love her," Ryan admitted.

"I'm so happy for you. My sympathies go out to Rebecca,

however." Miles had to give his buddy a friendly jibe. It wouldn't be a valid conversation between them if he didn't.

"I'll convey your sympathies to her tonight. Seriously, please be careful. At least until Rebecca gets a chance to meet you." Ryan had showed his concern and returned fire at the same time.

After the call, Miles donned his new shirt and left for Chez Parisienne for coq au vin and a nice bottle of Bordeaux.

The morning came early, accompanied by a level of discomfort that could only be delivered by a combination of overly rich food and an entire bottle of wine. Thankfully, Miles had until two o'clock to shake the cobwebs and be ready for the danger that lay ahead.

After a shower and a shave, he ordered a light breakfast from room service. He looked through his emails and was about to check in with his friends in Lakeville when there was a knock on his door. It wasn't room service as he had expected, but rather Agent Billingsley, who had been stationed in the adjoining room.

"Here's a jacket for you to wear to your meeting this afternoon. Be sure to call your special Uber driver when you leave the meeting."

This jacket was a casual one. Undoubtably the change of style was an effort to deflect any thoughts that his outerwear might hide a listening device. Once again, he was blown away by their attention to detail.

His room service breakfast arrived a short time later. After finishing it, he still had almost four hours until his appointment. Not feeling like going anywhere, he sat down in front of the

TV and channel surfed for a movie to watch. He came across one of his old favorites, *The Spanish Prisoner*. Its elaborate plot revolved around corporate espionage, which was incredibly timely given his recent investigation for Bobbie.

After finishing the movie, he felt motivated enough to go for a walk before making his way to Edison's office. His walk led him to Millennium Park, another one of Chicago's beautiful lakefront attractions. He bought a much-needed cup of coffee from a Starbuck's before crossing Michigan Avenue. A stroll through the sunlit park, combined with his caffeine-laden double espresso, was the perfect elixir for his still somewhat-cloudy mind. He found an empty bench where he could simply sit and watch the world go by.

He finished his coffee and people-watching at one thirty. It was time to catch a cab back to Edison's office. The ride got him to the office right on time. This time when he got to the door, he was greeted by the huge man from the previous day who immediately patted him down.

Miles gave him a sly grin. "No gun today, pal. You took all my bullets yesterday, so there was no point in bringing it along."

The huge man was not amused. He merely grabbed Miles by the arm and led him into Edison's office where Edison and the driver from the day before were waiting.

Edison greeted him with a less than enthusiastic "Welcome back."

"I assume you have my money," Miles said, cutting to the chase.

"We do. But first, Mr. Reese has asked us to deliver a message."

With that, the huge man wrapped his arms around Miles from behind and literally lifted him out of his chair. While the huge man held Miles so he couldn't raise his arms, the driver from the day before walked over and punched him hard in the stomach, knocking the wind out of him. Once he had barely caught his breath, the driver hit him again in the same spot. This time he followed up with a blow to the face. As he slumped in his chair, badly beaten with blood streaming from both his nose and mouth, Edison approached. He grabbed Miles's chin and pulled his head up so they could see eye to eye.

"The message you just received is how we communicate with people when we expect them to deliver on their promises. You do not want to see how we communicate with people who fail to deliver on those promises." Edison handed him a slip of paper with a phone number on it. "Call this number when you've fulfilled your promises. Now grab the paper bag on the table and get to it."

As hurt as Miles was, he was able to pull himself together enough to grab the bag and stagger silently out of the office. Once outside, he took a couple of deep breaths and then called for his ride. The car arrived less than three minutes later. He jumped in without saying a word.

"You look like shit," the driver said as they drove off.

It was a familiar voice. "Ken, we have to stop meeting like this!" Miles quipped, having just recovered his ability to speak.

"Hopefully under better circumstances for sure. Anyway, we recorded your whole ordeal and, coupled with the recordings from yesterday, I'd say your work here is almost complete. We're going back to the office for a full debrief, but after that I think you'll be able to return home."

"Home sounds great. I assume you'll be driving me back," Miles said hopefully.

"I can't. I'm flying out tonight to see my mom for her birthday."

"Does she still live in Newburgh?"

"She does."

Agent Caldwell pulled the car up to the back entrance of the FBI office. He turned around and extended his hand. "Hope to see you again under less strenuous circumstances and without a bloody Kleenex stuffed up your nose."

Miles shook his hand and replied, "I'd like that. Have a nice trip."

Miles got out of the car, grabbed the bag of money, and took the elevator up to see Agent Drummond. Apparently he had become one of the team, as no one batted an eye as he walked through the hallway to her office. When he arrived, a group of agents, including Agent Drummond, were sitting around a table in the conference room attached to her office.

"Well done, Mr. Darien." She handed him an ice pack to help treat the swelling on his chin.

"Do I get to keep the money?" Miles asked, having now recovered the balance of his sense of humor.

"Only if you want to join those guys in prison. Seriously, we're hopefully nearing the end of the line here."

The agents asked him a few questions to confirm the details of his encounters with Reese and his associates over the past two days.

"It appears we now have what we need to proceed with warrants for Mr. Reese and his loan-sharking operation. You still need to stay diligent until we can be confident you and your friends will be safe going forward," Agent Drummond said, granting him permission to return to the hotel to wash up and change out of his bloodstained clothes.

As he got up to walk out the door, she added, "For the time being we'll continue to provide on-site protection. In the next couple of days, we may need you to contact Edison again, but for now you are off duty."

Miles wasted no time in making his exit. Agent Maye, who would transport him back to the hotel and then on to Lakeville, led him back downstairs where they hopped into a more typical FBI vehicle. The agent parked in a loading zone in front of the hotel while Miles went up to his room to fetch his things. Agent Billingsley who had previously been in the room adjacent to his was waiting for him. Miles packed up his things, handed the agent his electronically enhanced jacket, and proceeded back downstairs to go home.

When he arrived home, no one was there. Agent Maye confirmed everyone, including Molly, was now at George's house. Miles deposited his bag in his room, briefly checked the mail, and then they were off to join everyone at George's.

Molly was the first to the door when Miles rang the bell. Olivia answered and gave Miles a big hug. Seeing the bruise on his chin, she asked, "Did they do this to you?"

"Yes, but I'm fine. The good news is, we're nearing the end of this saga. How is everyone here?"

"Come in and see for yourself," Olivia coaxed with a big Cheshire-cat grin on her face.

Sitting on the couch were George and Mrs. Sims. They both jumped to their feet when Miles and Olivia walked into the room.

"We have some news. George and I are getting married!" Mrs. Sims declared.

"I go away for a couple of days and look what happens." Miles put on his best mock-disapproval face, but his joy over the news wouldn't let him. He walked over and joined them in a group hug.

"George, I didn't know you were such a quick mover."

"What makes you think he was the mover?" Mrs. Sims shot back. They all broke out laughing. Even though it made his jaw hurt, Miles loved it.

After the laughter subsided, Miles asked, "So, what are the plans?"

Ms. Sims waved her hands in the air excitedly. "We'd like to wait until things settle down for Olivia, and for George's charter season to end. Sometime this fall. Do you think Ryan would come out for it?" she asked hopefully.

"He and his girlfriend are moving into a new place together in a couple of months," said Miles. "I'm sure he'd love to if their schedules permit." He figured since Ryan had become so attached to all of them, he'd definitely want to attend.

"Good. Then we'll invite him and his girlfriend too."

"Mom, you know his girlfriend is a famous actress, don't you?" Olivia chimed in.

"So I've been told." Mrs. Sims gave Miles a knowing wink.

"Enough of this wedding talk. I'm hungry." Not a shocking comment coming from George. He was always hungry.

Mrs. Sims and George had collaborated on that night's meal. George cooked up some freshly caught salmon filets. Mrs. Sims added a salad, baked potatoes, and Brussel sprouts. The agents joined them and even contributed some ice cream for dessert.

It was a welcome change for Miles, considering the earlier confrontation at Edison's office. After helping with the cleanup, Miles, Molly, and Agent Stevens returned to Miles's house. He was asleep before nine o'clock.

That evening, Edison picked up the phone in his office and called Reese to update him on the meeting with Miles.

"So, what do you think the likelihood is that Darien does what he's told?" Reese asked him.

"Pretty good, I'd say. We sent your message loud and clear. Besides, he's a rinky-dink small town PI who I'll bet has never had a potential payday like this one. He has every incentive to play ball." Edison was cock-sure he was right.

"What if he goes to the authorities?" said Reese.

"He's already in too deep." Edison doubled down on his assumption.

"You'd better be right. If you don't hear from in forty-eight hours, I want you to personally pay him a visit. If he hasn't done his job, you need to do yours. Understand?"

Reese's comment had a chilling effect on Edison. His boss didn't handle disappointment well at all, as evidenced by Stratford's gruesome demise. He vowed not to endure the same fate by making sure Reese's money had been well spent.

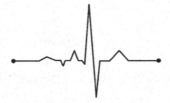

CHAPTER 38

T he night with his friends had done Miles a world of good. He awoke the next morning refreshed and, much to his surprise, having nothing in particular to do. His casework for Bobbie was complete and his undercover work for the FBI was either finished or, at the very least, in a holding pattern.

It occurred to him that he hadn't been to his office in a few days, so he recruited Agent Stevens to accompany him there. He would have gladly gone alone, but he realized it would be against the rules and foolhardy to do so.

The floor behind the front door of his office was littered with mail. Most of it was junk mail, but one item stuck out. It was a handwritten letter from Bobbie.

Dear Miles,

I want you to know how deeply grateful I am to my father for passing along to me the friendship the two of you shared. Rest assured, I plan to keep it intact always. That said, I've decided the time has come to finally allow my memories of growing up in Lakeville to remain just as memories.

So, I'd like to see if you'd be interested in purchasing the house. It could be done either on a land contract or by a traditional sale. Whatever works best for you. Please let me know if this is something you would consider. If it is,

I know we can come to an arrangement that fits well for both of us.

Just so you know, I chose to send you my thoughts in writing because I'm sure what would start out as a simple discussion would have become very emotional for me and likely for you as well.

Warmest regards,
Bobbie

P.S. I sent this to your office because it seemed weird somehow sending it to the house.

Miles was beyond surprised. He was sure Bobbie would want to continue her attachment to the house. It never crossed his mind whether he wanted to actually own the place. He did have the $50,000 windfall from the Jefferson/Shaw case coming his way. That would certainly make for a proper down payment if he chose to go through with a purchase. He laughed to himself. "So much for nothing to do today."

The subject of the Reese investigation was the number-one topic at Agent Drummond's morning staff briefing. After each of the involved agents provided their updates, she posed a question to the group: "We should have the warrants issued soon, but before indictments can be issued and arrests made, what do we do to protect those four people in Lakeville? Reese will likely double down on his efforts to make sure they can't testify."

After a brief silence, she answered her own question. "It's quite simple. We just kill Olivia Sims and Lyle Underwood."

The usually stoic group looked at her in disbelief.

"I don't mean actually 'kill them.' I mean we simply make it appear to Reese's people that his two targets have been killed. We have Mr. Darien provide fake evidence he killed Olivia. Then when he comes to collect the balance of the money he's owed for the first job, he promises to do the same to Underwood. As soon as we have Reese and his cronies arrested, they both come back to life."

One of the agents chimed in. "If we're going that route, we'd better get a move on it. Based on what we know, Reese will expect immediate results from Mr. Darien."

"Correct. We need to stage Olivia Sims's murder today. Ideas?"

They spent the ninety minutes developing a plan. Once they had agreement on how to proceed, Agent Drummond phoned Miles to lay out the plan her team had devised.

"Hi there, Audrey. Nice of you to check up on me."

"Actually, There a more pressing reason for my call. We need you to murder Olivia Sims today," she said matter-of-factly.

Miles was floored by the request. "What! Are you kidding me?"

"Calm down. I'm talking about staging her murder. We need to be sure the heat is off you while we proceed with the process of obtaining and executing warrants. Here's what we have in mind."

She spent the next several minutes detailing how she wanted things to go. After answering a few of his questions, Miles agreed to the plan. His response to Bobbie's offer would have to wait.

Miles grabbed a few of his forensic tools before he and his agent bodyguard headed to see Olivia. Along the way, he called his friend Jim.

"Jim, I need a favor."

"Again? I'm going to have to start charging you."

"That's fine. I'm sure the FBI will be happy to pay your bill."

"Sounds serious. What's up?"

"I need to stage a murder and I'm going to need a coroner's report to authenticate it."

"You're not serious. That's way more than a favor." Jim sounded understandably confused.

"Seriously, I can get you all the proper approvals you need. I really am working on this with the FBI. We just need to make it look like Olivia Sims has been murdered. I'm on my way to pick her up and bring her to your office. I can't take no for an answer. Her life depends on it."

Olivia and her mom were in the backyard pulling weeds from George's garden when Miles arrived.

"Hello, ladies. Beautiful day to work in the garden." Miles made a point of sounding cheerful given the request he was about to make of Olivia.

"Hey, Miles. Feel like getting your hands dirty?" Mrs. Sims asked.

"Some other time. I need to chat with Olivia privately if that's okay."

"Sure. Let's go inside," Olivia replied as she headed through the back door and into the kitchen.

"I have a rather unusual request. As you know, we're trying our best to arrest the people who are responsible for what happened to you. To do that, we need to pretend you've been murdered."

Olivia replied with a squint in her eyes and a tilt of her head. "Okay, I guess. What would I have to do?"

"You would have to come with me to the coroner's office and let Jim and I make you look dead for some pictures."

"That seems to be a reasonable request." She was relieved that was all they needed.

"Full disclosure, we would need to photograph your entire body," Miles sheepishly admitted.

"That's fine. Both of you have seen most of me already anyway," she said with a giggle.

"Thanks. Are you good with us leaving now?"

She nodded yes and, after saying goodbye to her mom, joined Miles and the agent in the car. On the way, Miles alerted Jim to get things ready and that they'd be there in ten minutes.

When they arrived at Jim's office, they went inside the building, leaving the agent at the door to stand guard.

"Miles, what sort of murder are we faking here?" Jim asked.

Miles explained the scenario. They needed photos of her body and an autopsy report to show Olivia had committed suicide by jumping off the Harbor Bridge. The effects of the fall caused her to lose consciousness, and she drowned. They needed to clearly show trauma from the fall, evidence of drowning, and that it was actually Olivia. Miles's intricate plan, if successful, would both help ensnare the criminals and keep Olivia safe while it unfolded.

"So, pictures and an autopsy report?" Jim asked.

"Exactly."

"I can't believe how clean and bright this place is," Olivia said to herself. "Not as creepy as I imagined an autopsy room would be."

Miles and Jim conferred about what Olivia's makeup should be. Once that was decided, Miles used the stuff he brought and some of the items in Jim's lab to give her face and body the proper ashen hue for the pictures. Jim instructed him on where to place the evidence of incisions he would have made if this were a real autopsy.

"Be sure to get a shot of the surgical scar from her kidney operation. It'll help prove it's really her."

Miles's coaching brought a "Really!" look from Jim, who said in no uncertain terms, "I know what I'm doing."

Olivia was a real trooper. She posed for every angle Jim needed and never flinched or seemed to be self-conscious. Once they were finished, Miles and Olivia adjourned to the lobby while Jim prepared his autopsy report. About thirty minutes later, Jim handed Miles the file.

"Thanks, Jim. We really appreciate it," Miles said as both he and Olivia shook Jim's hand. Then they drove back to George's house.

After dropping Olivia off, he called Agent Drummond.

"I have a very compelling autopsy report, complete with pictures, which shows the likely cause of death as suicide," he told her. "How do you want me to play this with Edison?"

"Contact him and demand to deliver the evidence but only directly to Reese. Say you're not interested in anymore 'messages' of the kind you received from his thugs. Also, be sure to ask for the money they owe you. And don't worry, we'll have you covered all the way."

Miles hardly felt reassured but promised to do as instructed and get back to her with details on whatever arrangements he was able to make. His next call was to Edison. He took a deep breath, collected his thoughts, and dialed the number.

"The first job is complete," he said as soon as Edison picked up. "I want to meet with Reese and get the next installment of what's been promised to me."

"It doesn't work that way," Edison pushed back.

"Make it work that way. I will not be subjected to your goons pounding on me for the hell of it. I have delivered what's been asked of me. Now you deliver what's been asked of you!" Miles demanded.

"I'll get back to you." With that, Edison hung up.

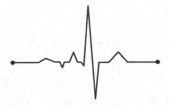

CHAPTER 39

M iles awoke Monday morning, hoping today would be the day this seemingly never-ending drama would finally reach its finale. He and his friends had certainly been through enough.

As he poured himself a second cup of coffee, he remembered he hadn't yet responded to Bobbie's offer to sell him the house. It was after nine o'clock, so he was sure it wasn't too early to call.

"Good morning, Miles," she answered. "I've been waiting for you to call."

"Sorry, I've been tied up with a case and also wanted time to think over your offer."

"No worries. So, where is your head at on buying the house?" Bobbie said hopefully.

"My head and my heart agree. I want to move forward. Do you have a price in mind?"

She suggested using the assessed value on the tax bill as the purchase price even though she acknowledged the actual value would be much higher.

"It works for me since I won't have to pay a real estate broker's commission. Sound fair?" she asked.

"It does. How should we proceed?" Miles was pleased with the offer. It was actually way more than fair. He didn't relish the thought of negotiating with his friend, so this worked out perfectly.

"I should have your check ready by the end of this week or

the beginning of next. As soon I know for sure, we can plan to get together to go over the particulars. When we do, I'd like to come in early in the day so we can handle the business side of things and allow me time to assess what I have stored there."

"Sure. Whatever works best for you. Keep me posted so I can put aside the entire day."

"Thanks, Miles. I'll be in touch."

This would be the first home Miles had ever actually owned. Even growing up, his family had always lived in a rented property. This purchase was more than simply a commitment to home ownership, it was a commitment to stay in Lakeville. That profound realization gave him an enormous sense of belonging.

Having decided to buy the house, he turned his attention to his long neglected chores. He hadn't thoroughly cleaned his place or done his laundry since all of this commotion over Olivia had begun. The laundry was doubly important now since he was almost out of underwear. He grabbed the overflowing laundry basket and carried it downstairs to put in a load. Of course, his phone rang when he was halfway down the steps. He set the laundry basket down to check the phone. It was Edison.

"Mr. Reese will see you tomorrow. Be in the lobby of his building at eleven o'clock. Bring proof you've done what you say you've done and come unarmed."

"Got it. I'll be there."

Bingo, Miles thought after hanging up. Tomorrow as the final act of this drama would do just fine. He dialed Agent Drummond almost subconsciously.

"What do you have for me, Miles?"

"Meeting's set for tomorrow at eleven o'clock at Reese's place. Do you have a new jacket for me to wear?"

"No need for that. The one warrant we've already obtained was for surveillance. His penthouse and the other key places in the building are already being monitored. You just go in, hand him the autopsy report on Olivia, get him to acknowledge what you've done, collect your money, and promise to take care of Underwood. Then you get out."

As she laid out the plan, Miles nervously paced the floor. All sorts of possible scenarios went through his mind. None of them good.

"Okay. But what if things don't go according to plan? I'm a sitting duck there."

"We have that covered as well. At the first sign you're in danger, we'll intervene. Oh, and I want you to take the train to Chicago. We'll have agents on board just in case."

"The train? I don't understand."

"Simple. I want to keep you out in public in case they're watching you. It'll also reduce the chance they're going to try something if the meeting isn't for real. Take your car by yourself to the Lakeville train stop. Then take a cab to Reese's from Union Station. After you're done there, take a cab back to Union Station. Go in one door and out another. Then take a cab to our office to debrief and unload the money."

"Got it. See you tomorrow." As fearful as he was about the possibility something could go horribly wrong, he was really charged up by all the cloak-and-dagger stuff.

Later that afternoon, Miles received a script outline from Ryan and Rebecca. It laid out the plotline, which was loosely based on Olivia's story. Highlighted were some areas where they felt Miles's input would be helpful. He emailed Ryan back with his commitment to work on it along with some questions.

Assuming all went well the following day, he wondered if the latest developments, including the fake murder, might be a good fit. If it were, he'd be sure to clear it with Agent Drummond before putting any of it into his script ideas.

It wasn't even dinnertime but he'd had a full day. An evening of leftovers and some old movie on Netflix sounded like the perfect way to relax. *The Maltese Falcon* proved to be the perfect selection. Miles saw much of himself in Humphrey Bogart's Sam Spade. At least his detective side.

With the big day ahead, Miles was in bed by ten p.m. He had both a morning train and a gang of criminals to catch tomorrow.

CHAPTER 40

Miles left the house in time to pick up coffee and a sweet roll on his way to the Lakeville train stop. As promised, he was followed closely by two FBI agents. If he hadn't known them, he wouldn't have detected their presence. The ride to Chicago was, as always, short and uneventful. In fact, once he arrived in Chicago he had some time to kill. So, he decided to walk along the Chicago River to Reese's building. Hopefully, he wouldn't be scolded for deviating from the plan. Even though the nickname of the Windy City didn't actually come from Chicago being windy, on this day it could have been. Miles had to hold the folder containing his report tightly to his chest. If it blew away, so would his whole plan.

As expected, when he arrived at Reese's building, Edison was waiting for him in the lobby. Without saying a word, they proceeded up the elevator to Reese's penthouse. As before, Miles was patted down at the door and then led to Reese's office. In addition to Reese, there were two other men in the room when he and Edison entered.

"Welcome back, Mr. Darien. Please have a seat." Reese was strangely cordial.

Miles obliged, taking the same seat at the wooden table where he sat the last time they met.

"Would you like something to drink? Coffee or water, maybe?" Reese continued.

"No thanks, I'm fine," Miles replied curtly.

"Okay, then let's get started." Reese motioned for Miles to share his evidence.

"This folder contains a full autopsy report on the death of Olivia Sims. You'll see it has been ruled a suicide. None of the evidence will point to me or ultimately to you." Miles did his best to deliver his explanation in a coldhearted manner.

Reese grabbed the report and, after examining it thoroughly, asked the first obvious question. "How did you manage to kill her, and have it be ruled a suicide?"

"You'll see in the report that her blood contained a high alcohol level as well as the presence of prescribed sleeping medication. I simply had a few drinks with her and dropped a sleeping pill into one of them. When she was barely conscious, I took her to the Harbor Bridge and pushed her off. You'll also see from the report that the cause of death was a combination of trauma from the fall and drowning."

Miles was relieved that he had gotten the explanation out without fumbling, considering his heart was beating a mile a minute.

"Okay, my next question is: how did you get this report?" Reese obviously wasn't yet fully accepting Miles's explanation.

"I worked for several years as a forensic scientist for the Lakeville Police Department. A buddy of mine in the coroner's office gave it to me."

It was, after all, the truth.

"So, he just gave it to you, no questions asked?"

"He did. It would become part of the public record eventually, so he saw no harm in it. Listen, you could not have more definitive proof than what I've given you. Let's transact our business and move on to the next order of business."

"There's been a slight change in plans. You see, we've already located Mr. Underwood and are taking care of the next order of business ourselves. Give me one good reason why I shouldn't simply have you eliminated and save twenty-five grand."

Miles could feel Reese's men slowly closing in around him. One of them also had his hand on the gun in his holster. Doing his best to keep it together, Miles answered, "Because I can be a valuable asset to your organization going forward. Look at the work I've done on this. I single-handedly dug up evidence leading me to your organization and then took care of a major problem for you. That should prove my worth."

"Not a good enough reason, I'm afraid. You're a once-and-done hit man, Mr. Darien." He turned to Edison. "Use my elevator key to take him down the main elevator nonstop to the basement and then get rid of him."

Before Miles could react, Edison and the two other men in the room wrestled him to the floor. As much as he struggled, they were still able to tie his hands and gag him.

Just as they started to drag him out of Reese's office into the hallway, there was sudden loud crash at the penthouse entrance. A squad of FBI agents in tactical gear and carrying assault weapons stormed in with its leader screaming, "FBI, you're all under arrest. Drop your weapons and put up your hands!"

Reese's men had no chance to win a shootout with the heavily armed FBI agents, so they did what they were told, releasing Miles and putting up their hands without a fight. All of them, including Edison, were in handcuffs a minute later. Then the agents quickly untied a most grateful Miles.

Agent Drummond followed her team in once the place had been secured.

"You all right?" she asked Miles.

"Yes, but barely," Miles replied, rubbing his wrists.

Their conversation was abruptly interrupted by one of the

agents who had just searched the penthouse. "Reese is gone," he said.

"Block all the exits on the ground floor, immediately!" Agent Drummond commanded into her walkie-talkie. She took off to examine Reese's office.

There was no sign of Reese or any exit he could have taken. Miles joined her in the office and began looking for some hidden passageway Reese might have used. He noticed one of the sections of the floor-to-ceiling bookcases seemed to be slightly out of alignment. Sure enough, with a little push, the panel revealed a secret doorway. Even in the heat of the moment, Miles had to chuckle. The hidden-doorway surprise was right out of dozens of spy novels and detective movies. Nevertheless, there it was.

Agent Drummond and three of her agents hustled through the door, guns drawn. Miles followed safely behind. The door led them down a short hallway to what appeared to be a freight elevator. It took several minutes for the elevator to arrive at the top floor, undoubtedly because it had just taken Reese down moments before. They all got into the elevator, and Agent Drummond pressed the buttons for the first floor and the basement.

At the first floor, Drummond instructed the two of the agents to get out and begin looking for Reese. She, Miles, and the third agent proceeded to the basement. Once there, Reese's escape route became obvious. Next to a collection of dumpsters was a lift device, which was used to carry those dumpsters up to the alley. The lift was in the "up" position, indicating Reese had likely used it to leave the building. Since there was no regular building exit at that location, Reese was able to leave undetected by the agents who were guarding the regular exits.

Agent Drummond gave the order for her remaining agents

to stand down, and then she called her office to have them monitor all airports and train stations in case Reese tried to escape the city using public transportation. She also told them to place additional security around Underwood and put a transfer to another facility in effect as soon as possible. Then her attention returned to Miles.

"How are you holding up?"

"I'm a little shaken, to be honest, but I'll be fine."

"Good. I'll have Agent Dougherty here take you back to Lakeville. We'll continue keeping an eye on you and Olivia Sims for a while, but I highly doubt you're in any further danger from Reese. Certainly, his attention must be focused on getting as far away from all of this as possible. With his substantial resources, I suspect he's totally focused on escaping prosecution by getting out of the country."

"I hope so. It would be really nice to get back to simply investigating cheating spouses and lost dogs." That brought a laugh from the usually-serious Agent Drummond.

"Miles, you've been a huge help. I can't thank you enough for putting yourself in harm's way as you did. If we meet again, I hope it's in less stressful circumstances."

"Me too, Audrey." They shook hands, and Miles followed Agent Dougherty to his car.

Miles and his escort drove back to Lakeville in silence. Miles did send a text, however.

"Olivia, it's all over. Take a deep breath and relax."

CHAPTER 41

Miles was never so happy to be back home. Molly greeted him at the door in full squeal, her tail wagging furiously. The prospect of filling the coming days with mundane tasks and drama-free events was incredibly appealing. It occurred to him that he hadn't checked his messages since leaving Chicago. When he did, he found two which were important. One from Bobbie asking if she could come to see him on Thursday, and one from Ryan asking him to call.

After texting Bobbie that Thursday would work, he called Ryan.

"Hi, Miles. What have you been up to?"

"As it turns out, quite a bit." Miles detailed all that had gone on since they'd last spoken. From faking Olivia's murder to the events at Reese's building, the lengthy retelling spilled out of him like a waterfall.

"Jesus! You must have soiled your underwear," Ryan exclaimed.

"Of course not. I'm a professional," Miles deadpanned.

"Seriously, you must have been terrified."

"I was. The contrast with the calm I'm feeling now is incredible. What's news on your end?"

"Obviously, nothing as exciting as what you've been through. I'm finishing up the last installment of my series for the *Times*. The plans for our new place have become a never-ending sequence of decisions. And, as you can see from the outline I sent over, we're making some headway on the script for Rebecca's show. Now that things have calmed down for you, why don't you come here for a visit so you can meet Rebecca and we can all work on the script?"

"I'd love that. By the way, Bobbie's coming here on Thursday. We're discussing my buying the house."

"You're just trying to keep up with the Duffy's, I suspect," Ryan teased.

"Actually, it was her idea. Regardless, I'm elated." Then Miles added another revelation. "Speaking of keeping up with the Duffy's, I have some wonderful news. George and Mrs. Sims are getting married in September, and they'd like you and Rebecca to attend."

"That is wonderful news. Send me the date and I'll run it by Rebecca. So, how soon can you make it here?" Ryan pushed.

"I'll try for Saturday. Stay for two, maybe three nights?"

"Perfect. Let me know once you've made your travel plans."

"Will do. See you soon."

The rest of the day was spent curled up on the couch flipping channels and devouring a huge bowl of popcorn. Never had such a waste of time been so well spent.

By Wednesday morning, Miles had already put aside the harrowing events of the previous day. He got up early and decided the first order of business would be to stop by the office, open the mail, and pay bills. Beyond would be a stop at the grocery store. Both he and Molly were out of food. He'd get all of his chores done before going to see Olivia, Mrs. Sims, and George.

His stay at the office was a short one. There was nothing of particular interest in the mail, so he went about paying his bills. That took all of twenty minutes, after which he closed up shop and set sail for the store.

When he pulled into the parking lot at Food Mart, he saw Olivia's Ford Fusion parked in the second row. There was an empty space next to hers, so he took it hoping it would reduce the odds he'd miss seeing her. It actually didn't take long to locate her in the store. When she saw him coming down the frozen-food aisle, she abandoned her cart and ran to him. After a giant hug, tears starting flowing down both of their faces.

"Miles, I don't know where to begin. You are literally my life saver."

"Yeah, but don't forget I supposedly murdered you, too." Miles's little joke brought a big laugh.

"I'm making dinner tonight for Mom and George. Will you join us? Molly's invited too." He knew she wouldn't take no for an answer.

"Sure, what time?"

"Six thirty. Red, by the way."

"Red?"

"The amazing bottle of wine you're bringing."

That brought a huge smile to his face.

They parted after another hug, and Miles went about collecting his groceries, Molly's dog food and the amazing red wine Olivia had demanded. By wrangling a dinner invitation along the way, he wouldn't have to figure out what to make for himself. Some days the sun shines particularly bright, he thought.

When Miles got to George's, he realized why Olivia had asked for red wine. She had steaks on the grill and baked potatoes in the oven. The dinner turned out be a celebration. First and foremost, a celebration that Olivia's nightmare had ended. Then of course, there was the excitement of the wedding. They toasted both events in equal measure. Miles's decision to bring two bottles of the red wine turned out to be a stroke of sheer genius.

"I'm going to New York for a short visit with Ryan on Saturday," he told them. "I'm really excited to finally meet Rebecca. She must be quite a person to have captivated Ryan as she has."

"He's pretty captivating himself," Olivia offered with a blush.

"How long has it been since you've been back there?" George asked.

"Several years. I'll admit, I miss it from time to time, but my life is here now. Besides, the only person there who I'm still attached to is Ryan, and he and I, as you know, are in constant touch. Maybe now that we're working on a script together, I may get there more than once this year."

"Script. What script?" Olivia demanded.

"Oops. With all that's going on I must have forgotten to tell you. We're going to submit a script for the season finale of Rebcca's show, *Compassion Clinic*. It'll be loosely based on your story and Ryan's essays about loans backed by human collateral."

"I can't believe it!" Olivia shouted, tears streaming down her cheeks. "Something good is actually coming out of all of this."

"Olivia should get royalties!" George declared.

"I'll work on that. By the way, Ryan would like to attend your wedding."

"Rebecca too?" Olivia asked.

"It will depend on both of their schedules. Once you have a firm date, I'll work on them."

"September eighth," Mrs. Sims answered. "Now get to work."

That night, Miles slept more soundly than he had in ages. The combination of red wine and the absence of the cloud which had hung over him for the past few weeks made for the perfect sleeping potion. He was awakened in the morning by the sound of a car door closing. Bobbie had arrived and he was still in bed. He hastily threw on a pair of pants and headed downstairs.

"Did I wake you?" she asked.

"I overslept. Sorry. Come in and make yourself at home. Actually, it is your home. At least for now." Even though he was only half awake, his sense of humor had already kicked in.

"Go and get yourself organized. I'll make us some coffee." Bobbie was always one to take charge.

"Thanks. Would you also let Molly out?"

She nodded and motioned for him to go upstairs. He could see Bobbie needed a moment to let go of the wave of emotion that had followed her through the front door, so he did as he was instructed. By the time Miles returned, the coffee was brewed, and Bobbie had recovered from her brief melancholy.

"Before we get down to business, how are things going with the case you've been working on?" she asked.

"I'm happy to say it's been resolved and my client is now safe from further harm." The thought of it brought a smile to his face.

"Happy to hear it."

Before she could continue, Molly was barking and scratching at the back door.

"Guess she doesn't want to be left out of the negotiations," Miles quipped as he let her in.

"Now that we have a quorum, shall we begin?" Bobbie said, calling the meeting to order. She pulled a copy of the property tax bill from her briefcase and pointed to the box which showed the assessed value to be $295,000. Bobbie then gave him a look that said, "Okay?"

"Frankly, I think it's too low. But if you're good with it, who am I to argue?" Miles replied with a shrug.

"We're agreed then. I brought an offer to purchase for you to sign. I set the closing date four months from today or sooner. I trust that will give you sufficient time to arrange for financing. I'm flexible if you need an extension. It also gives me some time to take care of the stuff I have in the basement." She handed him the offer to purchase, which he signed and offered her a handshake to seal the deal.

Miles was elated by how easily this was coming together. "With the check you're dropping off and some additional money I will put toward the down payment, it should be sooner, but feel free to take your time moving your things out."

"Great. Now the fun part. Here's your check for $58,600 covering your services and the bonus. Miles, you did both of us a lot of good with your work on this. Jefferson/Shaw has retained me to handle all of the negotiations as well as the settlement agreement with AccuTest. You will obviously be retained should any additional discovery be required. Now you must tell me how you so quickly discovered what happened and then tracked down Timothy Frost."

Miles explained about his working with the FBI on Olivia's case afforded him the opportunity to ask them for a favor. "I was pretty sure I knew how it all went down, and I would surely have gotten the goods on him eventually, but their resources dramatically shortened the timeline," he admitted.

"I assumed it was some law enforcement entity, but the FBI? Boy, you do travel in some high-level company." Bobbie was dutifully impressed.

Miles asked her if she'd like his help sorting through the boxes in the basement. She declined, opting to sort through her memories alone. She did, however, ask him to help bring the boxes upstairs once she was finished.

Miles had neglected his yard for a couple of weeks, and he knew he'd better tend to it before he received a citation from the city. "Give me a shout when you're ready. If I'm not in the house, I'll be outside cutting the lawn."

By the time he finished his yard work, Bobbie was ready to go. He helped her carry a few boxes to her car and shared another hug before she drove back to Madison.

Miles realized he hadn't yet made his reservations for Saturday's trip to New York, so he immediately went online and booked a nonstop morning flight to La Guardia from O'Hare. If the plane arrived on time, he'd be at Ryan's before two o'clock. He emailed Ryan a copy of the confirmation and included a note about having sealed the deal on the house.

Ryan replied immediately: "You're now officially a Cheese-head!"

CHAPTER 42

s Miles made his way to O'Hare on Saturday morning, an unusual anxiety set in. It wasn't meeting Rebecca. He was ecstatic about Ryan's new relationship. Goodness knows she filled a place in Ryan's heart that Miles could never fill. It finally dawned on him that it was New York. He worried that the force field which had once surrounded him and allowed him to navigate the city untouched by its frenetic pace and sensory overload wouldn't be there when he landed.

His flight boarded on time. There were no delays *en route*. After two hours in the air, his plane pulled into the gate fifteen minutes early. Miles would soon discover if there was a force field waiting for him outside baggage claim. It didn't take long for him to find out.

"Where ya headed?" the guy in charge of the taxi stand asked.

"78th between Amsterdam and Broadway," Miles answered.

"Welcome home, my man. Take the second cab," the guy said.

Obviously, the response proved he hadn't actually lost either his force field or his accent. He'd simply left them at La Guardia. As his cab crossed the Triborough Bridge spanning the East River, his anxiety turned into excitement. The city was brightly lit by the afternoon sun, allowing him to see the full length of Manhattan from the high point of the bridge. He spent the rest of the ride trying to recall the names of each site he passed.

When he arrived at Ryan's apartment building, Ryan was sitting on the stoop waiting for him. Even though it had only been a short time since they had seen one another, they embraced like long-lost brothers. So much had happened in the time in between.

"So glad you're here. Are you hungry?" Ryan asked.

"Actually, I am. What do you have in mind?"

"We're going over to Rebecca's. She has lunch planned before she begins the interrogation."

"Just what I expected. The interrogation, that is."

They stowed Miles's bags in the apartment and then jumped in a cab. The short ride gave Miles just enough time to fill Ryan in on the wedding plans.

"We'd really love to attend. Now that we know the timing, we'll work on arranging our schedules," Ryan promised.

After arguing over who would pay the cab fare, Ryan paid the cabbie and the two men entered the building and took the elevator up to Rebecca's condo. Ryan opened the door and the smell of something wonderful filled the air. They walked into the kitchen where Rebecca was putting the finishing touches on a frittata. She took the pan off the stove and headed straight for Miles. It was the first time in decades a woman had kissed him on the lips. The last woman had been his grandmother.

"So glad to finally meet you. I can't wait to get your take on who the real Ryan Duffy is." Her eyes sparkled when she mentioned Ryan's name. Miles knew immediately she was truly in love with his friend. He couldn't be happier for both of them.

They sat down to lunch and began exchanging stories. After the conversation turned from history to current events, Miles gave them a detailed account of what had transpired since Ryan left Lakeville.

"Have the authorities caught up with Jonathan Reese yet?" Ryan asked.

"No, and I'm not sure they will anytime soon. It's likely he's made his way out of the country. While I hate that he's escaped capture, his operation has been dismantled, which means no one else can be hurt by it. Olivia is safe now, and the fact that her mom and George have found one another is a wonderful postscript to the story. They are counting on the two of you being in Lakeville for the wedding on September eighth."

"We'll be there even if we have to come in just for the day," Rebecca promised.

After lunch, they spent the rest of the afternoon kicking around ideas for the episode of Rebecca's show. Miles offered his take on how the "Olivia" character might end up at the clinic and the various ways in which the crime could be investigated. They even discussed the possibility of Olivia playing the character she had inspired. He also supplied them with a list of procedures and terminology to add authenticity to the show's action and dialogue.

"I think we've done enough script work for the day," Rebecca declared, excusing herself to get ready for a mandatory dinner meeting with her publicist and a couple of journalists. The boys were on their own for the evening.

"I'd love to just bum around the village," said Miles. "A few drinks, some food, catch a little live music, just soak up the Saturday night action. You game?"

Ryan agreed, and they set off in search of the Village's bohemian vibe. They found plenty of it and awoke the next morning with the ultimate bohemian hangover.

Rebecca had made arrangements for the three of them to walk

through the new condo early Sunday afternoon. It was a good thing because both Ryan and Miles needed the morning to recover from the night before.

The minute they walked through the door, Miles was captivated. The place was beautiful. The open concept with the great room encompassing the modern kitchen, dining area, and expansive living room gave it a wonderful feeling of space with the spectacular view adding the entire Upper West Side as their front yard.

Rebecca guided Miles around the apartment, painting a mental picture for him of how each room would be laid out and decorated. She paid particular attention to the amenities she believed would make Ryan happy. With each moment they spent together, it became more and more evident how fortunate Ryan was to have this woman in his life. After the tour, they returned to Rebecca's to continue the discussion about the script. On the way, Miles received a text from Anne saying she could start work at the office the following Wednesday. He texted back his approval.

They ordered Chinese food to be delivered and worked on the script for the balance of the evening. Rebecca had an early location shoot in the morning, so they called it a night around nine o'clock.

"See you in Lakeville!" Rebecca pledged as she gave him another hug, this time accompanied by a kiss on the cheek.

The two men headed back to Ryan's place for a couple more hours to reminisce and have a night cap. In the morning, Miles would fly back to Lakeville with the hopes of latching on to a new assignment.

Miles's trip home mirrored his travel to New York, on time and stress free. He stopped by Mrs. Sims's house to pick up Molly before going home. Olivia had been caring for her over the weekend.

"Must be nice to have the house all to yourself now that your mom is living with George," Miles surmised.

"It is, but I enjoyed having Molly here to keep me company," said Olivia. "I heard from Janine, by the way."

"And?"

"Turns out she loves Rockford. She found a job and is moving there right away." Olivia was obviously very pleased for her friend.

"Good for her. I'm so glad her part in all of this had a positive outcome."

"And she and I will be as close geographically as we would be if she were staying in Chicago. Almost forgot. George asked that you call him when you get a moment."

"Thanks. Hope to see you soon. Come on, Molly. Let's go." Miles attached Molly's leash and headed out the door.

Once he had unpacked, he called George as instructed.

"Hi, Miles. Hope your trip went well."

"It did. Ryan and Rebecca have promised to do everything possible to attend your wedding."

"Cora will be so pleased. Listen, I know you're probably tired from traveling, but could you meet me at the boat this afternoon? I need your help with something." George sounded serious.

"Sure. What's up?"

"Stop by in an hour and I'll fill you in."

On the way to the marina, Miles worried some new crisis had emerged while he was in New York. While he certainly needed a new case to work on, he hoped this one didn't involve his friend being in trouble. When he arrived at the pier, George was already on the boat and waving for Miles to join him.

"Welcome aboard. Tell me a little about your trip." George's voice was cheerful, which Miles took to mean there was nothing ominous in the offing.

"I had a great time. Got to meet and spend some time with Rebecca. What a down-to-earth and caring person she is. I'm so happy for Ryan. The place they're moving into is fabulous. So, what do you want to talk to me about?"

"Well, here goes. You've been my good friend for a while now. Goodness knows what Cora and Olivia would have done without you. They care deeply about you. What I'm trying to say is, will you be my best man at the wedding?"

Miles felt genuinely relieved and touched at the same time. "George, it would be my honor. I have to say, when you called me to come down here I was sure you had something scary on your mind."

"That's not all I have to talk to you about."

Uh-oh, Miles thought.

"I have a little something I want to give you as a thank-you for all you've done for us." With that, George handed Miles a key chain with two keys on it.

"What's this?" Miles asked.

"Simple. One key unlocks the boat's cabin. The other starts the engine."

"I don't understand."

"My boat is your boat."

"I still don't understand."

"I'm giving you the use of the boat when I don't need it. You've spent many hours with me on it. By now, you've seen how it all works, including the Coast Guard regulations and safety rules you need to follow. Just leave it as you found it, particularly with a full fuel tank."

Miles was truly humbled by George's generosity. "George, I'm overwhelmed. I can't thank you enough."

"It's the least I can do. We're all family now. You've made it all possible. Shall we take her for a spin?"

With that, they started the boat intending to enjoy some time on the lake and a couple of beers. George also used some of the time to give Miles a refresher course just to be sure he was comfortable with all of the boat's systems and quirks.

Once back at the dock, Miles shook George's hand and again thanked him profusely for the incredibly kind gesture.

As Miles drove up his driveway, he realized for the first time in quite a while he'd be having a quiet evening alone at home. Alone except for Molly, that is. His mind wandered back over all that had happened within the past few weeks. He spent very little time reliving being shot at, beaten up, bound and gagged, and forced to jump from a moving car. He chose instead to focus on the friendships he forged with Olivia, Mrs. Sims, and George, the addition of Rebecca into his relationship with Ryan and, finally, the camaraderie he had forged with the agents at the FBI.

His phone dinged. It was a text from Ken Caldwell asking him to call when he had a moment. Miles responded immediately.

"Hi, Ken. So nice to hear from you. What's new?" Miles really hoped this was a social call.

"I just thought I'd call to see if you'd like to get together some time."

"I'd like that. Any ideas of when and where?" Miles tried to sound cool, but his insides were doing summersaults.

"Would you like to come to Chicago next weekend? We could see a show or something."

"To be frank, I've had enough of Chicago for a while. Why don't you come here?"

"What is there to do in Lakeville?" Ken wondered aloud.

Miles chuckled. "Do you like to fish?"

ACKNOWLEDGEMENTS

As always, I must begin by thanking my wife, Jackie, and my son, David, for their encouragement and for putting up with my incessant rants about the book I happened to be writing. I am also grateful to the rest of my family and my friends for their continuing support.

I have been so fortunate to have found a home at BQB Publishing. Terri and her staff have ushered me through the publishing process with compassion and a steady hand. In addition, I would be remiss if I didn't single out my editor, Caleb, who is both my collaborator and my teacher.

Finally, I must thank Miles Darien, who jumped off the page in *The Kingmaker's Redemption* to become the protagonist in *Human Collateral* and the foundational character for the series.

ABOUT THE AUTHOR

Harry Pinkus's passion for writing was ignited at the University of Wisconsin where he studied journalism and wrote for the campus newspaper, *The Daily Cardinal*. After many years as a partner in a marketing firm, he formed a consultancy to completely focus on writing for business-related publications, and creating marketing content and materials for both digital and print media. Coupling that passion for writing with his love of mysteries and thrillers has resulted in his first two novels, *The Kingmaker's Redemption* and *Human Collateral*.

"Writing these books has transformed my life by allowing me to creatively express my point of view through storytelling. It has redefined how I view the world and my place in it."

Harry and his wife, Jackie, live in Milwaukee, Wisconsin.

OTHER BOOKS
BY HARRY PINKUS

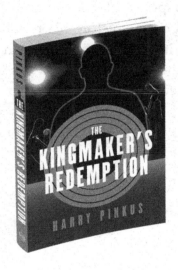

Fans of John Grisham will love *The Kingmaker's Redemption* with its intrigue and powerful courtroom showdown.

When political kingmaker Jack McKay chooses to change the arc of his life by representing a candidate he really believes in, he unleashes the full fury of his former client, Liberty Party leader Randall Davies. Davies becomes laser-focused on ruining Jack's career and his life by having Jack framed for a horrible crime he didn't commit. Randall's son, William, is the candidate opposing Jack's new client, Lindsay Revelle. Besides revenge, bringing Jack down would most certainly ensure the election of William Davies

When the Wisconsin Department of Justice launches a task force aimed at cracking down on child pornography around the state, Davies uses his sway over key individuals in Jack's orbit and their political connections to devise and implement a strategy using the DOJ's crackdown to implicate Jack in a crime he didn't commit.

The heart of the story is the struggle of Jack and his team to unravel the conspiracy aimed at destroying his life. Gaining his acquittal in a suspenseful courtroom showdown would not only prove his innocence, restore his reputation, and reinstate his parental rights, it would ultimately bring down the Liberty Party, their candidate, and Randall Davies in the process. If he fails, his life is ruined.